To Roger

Happy Reading

Mujilliard

J. RAPILLIARD works in further education in Liverpool. His main interest, apart from writing, is history and archaeology especially of the Viking period.

# The British Viking

J Rapilliard

---

# The British Viking

Vanguard Press

VANGUARD PAPERBACK

© Copyright 2008
**J Rapilliard**

The right of J Rapilliard to be identified as author of
this work has been asserted by him in accordance with the
Copyright, Designs and Patents Act 1988.

**All Rights Reserved**

No reproduction, copy or transmission of this publication
may be made without written permission.
No paragraph of this publication may be reproduced,
copied or transmitted save with the written permission of the
publisher, or in accordance with the provisions
of the Copyright Act 1956 (as amended).

Any person who commits any unauthorised act in relation to
this publication may be liable to criminal
prosecution and civil claims for damages.

The events and characters in this book are entirely fictitious and
no resemblance to anyone alive or dead is intended.

A CIP catalogue record for this title is
available from the British Library.

ISBN 978 184386 306 9

*Vanguard Press is an imprint of*
*Pegasus Elliot MacKenzie Publishers Ltd.*
www.pegasuspublishers.com

First Published in 2008

**Vanguard Press
Sheraton House  Castle Park
Cambridge  England**

Printed & Bound in Great Britain

# Dedication

To L. Gardner for her help, inspiration
and encouragement in the writing of this book.

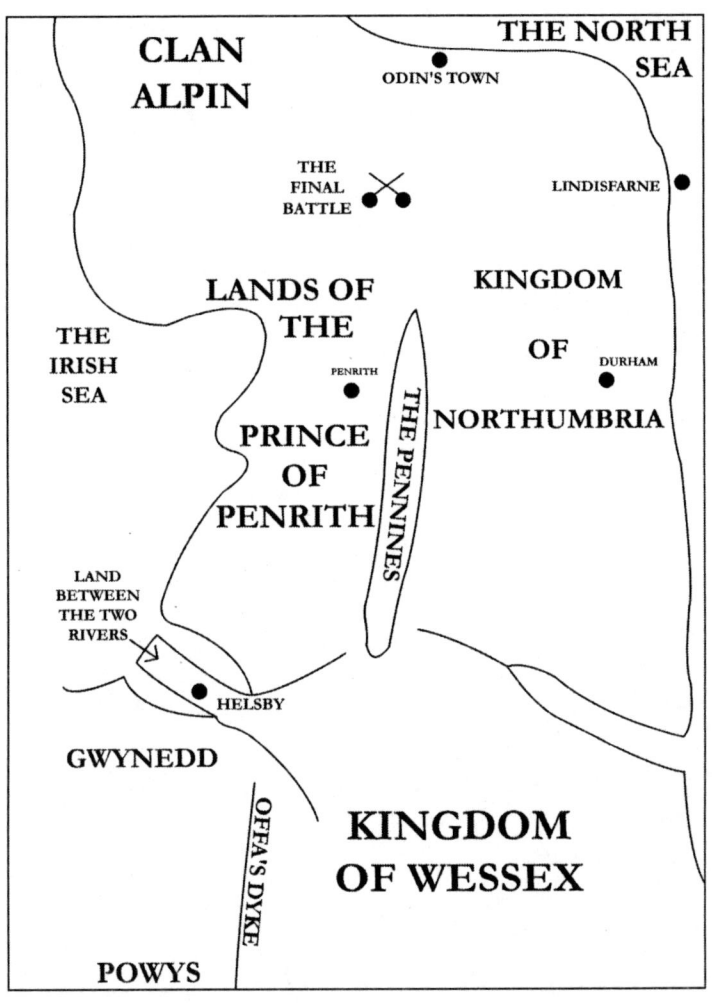

# CHAPTER 1

They call me Ap Thor, the son of Thor. Thor is my father. He is a Viking. We live on the outskirts of a village called Helsby because he is a blacksmith. It is close to the sea. My mother, Gwendwlyn, is British. She speaks Welsh. My father, on the other hand, speaks Norse. He was born in Ejksberg, many days travel by sea from here, the youngest in a family of eight, all brothers. He was brought up by his grandfather who also was a blacksmith and taught him the trade. I am fourteen years old, an only child with my whole life in front of me and I dream one day to travel and fight like a Viking.

My father knows how to make a sword sharp and strong that cuts deep and clean. He made his own many years ago when he joined his eldest brother Elgar in a foray to these parts. I like my uncle Elgar. I do not see much of him but when I do, he always has stories to tell me, stories of travel and battles, of foreign lands and raging seas. My father, on the other hand, speaks little and never about the past. I do not know whether he is happy with his fate or has any regrets. I do not think he was much of a warrior. He has not even told me how he and his wife, my mother, met or why they live together. She speaks little and always in Welsh. I can understand her and I speak some of the language but my father frowns when I do so. He wants me to be a true Viking and, at times, he thinks I should be a warrior and then he teaches me how to handle a sword and how to fight. I think he is a good teacher but, so far, I have not had occasion to prove myself as most of my time is spent helping my father at the forge. He has acquired quite a reputation and people come from near and far to have things made like shoes for the horses, farm implements, wheel reinforcements. However, it has been many months since someone has asked for a sword to be made because the land around us has become peaceful. The Saxons have stopped attacking this part of the country. They stay within their own kingdoms: Mercia to the south and Northumbria to the north-east.

The last time Elgar was here, only a few months ago, he spoke of his youth:
"Ap Thor, do you know how old I was when I left home?"
"No, I don't"
"About the age you are now. Do you know where my home was?"
"Father says it is a place called Ejksberg, far away from here."
"He's right. It is many days by boat but, when I was young, people were not coming this way. We were going eastwards. Ejksberg is not far from the sea. It is in a hollow between mountains. Most young people then would do the journey I made."
"Which was?"
"Well, early in spring, about a month after the thaw had begun for winter is very cold in that part of the world with snow and ice for four or five months, I and some local lads joined a ship that went east and up a river called Volga. When the ship could go no further, everyone on board lifted it out of the water and pushed it overland on a road made from tree trunks until we reached another river, called the Don."
"Aren't the boats heavy to carry?"
"We did not exactly carry them. How can I explain it to you? Vikings have been travelling that way for generations.

Some had settled along the river and are now known as Rus. At some point in the past, some of them had felled trees and made a wooden road upon which you just pushed the boat. It would take but a few days and then, on reaching that other river which I have just told you was called the Don, you would let the boat slip into the water and you could continue your journey."

"How long would it take?"

"All told, several weeks depending on the wind. Let me explain. On the Volga, you would be going against the river flow, so you might have to use the oars which was very tiring but would help develop the muscles in your arms for good fighting unless, of course, the wind was strong enough to push the boat and you would hoist the sail. Once on the Don, on the other hand, the boat would follow the river flow but, if you wanted to speed up, you would have to man the oars if there was no favourable wind."

"Why do such a long journey?"

"I'll tell you later but first let me continue with the journey as it happened. The Don would flow into a sea and crossing that sea, we would sail to a very big city named Constantinopolis. That's where we were heading to. As I told you before, all along both those rivers and the wooden road were Viking settlements, except that the people living there, while being Vikings or the children of Vikings, were not called Vikings but Rus. This was also a journey that many young Norsemen had done for centuries. It was considered a kind of rite of passage, the purpose of which was for us to learn the art of war, become a man and then settle somewhere. It was a well-travelled route and as we would go south, it would become hotter and hotter. Constantinopolis, our destination, was the capital of a large empire. The people there called themselves Romans and the empire was known as the Roman Empire of the East. Do you follow me so far?"

"Yes, but who were those Romans?"

"I'm not quite sure. Even though they called themselves the Roman Empire of the East, they were actually of different races. What I do know is that they did not like to fight. Their armies were made up of mercenaries. We, Vikings, formed the Varangian Guard and like all mercenaries, I signed up for a period of fifteen years."

"You spent fifteen years over there!" I said rather incredulously.

"Yes, and I could tell you lots of stories about that country and that Empire, but it would probably bore you. What I would say however, because I found it fascinating myself, is their tolerance of the various religions. You must have noticed that your father prays to Odin while your mother follow the Druids."

"I pray to Odin because my father says it is the only God. He has forbidden me to follow my mother's faith and I therefore know very little about it."

"The more the pity! Let me tell you how it was. Their official religion was Christianity because the Greeks, who formed most of the civilian population, were Christians, but other religions existed side by side. Their army was made of mercenaries many of whom were Vikings but called Varangians; they would of course follow the cult of Odin. There also were the Persians who would follow the cult of Baal. The Jewish religion was followed by the merchants who were bringing goods from all over the Empire and sometimes even from beyond its borders to the capital Constantinopolis. Soldiers from other lands, mercenaries like the Varangians, sometimes joined the secret cult of Mithras, the only cult apart from Christianity which believed in life after death for all."

"You're wrong, uncle, we, Vikings, live after death when we go to Valhalla and join Odin."

"No, Ap Thor, only the warriors who die in battle with their swords in their hands do. On the other hand, both the Christians and the followers of the Cult of Mithras believe that everyone will live after death."

"Don't you pray to Odin any more?"

My uncle laughed. "Of course, I've remained faithful to Odin but when you live in a country for fifteen years, you learn different things. Your outlook changes especially as I did not believe in isolating myself. After all, they may be right and I wrong, but Odin has always been my forefathers' God and I should stick by him."

"Right or wrong!"

"Right or wrong!"

We both laughed and our laughter reverberated through the empty countryside. We had been walking for a while. My uncle would only tell me about his life on walks away from my home. He did not seem to want anyone else to listen to him. This was helping to create a bond between us. Many of the things he would tell me appeared strange to me. I suppose that, one day, when I move away from home like he did and I try to make a life for myself, I shall come across strange happenings too. There seems to be so much to see and learn in the wider world. The question, of course is, when is my father going to let me go?

"Shall we turn round and go back home?" my uncle asked.

"No! Please tell me more about your life in that Empire of the East."

"Well!" said my uncle, pleased at my continued interest. "I, together with my fellow travellers, joined the Varangian Guard for the requisite period of fifteen years. While in training, we were stationed in camp not far from the capital. We even took part in some of the many official ceremonies presided over by the Emperor. When we were considered ready to fight, we were posted to the Eastern frontier. In the beginning, I did not see much fighting but after a few years the Empire started to be attacked in the East on a more or less regular basis. The attackers were Arabs who seemed determined to extend their rule over all and sundry fuelled by their religion, a new one apparently. Fighting was intermittent: A few months alongside one part of the border, followed by some truce. Then, fighting would restart along another part of the border. These forays became more frequent. Sometimes, fighting would flare in more than one place at a time. The army became stretched to its limits and the Empire began to lose land. The last two years of my fifteen-year stint saw continuous fighting and defeats. I got hurt twice but not seriously. So, you can imagine I was glad when I was given my retirement purse and my discharge. Many Vikings before me, over the years, once their military period had ended, would settle in the Empire or on its fringe. I decided against it. Having been witness to their determination, I believed the Arabs would eventually conquer the Empire and I did not want to see this happen during my lifetime and suffer for it."

"What did you do, then, Uncle?"

"I made the journey back North to Ejksberg. I was not alone. Many Vikings were thinking along the same lines, that the Empire would one day crumble and be overrun. The war would probably be a long one, lasting many years, and might even turn into a war of attrition. The general consensus, however, was that there could only be one eventual winner and somehow no one was thinking that the Roman Empire of the East would be that winner."

"Is there any way of knowing?"

"I'm afraid not. It might not even happen in my lifetime but I was not prepared to risk it."

"So, where did you go?"

"Where else but home!"

"Were you glad to see your family again then?"

"I thought I would be; but fifteen years is a long time and Ejskberg had changed a lot. So, upon my return, I felt like a stranger in my own land. I discovered that the Norse country around Ejskberg was crowded with people. There seemed to have been a population explosion making it virtually impossible for anyone returning to find land to settle on. Young men were not so keen to travel south any more as they had fifteen years before. Some preferred to stay put and for those in search of adventure, it would mean sailing the seas. Therefore, the direction of travel now was westwards. People with military experience were needed to lead the bands of men that were prepared to face the unknown and carve for themselves a place on some foreign land. Also, a few months before my return, my grandfather had died. His son took over the business and sent his cousin, your father, home."

"Why?"

"Things like this happen when people die. Anyway, there we were, the two of us at a loose end, drinking most of the time and waiting for an opportunity to turn up, and it did sooner than we expected when we heard that some local headman had acquired three boats and was looking for soldiers to man them. We contacted him. I had no difficulty in being accepted; I was a seasoned warrior with fifteen years' experience. In those days, people had heard of the Varangian Guard and treated with respect anyone who had been a member. It was not the same for my brother, Thor, your father. He had never fought before, neither was he a teenager any longer, but I managed to convince the headman, whose name by the way was Eldred, to take him on board saying that he would be useful to repair swords and any other implements that we may need to. After all, he had worked as a blacksmith for nearly ten years."

"Eldred?" I said. "I have heard that name before."

"Has your father mentioned it to you?"

"No, it was someone who came to the forge. He was talking about a famous Viking warrior in Ireland. Eldred the Avenger, he said. Must have had the same name."

"No, he's one and the same. Eldred made his name over there in Ireland. I might tell you his story some day but it's getting late and we should really go back."

We turned round and headed for home. As Elgar had stopped speaking, I asked him, "Please, continue your story. You are good at telling stories."

"All Vikings are good at telling stories. One day, you will be too and someone will listen to your saga just like today you are listening to mine. So, where was I? Oh, yes! I was convincing Eldred to accept your father. He did and we sailed, first Northwards and then due West. That was the scariest part."

"How?" I asked.

"You sail away from the land. As night falls, you are surrounded by water. Come the morning, you see no land. All day you move on, trusting in the Gods. Another night falls and when you wake up, you should be seeing land. We did. It was called Shetland and inhabited by the stone people."

"The stone people?"

He laughed at my surprise. "No, they are not made of stone, they are so called because they live in stone houses. In fact, everything is made of stone: the furniture, the beds, the plates, the streets between the houses. They also have their own customs that we, Vikings, respected. For instance, any boat was welcome to rest in any of their harbours provided the crew paid for the privilege. They could also buy food and water but were not allowed to land. After a couple of days, they would be expected to move on and that is what we did."

"Where did you go?" I asked.

"We sailed past a few more islands until we reached a larger one called Ireland. That is where Eldred wanted to go. You see, he had heard there was fighting going on there and indeed there was. Ireland was divided into tribes called clans and those clans were always trying to extend their territory at the expense of others. Many Vikings had been there before and had hired themselves to one or other of the chieftains."

"Chieftain?"

"The head of a clan was so called. He was a bit like our Headman, on a level with Eldred. The fighting, however, was not continuous: A few skirmishes, then a truce, possibly another battle and the war was over. So, we, Vikings, had carved a place for ourselves round a settlement we called Dublin where we could rest when we were not needed. Eldred took us there first. In fact we sailed right up to it. While we were waiting to be hired, I learned a few things about those Irish clans. For one, I was surprised to discover that Christianity was a religion that some of the clans had embraced, while the others remained true to their Celtic religion. The Celtic religion, as far as I could make out, was based on the worship of the rising sun. Your mother could probably give you more information as I believe the Welsh follow the same religion."

"My father insists that I pray to Odin," I said quite proudly.

"Odin is the God I pray to on the eve of battle because He was the God of my father and of his father before him, but I do not dismiss the other Gods out of hand, and I like to know about them. You should too. That's why I'm telling you about them. Take Christianity for instance. How could people as far apart as the Romans of the East and the Irish of the West follow the very same religion? Yet, there are differences: their holy men are called priests in the East and are married. In Ireland they are called monks and are celibate. Do not ask me why that is and just let me continue with my story. So, soon after we arrived, the

Christian clans formed an alliance to fight off, once and for all, the Celtic ones. They had their monks' full backing for that endeavour. We joined their alliance and, I dare say, so did every other Viking warrior who was in Ireland at the time. We saw some fierce fighting, but in the end the Celtic clans were defeated. Some crossed the sea but we did not pursue those. I suppose they now live somewhere North of here. Others surrendered and were incorporated into some of the victorious clans after their Chieftains had been killed either in battle or, afterwards, in cold blood."

"Did you do much fighting, uncle? Was my father with you? He never speaks of the past as you do."

"Yes, your father fought alongside me and Eldred. He was not afraid to fight if that is what you want to know, but he was just an ordinary fighter, not a professional one like me or Eldred for that matter."

Elgar saw that I looked crestfallen. I so much wanted to believe that my father had been a hero on the battlefield.

"I mean no disrespect to your father," my uncle said. "He was no coward and never turned his back on the enemy or fled the field of battle. In fact none of us ever did."

"So, when the fighting was over, what did you do?" I asked.

"We went back to Dublin, but by then the Saxons had attacked the British and the Prince of Powys was looking for soldiers to reinforce his army of native warriors. Eldred answered the call straightaway and he took with him all the Vikings that were fit to fight. I was not. I had a nasty cut on my leg. Thor, your father, did not want to leave me and stayed behind with me. Within a month, I had recovered and was ready to fight again. This time, I did not want to obey anyone and decided to form my own band. Other Vikings that had stayed behind because of injuries, had, like myself, recovered. I convinced some of them to join me. Your father of course did. In the end, there were some thirty of us altogether. We hired a boat and sailed for Britain."

"What happened then?"

"We hired ourselves to the Prince of Gwynedd. You should ask your father: It is as much his story as mine. But look, we have reached home and I bet our meal is waiting for us."

And so it was.

# CHAPTER 2

Since my uncle left, I have pleaded many times with my father to continue the story but to no avail. Today, he has gone to fetch some ore. He needs it whenever he plans to create anything new. He can manage without, just to do repairs. However, it is not all he wishes to do and, to be truthful, he can always find buyers because his workmanship is good, some say very good indeed. He buys the ore from a mine which is a day's distance from here, up in the hills on the other side of the river and, as we only have one horse, I cannot go with him. The forge is closed and will remain closed tomorrow as well, as the journey entails an overnight stay for my father. As there is no ferocious fire to be kept going, I do not need to spend the day at the forge. Instead, I can stay at home with my mother. The house we live in is more like a farm. It is a big rambling mansion with many rooms around courtyards. We only use one side of it, the animals occupy another and the rest is left to decay. It is certainly an old house, built many generations ago. When I was younger, I used to explore every nook and cranny, getting myself all dusty in the process, to my parents' dismay. My mother has lived here all her life. It was her parents' house.

Today, I spend the day with her, attending to the animals, giving them food, collecting eggs, milking the cow, harvesting a few vegetables. Farmwork is very hard and my father seldom helps my mother. She gets very tired but never complains. I think she is a little afraid of my father. When he is around, she seldom speaks, but today she has been quite chatty, telling me stories about the animals and the plants. Later on, after our evening meal, as we were resting around the grate with a slowly dying fire upon which the dinner was cooked earlier, I asked her what she knew about the house.

"Do you really want to know?" she enquired.

I was not quite sure what answer I was expected to give, so I simply said:

"I do!"

"How far back shall I tell you?"

"As far as you know."

"As any Briton will tell you," she began, "we, who now call ourselves Welsh, were the only people living in this land many, many years ago."

"How many?"

"As long as people had been living here, as the Druids would say. You know what a Druid is, don't you?"

"He is the man who leads your religious ceremonies, who sings and recites poetry."

"Well said!" she paused for a short while, sighed and continued: "A few generations ago, a foreign army overran the land. They were the Romans."

"Are you sure? My uncle fought for the Romans when he was in the East, he told me."

"I'm talking about here, where we live. I don't know what your uncle said. I am not like you, I cannot understand what he says when he speaks. It is a totally foreign language to me."

"My father speaks the same language, don't you understand him?"

"It is the language of the land he comes from. He is in a different country now. I don't see why I should learn to speak his language. Anyway, he has learnt some of mine. He needs to.

After all, many of his clients are Welsh like myself and they would certainly not speak Norse."

"Is that why you and my father hardly speak to each other?"

"There may be a grain of truth in this. As I was saying, the Romans conquered this land with their armies. They also built towns. There was one not too far from here. It was called Castrium. Their leading men built large houses at some distance from their town. This, believe it or not, was originally a Roman villa."

"How did you acquire it?"

"Some generations ago, the Romans left and my ancestors took over this place. It has been in our family ever since, until your father came, that is. He appropriated the forge and settled here."

"What about your family? I remember my grandmother who died a couple of years ago but no one else."

"Well! To continue the story: after the Romans left, came the Saxons who were worse because they killed our menfolk and moved the Britons away from the land they conquered. The Britons and the Saxons have virtually fought each other ever since until about the time of your birth. That is when the Vikings came around and fought on our side."

"So, we saved the day!" I shouted proudly.

My mother looked annoyed.

"You consider yourself a Viking, then?" she said. "But you should remember that British blood runs in your veins too. You're no more a pure Viking than a pure Briton. You're actually a British Viking and you should never forget both your origins."

I did not know what answer to give her. I had spent so much time with my father soaking up the Viking way of life and their Gods, how warriors who die on the field of battle can go to Valhalla and live there happily, that it had not occurred to me until then that there was another side to me, a side I had inherited from my mother. Her people had their own Gods and traditions and I knew very little about it.

"Don't stop! Tell me more!" I said.

"What more is there to tell? That we, as Welsh, lost battle after battle? That the Princes of Powys and Gwynedd could not unite and fight together? Yes, the Vikings came, but the price we had to pay for their help might have been too much."

"What do you mean, too much?"

"Their reward was land and silver and they now live among us."

"But you married one! How can you complain?"

"I was forced to in a way. Do you want to know how it happened? I don't think you are too young to know. Mind you, I'm not sure your father would approve my telling you, but never mind. It all started about three years before I set eyes on your father. The men of Powys were defending their border as best they could. The men of Gwynedd were staying within the confines of theirs. They had not yet been attacked, so they decided to remain neutral. I believe the outcome would have been quite different if they had joined in the fight. Anyway, the Prince of Powys realised he needed help. He had heard about the Vikings hiring their services to one clan and then another in Ireland and so sent for them. With their help, he won a few skirmishes. It is then that the Saxons decided to attack Gwynedd. Every man was called to defend the land. So, my father and my two brothers left to fight in the war."

She stopped for a minute or two while she shed a tear, then continued:

"My younger brother, Gwendwr, was captured and we've never heard from him since. We do not know whether he is still alive, a slave to the Saxons. Thankfully, we do not have slaves like they have. You did not know that, did you, Ap Thor?"

"No, I didn't. Is there any way of knowing his fate now there is peace?" I enquired.

"Do you think that neither my father nor my elder brother ever tried to find out? They did while still in the army, just after peace came. They may both have been hurt but there was no reason why they should not try to find Gwendwr. Their injuries were also the reason why they had not reached home when the Vikings came. No! Don't say a word! Let me explain first and then you can ask me all the questions you want. Where was I? Oh, yes! The war started badly for Gwynedd, but then suddenly out of nowhere a band of Vikings arrived from Ireland and offered their service to our Prince. They were led by a man called Elgar. Yes, the same Elgar who is your uncle. Their offer was accepted and, in exchange for their help, they were told that, when the war was over, they could have any land they wanted provided it was somewhere in between the two rivers. I know these parts where we have lived for generations were under-populated but, nevertheless, it was quite a shock to see them arrive. As you know, the greater part of them settled south of here and built the village of Helsby. A few scattered north and west and the remainder returned to Ireland having taken the Prince's booty instead, your uncle among them."

Gwendwlyn, my mother, stopped deep in thought. I said nothing, I just waited for her to continue:

"At that time, neither your grandmother nor I had heard any news of my father or of my two brothers. We were just two hardworking women who were trying to keep the farm going in the absence of their menfolk. There was little we could have done against any attack and we could even had been dispossessed. One morning, we saw smoke coming out of the building which is now the forge. We thought the Vikings had put fire to it as a prelude to a general attack. We knew they had arrived in the countryside around us a couple of days before. Your grandmother and I decided to make ourselves known, hoping they would spare us and the farm. Imagine our surprise when we saw your father and his brother repairing the building and stoking up the fire. I had never seen a working forge before. Your grandmother remembered it had been used occasionally in her youth, so she realised what was going on. I think that Thor and Elgar were just as surprised to see us as we were to see them.

"I blacksmith. I Thor. He brother. He Elgar." was the way your father introduced himself and his brother, trying as best as he could to speak our language.

"This is our farm and our land," replied your grandmother.

There was a moment of silence when none of us knew what to do or say next. Then Elgar spoke:

"My brother is a very good blacksmith. You have no blacksmith. Let him be your blacksmith. You keep farm."

"Agreed!" said your grandmother and we walked away. I do not think we could have done anything else at the time. Of course, we had hoped our men would return and sort it all out. But, it did not happen. We heard from nobody and we dared not leave in case the farm was stolen from us. What frightened us the most was the number of people who came to have things done at the forge, especially in the beginning when these were only Vikings. After a while however, a few of my compatriots came too. We were able to speak to the latter but none had any news to give us. No one ever came to the farm except for Elgar when he wanted to buy some food. Then, one day, he told us that he was going back to Ireland but that his brother was staying on. And that, my son, is how it happened."

I was not convinced. I needed to question her further:

"Surely, mum, that's not the whole story. You have not told me how you got married to my father nor whether you ever heard from your father and brothers again."

"That's true enough. Let me continue, then. Almost a year had gone by. We were struggling running the farm on our own. There had not been any news of our menfolk. There was no doubt either that Thor was making a huge success of the forge because of his excellent workmanship. The neighbours would only come when they wanted something made at the forge which was not too often. They might then call upon us but otherwise they did not seem to care too much about us. In those circumstances, my father should have been here to arrange my marriage to some suitable farmer. My two brothers should also have been here to keep the farm running smoothly. I as well as your grandmother could see that we were going downhill. There seemed to be only one solution. We discussed it for many an evening. After about a month of deliberations when we could think of no other solution, your grandmother invited Thor to come round and share a meal with us. When he came, he brought with him two small bracelets.

"I made them today," he said as he gave one to each of us.

"Let's sit and eat," your grandmother replied.

"We ate in silence." Gwendwlyn continued her story. "It was not up to me to initiate conversation and your grandmother seemed to waver in the decision we had made. I could not tell whether Thor had guessed the purpose of our invitation. All I could see was that he was enjoying his food. We had not made anything special: just a good, thick stew. At the end of the meal, Thor was the first to speak as best he could in our language which was foreign to him:

"That was a very good stew but I don't think you invited me just to taste your stew."

"No, we did not," your grandmother replied. "My daughter and I have been talking. She has no husband, you have no wife…"

Again, Gwendwlyn paused as if to collect her thoughts before she continued:
"Thor burst out laughing. That was unexpected to us. We could but wait. Then, he spoke:
"I am a very lucky fellow. I have been thinking of saying the very same thing to you for a while but I thought you might have been offended. I did not think you liked me very much. People do not usually like blacksmiths. They say they do when they want something repaired. Otherwise they would not be bothered with us. My grandfather always said so and he was right. He taught me everything I know. I lost a good master when he died."
"Is this why you became a soldier?" your grandmother asked.
"No, not exactly, it's more of my brother's doing. I just followed him here but I'm not as keen as he is about fighting. I preferred to settle down at my trade. That's why I'm here and he's gone."

Gwendwlyn sighed a long deep, thoughtful sigh while looking at the dying fire before continuing:
"The die was cast. Within a week, Thor and I were living together. He used to live at the forge, but he repaired this part of the building where you have always lived and when the job was done, he moved in and I joined him. Nine months later you were born and three months after that my father and my elder brother returned."

# CHAPTER 3

That night I slept badly or rather I found it difficult to fall asleep. Until now, I had not been aware of the differences between my parents. I have always seen them together, going about their respective tasks around the forge, the farm and the home. For me, it was a happy home. I could not imagine any child wanting a better life. My parents were kind and considerate but, as a matter of fact, they now appeared to me to be as different as chalk and cheese. I am sure they both loved me but, did they love each other? My father only speaks of things Viking. My mother prefers to dwell on the traditional way of life of her people. She thinks of my father as a stranger who has come and appropriated the home of her forefathers. I do not think that she has told me the full story. For instance, what happened when her father and brother returned? I do not remember any of them and yet she told me it happened after my birth. Why? Was I too young? My uncle Elgar, in a way, did the same: he only told me part of the story, stopping when he and my father left Ireland. Why could they not bring their stories up to the present day? Are they hiding some big secret from me? I believe so and as I am not a child any more, I think I should therefore be told the truth. How could I find out? Whom should I ask? Or, more to the point, who is more likely to tell me the truth? And what if both tell me a different truth? Whom should I believe? These are difficult questions for a fourteen year-old boy. I kept reminding myself of the conversation with my mother and I just could not sleep. But, in the end, I must have fallen asleep towards the morning for, when I woke up, the sun was high in the sky.

I got up, had something to eat and went looking for my mother. I found her in the fields by some hedges; she was collecting berries.
"Mother," I said, "let me help you."
"No, go and wait for your father."
"I need to ask you a few questions."
"I don't want to answer any questions. Can't you see I'm busy? Anyway, I suppose it concerns what we talked about last night, doesn't it? Well, forget it."
"Why?"
"I don't have to give you a reason. Go and wait for your father!"
I did as I was told. I walked down the road, past the crumbling remains of the uninhabited part of our house, past some fallow fields full of overgrown weeds that had been neglected by us, then I ascended a hillock to my right, on the top of which were a few large stones; some were still standing but a couple had fallen on to their side. Every time my father had been away, on the day he was due to return, I would climb on top of one of those stones and keep a look out for him. Then, as soon as I would see him, I would run down to the road and surprise him. On this occasion, because my mother had sent me away, when I reached my observation spot, it was still early in the day. From my position, I had a good view of the river and of the countryside on either side. I liked that spot. I could feel the wind, see the sun reflected on the water, be aware of the wider world existing beyond the confines of my home. I also liked to watch the sun go down behind the horizon. Usually, the sky would change colour: from blue to pale yellow, ochre and then red. At the same time, I would look towards the south in order to

catch sight of my father riding back from his trip to the mine. I could almost tell when that would be; it would usually happen when only the top half of the sun was still visible over the horizon, giving us just enough light to see us safely home.

Large dark clouds were gathering in the sky, meaning that few stars would be visible. They might also hide the moon, making the night very dark indeed. I began to worry. I could not see my father coming home and the sun had almost entirely disappeared behind the horizon. I could stay no longer. I had never before had to walk home in darkness. I ran down the side of the hillock and reached the road as dusk turned into night. The wind gathered pace. More and more clouds were fleeting across the sky obscuring the moon most of the time. Then, it started to rain. At first, only a few drops, but soon it poured. At the same time, lightning illuminated the sky, followed almost immediately by a loud clap of thunder that reverberated all around me. Fear came over me: I was in the presence of the Gods. What did they want with me? Where was my father? I began to run and did not stop until I reached home, soaked to the skin and out of breath.

"Have you been running alongside your father's horse?" my mother asked.

"My father is not with me," I replied when I was able to recover my breath.

"Not with you?"

"No!"

"Dry yourself first and then eat."

I obeyed immediately. Outside, the storm was gathering pace. When the meal was over, I was the first to speak:

"What do you think has happened? Are the Gods angry?"

"Storms are part of nature. They have nothing to do with the Gods."

"That's not what my father says."

"And you would believe your father, wouldn't you?"

"I believe in my father's Gods, yes. He believes in them, why shouldn't I also?"

My mother sighed before she stated:

"My Gods are in the trees, in the grass, in the plants around us and in the rising sun. I believe in them, why should not you?"

I did not answer. There was a great deal of truth in what she had said. Which were the best Gods? My father's or my mother's? Whom should I believe in? Did they exist side by side? I did not like it when I had to choose between different beliefs. Somehow, I preferred to listen to my father but I also knew it would upset my mother and this made me feel bad. I did not want to be drawn into an argument so, I just kept silent. After a while, I asked her:

"Why don't you tell me what happened after your father and brother returned? We could spend the rest of the evening around the fire like yesterday."

"We could, indeed. But, perhaps, I do not wish to do that."

"Why not?"

"It could be so painful for me to remember. It still hurts inside after all those years but, I suppose, I shan't have peace with you until I tell you. So, I'd better continue the story. This is what they told me: they both had been hurt in battle and had to recover before they could travel. Also, they wanted to find out what had happened to Gwendwr. Let me tell you how it all began. It had been one of those long drawn out battles that lasted more than a day. Neither side could gain an advantage, nor would either side withdraw during the night. This particular battle which both my brothers and my father were involved in lasted for three whole days. The Saxons continuously sent fresh troops in. By the end of the first day, our troops were forced to withdraw a few yards, leaving behind their fallen comrades.

That is when Gwendwr disappeared. The following morning, the battle resumed early on and the Saxons were pushed back. In a lull in the afternoon, my father looked among the dead but could not see Gwendwr. The only possible assumption to make was that he had been taken prisoner. My father then decided to fight alongside his remaining son as fighting started again towards evening. He saw his son being hacked in the legs and fall to the ground. He himself was hurt trying to protect him. Fortunately, the rest of our men moved forwards, allowing my father to drag my brother away from the battlefield. The latter could not use his legs at all. The muscles in his thighs had been cut through and he had lost a lot of blood but had survived. Night again stopped the fighting. At dawn the following day, the two armies stood facing each other but neither wanted to be the first to attack. Towards the end of the morning, the Saxons started to walk away. Our commander thought it prudent not to give the order to attack or pursue. He, however, sent someone with a flag of truce to try and negotiate an exchange of prisoners. The Saxons did not reply. They seldom did. A few days later, our men withdrew to their winter quarters."

Gwendwlyn stopped for a short while before she continued the sad story:

"My brother was too feeble to move and anyway he could not walk. My father collected a few branches, made a kind of stretcher with them, put his son on top and started on the journey back home, pulling it behind him. As he had been hurt himself, he could neither go fast nor without stopping every so often. He soon lost sight of the army as he could not keep up with the men. However, he continued on his journey, begging for food and shelter on the way. A month later, he caught up with them. It was evident that his son would never walk again but my father wanted to find out what has happened to his other son, Gwendwr. So they stayed with the army hoping that some negotiations might be started between the Prince of Gwynedd and the Saxons. It did not happen. At the end of winter, a new campaign started. My father then decided to drag his son home. It took him the whole of the summer. That is why they only arrived back after your birth."

My mother remained silent for some time and I did not know what to say. She was the first to speak again:

"My brother only survived for a few months. He never regained the use of his legs and could only drag himself on the floor of the house. He died during the following winter. As spring came, my father decided to fight again and left me and my mother to rejoin the Prince of Gwynedd's army. We never saw him again. We later learnt that he had been killed during the first battle of the new campaign. That is why you do not remember any of them. You were too young then, just turned two years when he left. That also was to be the last campaign. Since then, the Saxons have kept to their side of Offa's Dyke and we have enjoyed over ten years of peace."

The fire in the grate had almost died but it still gave enough light for me to see a few tears roll down my mother's cheeks. I said goodnight and went to bed. The following day I made myself scarce, going early to that hillock from which I could look out for my father. The road was full of puddles, but the rain had stopped. It was still fairly windy: I could see ripples on the surface of the river. It was difficult to tell the time as the sun had not made an appearance. The clouds were not so low-lying as they had been the day before, and, so far, the rain had held off. My mind, however, was rather devoid of thoughts as I looked blankly ahead of me while sitting upon my usual stone when, suddenly, I saw something moving from the direction of the south. I ran down to the road. It was my father!

I felt glad, relieved and elated all at the same time. I could also see there were two large bags hanging on either side of the horse. They were filled to the brim. A third one laid on top of them across the back of the horse with my father sitting behind it. As soon as he saw me, he reined in his horse, jumped down and holding the bridle he walked alongside his mount. I ran towards him.

"Steady!" he said. "You'll frighten the horse."

"I expected you yesterday. You don't usually bring back so much material, do you? Is this why you're a day late."

"So many questions! No, I don't usually buy that much in one trip but war has started again. There were many people at the mine, I had to wait my turn. I also bought more ore than usual as there's bound to be a demand for swords. Tomorrow, we'll make a few and I expect you to help me. You'd like that, wouldn't you?"

"Of course! But," I asked, "will you go to war?"

"No! I am needed here as a blacksmith. Other people, younger than I, may go if they wish."

"Like me, you mean."

"You're too young. Anyway, you have no experience."

"Father, you showed me how to handle a sword and how to hold a shield and we have had a few mock fights."

"I know, but that is not enough, not against the Saxons."

We walked the rest of the way in silence right to the forge. Once there, we dropped the three bags of ore and took the horse to the stable before we made tracks to the house where my mother and our dinner were waiting. No words were exchanged even then. We just ate and I went to bed early.

The following morning, my father woke me up at the crack of dawn.

"We have plenty to do today," he said and, almost as an afterthought, he added: "You've got to get used to an early start if you want to become a soldier."

I jumped out of bed and followed my father outside. He had mentioned the magic word 'soldier' and I was all for it. We started the fire, cleaned the water tank and filled it with clean water from the well. We prepared the mould and heated up the ore. A few hours later, the first sword was receiving the final hammering, followed by sharpening with a stone. All the time, we just worked and did not speak. I liked it that way when we worked and sweated together, my father and I, and I was happy. When the first sword was finished, I could not help myself. I grabbed it and made fighting gestures with it, thrusting forward, slicing sideways. My father said nothing. He did not try to stop me either. When I eventually stopped, slightly out of breath and with a large smile on my face, he said to me:

"You have the making of a warrior. I do think that, when you are old enough to fight, you will make us Vikings proud."

I felt like walking on air for the rest of the day.

# CHAPTER 4

A few months later, at the beginning of winter, my uncle Elgar again paid us a visit. He had been in the thick of the fighting that had lasted all summer between the armies of the Prince of Gwynned and the King of Northumbria. Gwynedd is where we live and I am glad that my uncle had been fighting for us. Northumbria is the Saxon Kingdom to the North-East of us. On his first night home, we were all sitting down to a meal. My uncle had caught a couple of rabbits on his way and had given them to my mother. Therefore, the meal consisted of rabbit stew. Stew seemed to be the only meal my mother knew how to cook. Usually, it was just vegetable stew with the odd ground grain added in it to thicken it. I ate little because rabbit is not my favourite. Meals are usually eaten in silence and I hoped that, tonight, it would not be too long before we had finished and I could chat to my uncle. I was desperate to talk with him: I wanted details of his recent fighting, what it has been like, but, also, I was hoping he would continue the talk from last time and that I would learn more about his and my father's past. I had tried to get my father to be more open about his past and to continue Elgar's story which, as the latter had said, was as much his story as my father's but to no avail. In answer to such a request, the reply was:

"Let's concentrate on our work, let's not talk."

As my father liked to eat his meals in silence, my mother and I usually conformed to the mealtime ritual. Therefore, I was very surprised when, half way through the meal, my father asked his brother:

"Is the war over?"

"Far from it!" my uncle answered. "It is only a lull during the winter. Both sides need to regroup and recuperate. There has been some fierce fighting during the autumn, even worse than during the summer. There will be a need for more men when fighting restarts in earnest next spring."

"May I come?" I asked.

"You're too young," my father replied.

"I want to be a warrior like my uncle and like you were, dad."

"I know. Your day will come, son. But, for the present, you help me at the forge."

"Is it so busy that you need his help?" Elgar enquired of my father.

"Don't try to encourage the boy!"

"I'm not. For one thing, he needs training. What kind have you given him so far, Thor?"

"How to hold a sword correctly."

"Not much of a training, then!"

"I could show you tomorrow," I said.

My mother was trying to follow what we were saying but I doubted she could really understand. So, I spoke in Welsh to her:

"Uncle is offering to train me as a soldier."

"Is it what you really want?"

"Yes, mum!"

"What are you two talking about?" interrupted my father. "I told you many times before not to talk Welsh in front of me."

"Surely, there's no harm in that," said Elgar. "Your wife has a right to have her say in your son's future. I wish I could speak both Norse and Welsh as your son does. It does not make him less of a Viking."

My father gave no answer and after a short silence, Elgar continued:

"Whether this young man here goes to war next year, the year after or the year after that, it is never too soon to start proper training and this is what I suggest: I will not be staying here. I have decided to spend the winter in Ireland. I want to meet Eldred again and some of my former comrades. I hope that some of them will follow me when I return. I shall probably be spending most of my time in Dublin. Ap Thor, here, should come with me. We, soldiers, have to keep fit and exercise. Your son should join us. It would be the best training he could possibly get. He would be totally immersed in the Viking way of life. That's what you want for him, isn't it, brother?"

"Of course!"

"That's settled then," Elgar decided bluntly. "We'll say no more about it: nephew, you're coming with me!"

Two days later, we were on our way. I had never been on a boat before. It felt strange. There was a slight rocking movement. We were seated in rows. There was an oar in front of us. I was sitting on my uncle's right next to the side of the ship. My uncle grabbed the oar and told me to do the same. We pushed it out against the river bank and the boat slowly moved into the river stream. We were on our way. An order was barked out, which I did not understand. The oars splashed into the water. We had to row. It was hard work but my uncle did not seem to mind. After a while, he whispered to me:

"How are you doing?"

"I'm fine," I whispered back.

"Be ready!"

"For what?"

Before my uncle could answer, the boat rocked violently. We had reached the sea. The sail was hoisted but we continued to row. We wanted to make good progress. As night fell, we made for some cove and spent the night on board the ship. The following day we reached Ireland. I felt tired, hungry and cold as we disembarked. I was used to the quiet of the countryside and I was taken aback by the crowds of people that were around us. My uncle did not seem to mind the bustle and forced his way ahead, with me following behind as best as I could. Eventually, we stopped and entered a house. It was smoky inside but warmer. There was a big fire in the middle of the room with a cauldron on top of it. My uncle walked up to a big woman in one of the corners of the room while I could not resist staying by the fire. I saw my uncle give something to the woman and receive a couple of bowls in exchange. When he joined me, he handed one of the bowls to me and said:

"Fill it up!"

I did not understand what he meant but I saw him pick up a ladle and pour himself food out of the cauldron into his bowl. I did the same. On one side of the room was a table with a couple of rickety benches. We sat there and ate in silence. The warmth of the watery concoction that passed for a meal soon had me feeling better.

"What is this place?" I asked my uncle.

"Dublin, where we're going to spend this winter."

"I mean this house."

"This is where we're staying: We'll sleep in the room next door and have our meals in this one."

"And the other people?" I whispered to my uncle.

He laughed.

"This is a public house where travellers eat and sleep together. I see, Ap Thor, there are many things you need to learn."

"I thought I was going to learn how to fight," I said, rather downhearted.

"Did you expect a military camp?"

"Yes!"

"You're not ready for that yet and I have seen enough of them. For me, this is something of a holiday. Believe me, you will get plenty of exercise, meet people, become a man. I assure you, you will not get bored."

"But, we'll stay together, won't we?"

"Not all the time! You will have to learn to fend for yourself, make your own friends. Oh! Please! Don't look so despondent! You wanted adventure, you're getting it. Don't complain!"

I looked around, it was not as I had imagined it. For a start, I felt there was not a single person in that room that I could befriend. As the evening wore on, I observed more people walking in, sitting down and eating. They were all talking at the same time. The noise and the heat combined with the tiredness I was feeling after two days at sea made me fall asleep at the table.

I woke up late the following morning and found myself lying on some straw. There was nobody around. I got up, picked up my sword, which I found had been laid next to me and walked to the other room. The fat lady was still sitting in her corner. The fire in the centre of the room was still giving up vast amounts of smoke with the same cauldron on top of it.

"Eh! Sleepy child! Elgar will be back later," the fat lady shouted from her corner. "Come and get your bowl!"

I walked to her, picked up the bowl and noticed that there was a piece of very dark, almost black, bread at the bottom.

"Is that my breakfast?" I enquired.

"Top it up with stew from the cauldron!"

"How do you know my uncle's name?"

"Elgar always stays here when in town."

"Did he say when he'll be back?"

"You never ask that question of Elgar: he's a law unto himself. Now, be a good boy, go and eat and let me be."

There was little I could do but retreat with my bowl. I very much resented having been called child and boy. I hurriedly ate my breakfast and made my way to the door. Before I could get out, the fat lady in the corner shouted at me:

"Did Elgar tell you my name?"

"No, he didn't."

"I'm Grunhelda. Are you going out?"

"I'm not staying here."

"Please yourself! But if you get lost, ask for Grunhelda's place. Everybody knows Grunhelda's place."

"Thanks," I replied and went out. The air was crisp but there was a foul smell about. I could see the sun high up in the sky and I worked out that it must have been around the middle of the day. I walked straight ahead. I thought there was thus less chance of my getting lost as, upon my return, I should be able to retrace my steps in the same straight line, except that the road forked here and there. All the time, I was looking around me at the strange sights. I had been to Helsby a few times with my father or mother but it was a small place, nothing to compare to Dublin. People were shouting, trying to sell various wares or food. I ignored those. At last, I reached the edge of town. A few feet past the last house stood a small young man, dressed in a cloak right down to his feet. He did not look like a Viking. He, too, was shouting in spite that he did not seem to have anything to sell. As I came closer, I realised he was shouting in Norse with a strong foreign accent. He was repeating the same sentence over and over again:

"Listen to the voice of the true God."

Nobody was stopping. I did not either but I did wonder what else he would have said if anyone had stopped. The reason I did not stop was because I had caught sight of a field full of Viking warriors fighting each other. I, at once, thought that it must be one of the exercise grounds my uncle spoke about and where, he had said, I would get my training with him. So, I decided to have a closer look. It was a fairly large ground covered with trampled grass. To one side was a huge boulder towards which I made my way and, leaning against it, I watched the men fight.

"You should not just be standing there watching," an elderly man suddenly said to me. "If you're looking for a partner, I'm your man."

"Actually," I said, and I knew I was lying, "I'm waiting for my uncle."

"I'm looking for someone to partner me. Why don't you until he comes?"

I assented and we both drew our swords. At the beginning, we were exchanging blows like my father had taught me. Soon, however, it became more challenging. For a while, I managed to hold my own but I had a deep suspicion that I was going to be beaten. He was moving his arm faster and faster. Suddenly, he made a kind of circular move and my sword went flying into the air. As soon as it fell to the ground, as I was bending down to pick it up, he put his foot on it and said:

"This is mine."

"No, it is my sword."

"You just lost it."

"You wanted me to partner you. You said nothing about me losing my sword to you."

Our argument was beginning to attract a crowd. I could not possibly give in. Before I could say anything else, he gave me a strong push that nearly had me flying and then, he picked up my sword. I was getting angry.

"This is my sword," I said. "I made it myself."

There were some guffaws from the crowd. He was now showing off by asking me:

"What do you mean, made it yourself?"

"My father is a blacksmith and taught me how to cast a sword."

"And you cast your own sword, little blacksmith!"

The crowd roared with laughter.

"Give me back my sword," I said as firmly as I could.

"No! Let's see if you're as bad a blacksmith as you are a warrior." And with these words, he raised my sword as high as he could and with the maximum force, he struck the stone with it. My sword did not break. It actually cut through the stone and remained wedged in. The crowd became silent. My former partner tried to pull it out but could not.

"Well!" he said, "it looks like the stone has got your sword instead of me. You'll just have to make another one."

I went to get hold of my sword in the hope I could retrieve it. Seeing this, the crowd that had begun to disperse, turned round and came back to watch. I could hear them cracking jokes at my expense and renewed laughter. I, on the other hand, was applying a trick that my father had taught me: he always added flexibility in the manufacture of a sword. This, he said, would make it more resilient and less likely to break. Also, if it were to get stuck into something, by slightly shaking it, it should disengage itself. I could feel it moving ever so slightly. I was concentrating so much I had not noticed that a tall and heavily built Viking with naked arms full of battle scars and armlets, and with a heavy mane of shoulder-long hair that was beginning to turn grey, was approaching me. He tapped me on the shoulder and said:

"You're wasting your time."

"With Odin's help, I shall get my own sword back."

Hearing those words, the crowd roared with laughter while I, realising I was beginning to succeed in my endeavours, gave a strong tug that released my sword and almost hit the big fellow on the nose in the process. There was total silence as I was standing there, motionless, with the point of my sword less than an inch from the tip of his nose. He was the first to speak:

"Are you challenging me? Do you know who I am?'

"No, I am not challenging you and no, I do not know who you are."

With those words, I put my sword back in its scabbard and expected some reaction from the crowd. There was none. I began to worry.

"Wise move!" said the big fellow. "My name is Eldred."

"My uncle is looking for you," I replied.

"Big Deal! You found me instead."

"Elgar's my uncle's name. He had fought alongside you. He and his brother, Thor, my father, have sailed on your boats from Ejksberg. Surely, you remember them?"

"Elgar! Of course, I do! So, he's back in Dublin, is he? Where is he staying?"

"At Grunhelda's place!"

"Of course, I should have guessed. He can't keep away from that woman." And seeing the surprise on my face, he added: "She was quite beautiful when she was younger. She had a lot of admirers then but, after the birth of her son, she started to take less care of herself. Some said he's Elgar's but it was always denied and, to tell the truth, his father could be any of a number of men, some still alive and others dead. Let's not go there. Tell your uncle to meet me here tomorrow morning. I'll be glad to see the old swine again and tell him from me he'd better keep the appointment for I'll soon be gone."

"I'll tell him."

"What's your name?"

"Ap Thor!"

"Funny name for a Viking, that!"

He walked away. The crowd had dispersed long ago and I found myself alone again. It was time to make tracks. I walked towards the town and passed that young man who was still shouting:

"Listen to the voice of the true God."

Then, I lost my way. I had to ask for directions. The first person I talked to, replied:

"You don't want to go there. It's no place for a young man."

A bit further along, I came upon a couple of elderly warriors and decided to ask them. They looked at me in a strange way.

"Why?" one of them asked.

"Because that's where I"m staying with my uncle."

"Really! What's your uncle's name?"

"Elgar!"

"Not Grunhelda's Elgar by any chance?" enquired the other.

"Yes!" I said, remembering what Eldred had said about the two of them.

"Then, you'd better come with us!"

Some ten minutes later, all three of us were walking into Grunhelda's place. I walked straight to her in her corner and asked for a bowl. At the same time, I took a good look at her as I had been intrigued by what Eldred had said about her. I must have stared, because she snarled:

"What are you looking at?"

"Nothing!" I said, taking the bowl and walking away.

As the two warriors were following me for their bowls, she asked them:

"What have you told the boy about me?"

"Nothing!" they said in unison.

"Don't tell me that! Liars! Get out of my sight!"

As the two warriors sat by me at the communal table, one of them asked:

"What's up with her?"

"Are you staying here?" I asked "I don't remember you from last night."

"I don't think you remember anything from last night, do you?" said the other fellow.

"You were fast asleep when we came in," added the first.

"Oh!" I replied. "I think I was dog tired."

The inn was beginning to fill up. People knew each other and talk and laughter filled the room. I was being left alone. After a while, I felt sleepy like the night before. I tried to keep awake, expecting to see my uncle walk through the door any minute. He did not, I gave up waiting for him. I just went next door, lay down on some straw and fell asleep.

# CHAPTER 5

A rather loud noise was waking me up. I did not want to open my eyes but, seeing daylight around me, I forced myself to get up, that is when I recognised the noise: it was heavy snoring. It came from the only other body in the room, some distance from me. I moved to the other room and asked Grunhelda in her corner whether she knew where my uncle was.

"Can't you hear him?" she answered.

"That's him who snores?"

"You're spot on!"

"I need to wake him up."

"You'll need your sword for that."

"What do you mean?"

"The only way to wake him up is to prod him with the tip of your sword but be careful: stand away when he wakes up."

"Why?"

"He might run you through with his own sword thinking he's being attacked." Her words were followed with a burst of laughter that made her whole body shake. I was beginning to hate that woman. She never seemed to have a kind word for anyone. She was always surly and sort of aggressive. I did not give her an answer but went back into the sleeping quarters, stood over my uncle and prodded him with my foot.

"Let me sleep!' he said.

"I can't. Eldred is waiting for you."

"Where?" he asked, jumping up.

"At the exercise field!"

"When?"

"This morning!"

"Have you had your breakfast?" he asked me as we walked out of the sleeping quarters.

"No!"

"Two bowls!" he barked at Grunhelda. "And why couldn't you wake me up instead of sending my nephew? Why did you let Eldred get away?"

"What has Eldred to do with it?" she asked.

"Uncle!" I said as I tried to interrupt.

"Shut up! I'm talking to Grunhelda."

"What nonsense are you talking about, Elgar? You know Eldred would never come here."

"I saw Eldred yesterday and told him you wanted to see him," I finally managed to say.

"Appie! How did you recognise him?"

Appie was a nickname he sometimes used when he was talking to me. I never knew what to make of it. I hoped it was kind of affectionate.

"There, Elgar, you were blaming me. You have not changed in all the years I've known you. Always blaming Grunhelda! Grunhelda is wrong, always wrong with you. I don't know why I'm putting up with you. I really should bar you. This is a respectable establishment…"

Elgar interrupted her with a laugh, then he said, "you can't forget me, that's why."

"Don't flatter yourself!"

"Then, it's my money."

"What's up with you two?" I interrupted.

"None of your damn business!" they both said at the same time. Then, they burst laughing. I was disconcerted. I ate my breakfast in silence and so did Elgar. When he had finished, he got up and, as I did not move, said:

"Are you coming?"

I followed him outside. He walked fast and I had difficulty keeping pace. Neither of us spoke until we nearly reached the exercise field.

"You never told me how you recognised Eldred but it shows courage to have spoken to him. Others would not. I am proud of you."

Before I could reply, someone in the crowd shouted: "Are you going to fight the stone again today?"

I turned crimson and my uncle looked at me quizzically.

"What have you been up to?" he asked but, before I could answer, someone shouted his name in a booming voice. It was Eldred.

The two men embraced with much slapping of backs. Eldred was the first to speak:

"Elgar! It's been too long. What have you been doing all these years? Don't tell me! Fighting and fighting and fighting. I heard the Saxons and the Welsh are at it again. Did you get much booty? Spent it all, I suppose. It would be just like you! And what about this young man? Did you not teach him to have proper respect for his elders? He nearly cut the tip of my nose yesterday. Oh, from the look on your face, I can see he has not told you. Well, let us not stay here. Drinks are what we need. Come on, I know just the place."

They started to walk and I followed them, but Eldred would have none of it. He turned round and said:

"It's going to be men's talk. You stay here and exercise."

A group of men were doing exercises but not actually fighting. I joined them. I could not really understand what they were doing but I was trying my best to imitate them. After a while, the one who seemed to be their leader, said to me:

"You've never been on a battlefield, have you?"

"No. I haven't. How can you tell?"

"These are manoeuvres. We've never seen you before. Where do you come from?"

"My uncle brought me here. I was supposed to train with him but he keeps spending time with mates of his."

"What's your name?"

"Ap Thor!"

"I've never hear Ap before. What kind of name is that?"

"It means son of. It's Welsh."

"If you're Welsh, what are you doing here?"

"My father is a Viking like you. I consider myself a Viking too."

"You can stay for today. Actually, we need someone for practising with the sword to make up a full team. I hope you know how to handle yourself."

"I do!" I said firmly and fully convinced I could hold my own. However, I was not prepared for what happened next. We split into two groups facing each other, drew our swords and a kind of mock battle began. I was hemmed in between two burly veterans and the man facing me, while still young, looked battle weary. I did my best. I sweated in spite of the cold air. I grew tired, yet nobody else seemed so. It was a relief when the leader shouted for us to stop.

"We're going for a run," he said, "are you joining us?"

"I don't think I could run," I said, trying to catch up my breath.

"If it had been a real battle, you'd probably be dead by now, and if it was a rout, you could not run to save your life. You've got a lot to learn still."

And with those words ringing in my years, they ran away, showing no sign of tiredness. As for me, I dragged my poor, aching body all the way back to Grunhelda's place. Once there, I went straight to the second room, fell down on the straw and into a deep sleep in spite of the fact that it was only the middle of the afternoon.

When I woke up the following day, most of the sleepers had gone out. I felt very hungry and went straight for a bowl.

"Fill it up!" said Grunhelda. "Then, come back and sit by me. I need to know something."

I did as I was told, sat myself as comfortably as I could and began to eat.

"Why did you come to Dublin?" she asked.

I continued to eat. She grew impatient:

"Why don't you answer me?"

"I don't think I quite know the answer."

"Is Elgar really your uncle?"

"Of course, he is my uncle. What kind of question is that?"

"I don't think I know your name. I heard Elgar calling you Appie but that can't be your name. It doesn't sound Viking."

"How can you tell?"

"I'm a Viking through and through. I came over here with my brother even before this town existed. He was one of the first to die. I had to make a living as best as I could. Many Vikings wanted me. I accepted them all as I could not choose one. I liked drinking, still do. Men want women and I was available. Mind you, I enjoyed it. They also looked after me. They built me this house and they still call on me. Surely, Elgar told you all that."

"No, he did not, but Eldred did."

"Eldred! That was a man!"

"He's called the Avenger. Why?"

"Do you know Eldred or don't you?"

"I know that my father and uncle came on his boats and fought under him, but I only met the man a couple of days ago."

"When Elgar introduced you to him?"

"No, when I nearly cut the tip of his nose."

"You, what?"

"It was an accident. I never meant to hurt him."

One of the guests, who was waiting for Grunhelda to give him a bowl so he could have his breakfast, interrupted by asking me:

"Are you the young lad who pulled his sword out of the stone?

"I am," I said simply, wondering how he could have known.

"What now? What have you been up to?" enquired Grunhelda, who did not seem pleased by the interruption. She threw a bowl at the guest and told him: "Leave us alone."

The guest took no notice as he addressed me:

"That was quite a feat! I had no idea that you were staying here."

"Get lost!" Grunhelda growled and this time the guest moved away.

"There's nothing to it," I said and told her everything as it happened, concluding, "now, it's your turn. Tell me why Eldred is called the Avenger."

"Nobody speaks to me like that! I say what I want to say and no more. Elgar and I have come a long way together and you should show me the same respect that you show your uncle."

"Why? Because of your son?"

She became livid with rage and shouted: "Get out of my sight!"

I ran out of the house and bumped into my uncle. He was drunk. I took him by the arm and led him away. I was unhappy with him. I needed answers. He had cared very little for me since we had arrived. His present behaviour was so different to what I was accustomed to when we were at home that I needed to know why. I had no idea where we were going. All I wanted was for him to sober up and answer my questions. I was in for a surprise for, suddenly, he pulled me into a house. Inside were men drinking and half-naked women sitting on their laps.

"Come on, Appie," he said, "it's time for you to become a man."

"I am a man."

"If you say so, but I doubt it. At least, have a drink with me."

"Why not? But, we talk, man to man, agreed?"

"Are you picking a quarrel with me?"

"I have many reasons to pick a quarrel with you."

"Appie, do you know how we, Vikings, settle quarrels? With the sword! Are you ready to fight me?"

"Uncle! What's the matter with you?"

"Can't you see? I'm pissed out of my brains."

I walked out, leaving my drink unfinished. To my surprise, he followed me.

"Come back in!" he said.

"No!" I replied firmly. "Not when you're in that state!"

"I'm a soldier. That's what soldiers do: they fight and drink and bed women. You want to be a soldier, you do the same."

"Is that why my father never goes to war with you? Is that the way my father expects you to train me?"

"No, it's the Viking way. But you're not a true Viking, are you?"

Those last words cut me to the quick and I walked away. He went back inside. I now was in a dilemma: I could either stand my ground and find myself alone in a strange city or give in and get drunk with my uncle. I was also angry with myself for both Grunhelda and Elgar getting the better of me that morning. I needed to work out my frustration. Unconsciously, my steps had been taking me in the direction of the exercise field. I only realised it when I heard the same young man I had seen before, shouting:

"Listen to the voice of the true God."

I stopped for a fraction of a second before continuing on my way. I became aware, however, that as I did so, he smiled at me. I was not in a mood to listen to what might turn out to be nothing but rantings and, in my state, I would probably have picked a quarrel with him. If he was some kind of priest, I needed to show him respect like my mother told me to always show respect to the Druids, even if I did not follow their religion. In no time at all, I reached the field. To my surprise, Eldred was there. He was talking and everyone was listening:

"...and a time for peace. I have fought many battles and so have many of you. Some have followed me and most of you have seen many good men die. Those have gone to Valhalla. I have not been so lucky. I bear the scars of many cuts but Odin has been a good protector. We, Vikings, are travellers, fighters and settlers and I think it is time for me to become a settler. Not here, not in Ireland. Fellow Vikings have discovered the islands of Eisland and Groendland. They are ours for the taking without the need for fighting as they have been found to be uninhabited. We are even told there are more islands still to be discovered to the West of them. I am going and anyone of you is welcome to join me. Bring women with you too, they will be needed to keep the fires burning in our hearths. My boat sails the day after tomorrow. For those who do not wish to come, it's goodbye.

You will probably enjoy peace with your neighbours now but, if you want fighting, you will need to go over to Britain and hire yourself to the Welsh Princes in the defence of their lands against the encroaching Saxons. I have said my piece, let Odin protect you all."

There was silence for a while. One of the Vikings standing close to me said:

"This is the end of an era."

A few grunts of approval echoed his words. I felt bold enough to ask him:

"How?"

He turned towards me, looked me up and down and said:

"You're too young to understand. Do you even know who he is?"

"I do! He's Eldred whom some have called the Avenger. My uncle has fought alongside him."

"Where is your uncle now?"

"Drinking in some tavern."

"Shame on him! He should be here with us. I'm going to that Eisland. Life here is not what it used to be. Will your uncle be going? Will you be going?"

"More to the point," said an old man, "what's your uncle's name?"

"Elgar!"

"Elgar the Drunkard!" exclaimed the old man. "We should not be surprised!"

I was disconcerted by this remark. A few days ago, I would have been angered if anyone had so called my uncle but, now, I was too painfully aware he was speaking the truth. His behaviour over the last couple of days had been such a big disappointment to me.

"And who is your father?" Asked the old man.

"Thor!" I said.

"Don't know him. Is he with you?"

"No! But tell me: How did Eldred acquire the name of the Avenger?"

"Has nobody told you?"

"No!"

"Quite simple, really. When we first came here all the Irish clans were fighting each other. There was money to be made and booty to get by hiring ourselves to this or that chieftain. To complicate matters, some clans were Christian and some worshipped the sun. Usually, a Christian clan would be fighting a pagan one. It turned out that we, Vikings, were being hired by the Christians and, thanks to our help, they won. Some of the losing clans crossed the sea into Britain while others submitted to the victors. The result was peace but not for long as a few rebellions started. As long as it was purely an Irish affair, we did not intervene. However, when the rebels started killing Vikings, Eldred did not wait any longer. He recruited a few men and wherever a Viking had been killed, he destroyed the nearest village, killing the inhabitants and moving on to the next. He did a full sweep of the country. That's when he acquired his nickname."

"Thanks!" I said.

"That's not all," continued the old man. "The clans started fighting each other again and we, Vikings, got hired again. Only this time, Eldred had acquired such a reputation that, if any chieftain would hire him, his opponent would sue for peace and refuse to carry on fighting. Within a few months, nobody dared attack anybody. Fortunately, the Welsh called for our help as they were once more attacked by the Saxons. And that, young man, is the full story."

"Thank you! I'm so glad that someone has, at last, told me what I was dying to know for so long."

"So, do you have any plans?"

"For today? I was only thinking of training here."

"With whom?"

"Whoever is willing to partner me."

"Will I do?"

A broad smile came across my face. We drew our swords. I was no match for him but he did not try to take advantage. Instead, he gave me advice, suggested moves and showed a great deal of patience. We stopped now and then to rest for a few minutes before raising our swords again until evening came. He was the first to call it a day:

"Thank you for a wonderful day. There is a lot of potential in you. Fighting is not all brawn. Use your brains sometimes. Try and guess what your adversary is going to do. Change your tactics. Don't handle your sword in always the same way. Confuse your opponent. This will help you to stay alive. Now, shall we walk back to town together?"

"I'd be delighted. I'm ever so grateful to you for sharing your knowledge with me."

"Don't mention it! I won't see you again because I'm going with Eldred. Also, you should be with people of your own age. I know of a young man who would be the ideal companion for you: He is called Grunwald. I admit he is mischievous but also wise beyond his years, probably because of his mother. I have not seen him for a while but he's around, I'm sure. Tomorrow, go to his mother's place and stand your ground firmly until you see him. Don't take any notice of her shouting for she'll probably shout at you. She does it to everybody all the time. Her name is Grunhelda. She runs an inn. Just ask for Grunhelda's place. It's further down this street but here is my house so, I must say goodbye."

# CHAPTER 6

More than half the day had already gone by and I was still sitting in the same position at the table that I had occupied since breakfast time. People might think I was waiting for my uncle who, by the way, did not return last night but it was not so. Instead, I was looking at every person that went in or out hoping to see one who would be young enough to be Grunhelda's son. The suggestion that I should make friends with him, given me the day before, had taken hold of me. Of course, the best course of action would have been to ask Grunhelda to introduce me to her son but, somehow, I could not find the courage to do so. My uncle might have helped out but he had not yet returned and, after yesterday's argument, I could not be sure whether he would accept to act as a go-between. I also felt a bit guilty in the way I had reacted towards him. I think it was because his behaviour had taken me by surprise. This was so unlike him back home. It was as if I did not know him at all.

Grunhelda was unusually quiet. I had not heard her shouting at anybody that day, nor had she said anything to me for staying on alone with her in the room. This should have encouraged me to approach her but it did not. Instead, realising it was nearly the middle of the afternoon, I opted for an early meal. My bowl was still in front of me. I went to the cauldron and filled it up. It was cosy and warm by the fire if rather smoky. As I stood there, basking in the warmth, Grunhelda spoke:

"Early dinner?"

"Can I ask for your advice?" I said as I walked towards her and sat on a nearby stool.

"What is troubling you?"

"Many things!"

"Such as? Let me guess: Your uncle's absence must be one. I'm right, am I not?"

"I walked out on him, making it plain I did not approve of his behaviour."

"What has he done now?"

"He took me for a drink to a place with half-naked women."

Grunhelda burst out laughing with that kind of laugh I had seen once before when her whole body was shaking. When she recovered, she said:

"I bet he thought he was doing you a favour."

"How so?"

As she looked up at me. Her eyes were gazing directly into mine. They were a beautiful shade of blue. She smiled and her smile for once was kind. At that moment, I realised she must indeed have been beautiful in her youth as people said she was.

"No! He should not have!" she said and added: "But that's Elgar for you! And you're still young, very young, aren't you?"

"I'm nearly sixteen."

"What made you come here with your uncle at such a young age?"

"I want to become a warrior, not to be a blacksmith all my life like my father."

She burst out laughing again, then exclaimed:

"Elgar's brother a blacksmith! Who would have thought? Wait a minute! Has your father ever been in Eldred's band of men? I think I recall there was a blacksmith in that band. Quite a peculiar fellow! Staying quiet, always overshadowed by someone else. What's your father's name?"

"Thor."

"Does not ring a bell!"

"My father did come with Eldred and my uncle. Was he ever one of your admirers?"

"Steady! You're getting too personal now. Anyway, who told you about admirers?"

"I was told you had plenty and that both Eldred and my uncle were among them, weren't they?"

"I suppose Elgar has babbled about me. What did he say? Don't be shy, tell me!"

"He has not, actually. Eldred is the one who babbled."

"Oh! I would have thought he would have completely forgotten about me."

"Apparently not!"

"Anyway, how is it you're such good pals with Eldred?"

"We are not. Anyway, he's leaving tomorrow."

"Where to?"

"I'm not quite sure. Eisland or Groendland."

"No! I know that quite a few people are going. This town is emptying as the weeks go by but I would never have thought that Eldred would follow that trend. I'm not happy about it, not happy at all."

"Why?"

"Mind your own business!"

"As you wish! I have, however, been pondering all day about a question I'd like to ask you. I've come here because my uncle said I could get a decent military training for when eventually my father would let me go fighting. Elgar, as you can see for yourself, has virtually abandoned me."

"And you think I can solve your problem? Am I your nanny?"

"No! You've misunderstood me. Let me finish. I went to the exercise field and managed to find partners but I also got into scrapes. Yesterday, I got a decent old man. When he had finished, he said I should find a companion of my own age."

"That's very sensible advice."

"He suggested your son, Grunwald."

She did not answer but looked at me in a way that made me feel very uncomfortable, all the more so because it was not the reaction I was expecting. The old man did warn me that she would probably shout at me but that I should stand my ground. It did not happen that way. She did not shout, but her silence could be more terrifying. I still had some food left in my bowl, so I decided to finish it. It gave me a reason for not looking at her. Having done so, I was on the point of getting up to get some more, when she spoke:

"You're incredible! Absolutely incredible!"

"What have I done now?" I asked, still unable to make out whether she was angry or not.

"You're so gullible I cannot be angry with you."

"I don't understand."

"I don't allow people to mention my son to me."

"Why?"

She emitted a brief, mocking laugh but said nothing.

"Is he dead?" I asked, as I could not think of any other reason for her attitude, and added: "If he is, I'm sorry to have mentioned him."

"He's alive and well and I'm very proud of him. However, I like people to keep out of my business. Surely, you must have heard stories about me. I do not like my past to be thrown back in my face, especially where my son is concerned."

"But you've done nothing wrong, have you?"

"Is that what you think? Then, surely, you don't know the full sorry story."

"Tell me!"

"Refill your bowl and promise me not to interrupt."

"I promise," I said as I got up. I hurried to the cauldron and back again because I was afraid she would change her mind and also because I was very curious to learn more about her life. As soon as I sat back next to her, she began:

"When I was about two years older than you are now, a man, back in Norway, fancied me, in fact he had an obsession for me. I could not stand him. I wanted to have nothing to do with him. My parents told me that I had no choice but to go and live with him. I refused. One of my brothers who was planning to leave for these shores offered to take me with him. I was glad of this escape route. I had to dress as a man and join the others in rowing the boat but I did not mind. I was soon found out. What could be done when I was far out to sea? Nothing! Also, my brother would not have me returned. So, nothing more was said and once we landed, I followed him as he fought here and there until he was killed. It was about the time when this settlement was being created. People were saying I was beautiful. It made me more welcome. Then came Eldred and his band of men. I felt attracted to Eldred but he made it plain that, if I wanted to be with him, I would have to share him with his men. I was young. I had never felt anything like it towards any man before, so I accepted his conditions. They were all heavy drinkers and I joined in their bouts. It also helped with this kind of life. I travelled the length and breadth of the country with them as they hired their service to this or that chieftain. Between the fighting, we always came back here, to Dublin, for more drinking and revelling. How I loved that life! I was never alone. There was always someone in my bed. You need not look at me like that! One day, you will enjoy women too! A couple of years went by, I was getting more drunk every day, and the more drunk I was, the more I craved men. Then I became pregnant.

By whom, I don't know. As soon as he heard about it, Eldred's attitude changed: from sharing me with his men, he now wanted me for himself only. He said he would care for the child but I would have to do as he told me. He would have been a good father to Grunwald but I was young. I liked the life of drinking and being wanted. So, I refused. He told me to stay away from him and his men. I was shocked but so were they and Elgar even more so. Elgar would have made the worst father ever and I told him so. I also told him I did not have a clue as to who among them was the real father. He could have been anyone of them. They would all have to accept this fact and leave me to raise the child on my own. Consequently, they did the decent thing: they rallied together and built this house for me. I've lived here ever since but Eldred never came nor spoke to me again."

She sighed. I kept silent. After a while, she continued:

"After the baby was born, this place became known for its drinking parties. People were coming to see me, to drink with me, to sleep with me. These were the wonderful years of my life. All that time, I was raising my boy up and because of this I had to do with very little sleep. After a few years, my body could not cope with this life any more. Instead of being the life and soul of the party, I began to fall asleep after a few drinks. I also put on weight. Fewer and fewer people came for me, the partying time was over. They were now coming for bed and board and this house just became another inn. A few, like your uncle, kept coming back, year after year, and I'm pleased to see them, to know that I am not forgotten, but also sad when they tell me that one of their comrades had died. Others come because of the stories they have heard. They want to see for themselves, to speculate who my son's father is. That's why I made a rule that no one staying here speaks about him. And this rule applies to you."

"There's something I need to know."

"Whether you can meet him and spent time with him? No, you cannot, because he is not here. A few months back, he decided to sail to Groendland. That's why I am not happy about Eldred sailing there as well. I don't trust that man any more and I would not like anything to happen to my boy because of him."

"That's not what I need to know."

"What is it then?"

"Could my father be his father?"

She looked at me in a very strange way. Her answer was quite unexpected:

"Do you have any brothers or sisters?"

"No."

"An only child! Eh! Just like mine! No! I don't think your father could have been the child's father. I don't remember him. If there had been the remote possibility that he might, I would have remembered something of him. No, you do not have a half-brother."

"Cousin, then?"

"Possible! I do not really know and I'm not making this up. Yes, your uncle could be his father but also he may not be. Please, don't tell Elgar any of this. I have spoken too much. You must forget what I have said. Now, people are arriving for the night, don't let them see us talking together."

She laid back against the corner walls in her favourite position, a vacant stare in her eyes. She had once more become the landlady of Grunhelda's place and not the mother who had just been speaking to me.

# CHAPTER 7

I woke up the following morning unresolved as to what to do next. It goes without saying that my uncle had not yet returned. I did not know whether he was punishing me for having refused to join him in his drinking bout or whether he was trying to see how I would cope on my own. The truth was that I was not coping very well. It was, however, clear to me that I only had two choices: either to remain sitting at the table waiting for him or to go to the exercise field.

If I were to choose the former, I would be under Grunhelda's glare all the time. After our talk of the day before, I did not think that either of us wanted to speak to the other. On the other hand, if I were to go out, anything could happen to me and, after the experiences from the past week, I was becoming wary of who I would meet. Then, suddenly, I remembered it was the day when Eldred and others were sailing away. I rushed out and made for the quayside. It was a cold day with dark clouds hanging low. I was too late. The quayside was deserted, the harbour devoid of boats. I could just make out a few sails in the distance. I felt miserable. As I stood there, looking into the distance, I became aware that many things had not turned out the way I had expected. Nothing I had experienced so far fitted with my uncle's stories of his adventures, nor did his behaviour, for that matter. I do not know how long I remained rooted to the same spot when a sudden gust of wind made me shiver. I felt cold, very cold. I knew then I had to move but, because of the way I was feeling, I did not want to be among people. So, instead of walking back into the town, I directed my steps towards the open countryside adjoining the harbour. I walked briskly for a while before turning right. Subconsciously, I was making my way to the exercise field. It was almost deserted when I arrived. I went to the boulder and leaned against it.

After a while, it began to rain. People left the field and, once more on that day, I was alone. I was also getting soaked but I did not seem to notice or care. How long I stayed there, devoid of all thought, feeling total emptiness, I could not say. What brought me back, was the sound of a voice, which at first I could not understand. It kept repeating, slowly in what appeared to me to be a foreign accent:

"Do... you... need... any... help?"

I looked up and saw a small, thin young man, as soaked as I was, standing close to me. He was not dressed like a Viking. I put my hand on the hilt of my sword. He moved back a step or two.

"What do you want? What are you doing here?" I said. "You're not a Viking, are you?"

"No, I'm Irish. My name is Aidan."

"I don't care about your name. Wait! I've seen you before. Oh! Yes! Now, I remember – You're that fellow who stands outside the town gates shouting something about a God. How do you happen to be here?"

"You speak too fast. I do not understand you."

I felt rather unlucky that the only person that would speak to me could not speak my language. Then, I remembered my mother having told me once that Welsh and Irish were both Celt and were virtually speaking the same language. I did not quite believe her then. Now was the time to test it. So, speaking in my mother's tongue, I said to him:

"What do you want with me?"

"You speak my language!" he replied with surprise in his voice and this time in Irish.

"My mother's Welsh. My father's a Viking. Make no mistake, I, too, am a Viking. So, again, I ask you: what do you want with me?"

"I saw you alone. I thought you might have been hurt. I wanted to help."

"How did you happen to walk this way?"

"It's my way home. I live by the edge of the cliff over there. It's not far. Why don't you come with me out of this rain?"

I hesitated for a short while. I looked up at the sky. There was no sign that the rain would stop. It would soon be dark. If I followed him, I would not be able to go back to the inn that night. I smiled at myself at the thought of Elgar possibly waiting for me. This was enough for me to decide.

"Show me the way!" I said.

We walked in silence for a while. Soon, we could hear the sea splashing against the rocks at the bottom of the cliffs. Aidan was the first to speak again:

"We're nearly there. I built my church and my home in a hollow and covered them with turf. I call it a church but it is very small, more like a chapel. My home is just a small room and I'm afraid I can only offer water and gruel by way of refreshments."

"Who lives with you?"

"Nobody! I felt called to the service of God. My parents were very proud when I decided to become a monk. It's an honour among us, Irish, to be called by God to serve Him."

"How did God call you?"

"It's difficult to explain. It's as if you hear an inner voice telling you what to do. Then, you speak to other monks and they help you find your way and your destiny. But, here we are. This is the chapel, come inside with me."

I followed him in. The floor was made of beaten earth. At the far end, was a slab put over two stones with a cross, made of wood, upon it. Aidan knelt in front of it, touched himself in four places with his right hand, said what seemed to me to be a prayer, made the same gesture again and got up. He then took me by the arm and led me out and into a small, adjacent room, half of which was filled by the bed upon which we sat. As promised, he handed me a beaker filled with water and a small bowl inside which was some cold, thick gruel. We ate in silence. When I had finished, I asked him:

"What made you decide to live like this?"

"All monks make a vow of poverty. We are not interested in acquiring goods or in the comforts of the flesh. We dedicate our bodies and souls to the service of God and his son, Jesus Christ."

"Why are you here? And why are you standing outside our town every day?"

"When I was a boy, I played with my neighbour's children. They were Vikings. I learnt to speak some of their language and that is why, after I had been ordained, I was given the order to build a church close to Dublin and to do my utmost to convert the town to Christianity. I feel I have failed miserably. No one ever spoke to me."

"I nearly did once, but I moved on. I think you smiled."

"I always smile at anyone who looks at me in the hope he may wish to hear about my faith. Do you want to learn about Christianity?"

I nodded. He spoke non-stop for a very long time. The drone of his voice made me sleepy. I tried to fight against it but to no avail. When I woke up, the sun was shining brightly. Some of its rays were penetrating the room and making it look quite pleasant. I stretched myself out and realised my sword was still hanging from the belt round my body. I must have forgotten to remove it before I fell asleep. I got up and went out. I peered into the chapel and there was Aidan standing close to the altar, moving his arms and praying aloud. I leaned against the door lintel and watched him. He seemed oblivious to anything around him and I did not wish to disturb him. At last, he knelt on one knee for a brief moment, made that gesture when he touched four parts of his body with his right hand, got up and turned around. When he saw me, a large smile illuminated his face and he walked towards me.

"What is that gesture you keep doing?" I asked him.

"It is the sign of the Cross. You were tired last night. Do you remember anything I said?"

"You were explaining your religion to me, weren't you?"

"Do you wish to know more?"

"My father's God is Odin. He says that, as his son, Odin should also be my God. My mother's God is the rising sun whom the Druids pray to from within their stone circles. My father let her practice her religion but has forbidden me to follow it. He would not approve of me following yours. My mother, on the other hand, always says that priests, of whatever religion, should always be treated with respect. From what you told me last night, you are a Christian. My uncle, when fighting in the East, met with Christians but he remained faithful to Odin, the God of his forefathers and mine. I wish you well but I do not think any Viking will ever listen to you."

"Even if Christianity is the only true religion and God is the only God there is."

"How can we know?"

"That's where faith comes into it. You need to believe. Every Irishman believes that Jesus is the Son of God who came upon this earth to redeem us sinners."

"You mean, those who live in Ireland."

"That's where Irish people live, in Ireland."

"Not quite true! When my uncle and father both came to this island, there was fighting between the various clans. Some were Christians and some were pagans. The Christian clans hired us, Vikings, to fight on their side. The defeated pagan clans crossed the sea and settled in Northern Britain. For all I know, they might still be pagan."

"I know nothing about that."

"You must have heard of Eldred the Avenger."

"Yes, but I'm not sure I know what he did."

"He is a leader of men, well respected among us. My uncle is proud to have fought alongside him."

"You always talk of fighting. Let me tell you: he who lives by the sword perishes by the sword."

"Eldred is still alive. He has just left for Eisland, to settle there."

"I know, for many an Irish girl had gone the same way as the Vikings to those far away places of Eisland and Groendland. Their children will be raised as Christians. To ensure this, a couple of monks are travelling with them."

"Thanks for your hospitality but I feel it's time for me to leave."

"We need to talk some more. If not today, do come back and see me again."

"I doubt it for I have come to a decision: Ireland is not for me. It is not where my destiny lies. I shall be going home as soon as I can."

"Think about what I said and I shall be praying for you."

I set off and Aidan went back inside the chapel. The sun was drying the land and making the day pleasantly warm. I was in no hurry. I had made my decision. I felt better for it. I stopped and turned round. I could see the sun being reflected by the sea in thousands of shining little suns. There was no wind. I could just about make out Aidan's chapel and home under the turf. The whole view was so peaceful that I stood motionless for a few minutes. I wanted to retain this sight among my memories of my time here. Somehow, I had the feeling that I had reached a turning point in my life. I did not want to be a warrior without ambition like my uncle Elgar. I wanted to be a well-respected leader of men like Eldred. This I could only achieve by returning to my home and defending it against the Saxons. I would be Welsh with the Welsh and Viking with the Vikings. I had a double heritage and that would be my strength.

I started walking again. Soon, I had reached the exercise field. There were only a few people going through the motions of attack and counter-attack, of parrying and thrusting. They did not notice me as I made my way to the boulder. The mark made by my sword on the first day I came here could still be seen. However, I doubted that anybody would ever notice or remember how it happened. I passed my hand over the spot as if to wipe out the past and resumed my walk. It was strange, as I approached the town gates, not to see or hear that young man shouting 'Listen to the voice of the true God'. I briefly wondered what he was doing and whether he would ever come back to this spot. I entered the town. It was less busy than usual. As I walked past the inn where I last saw my uncle, I decided to put my head round the door to see if he was still there. The place was deserted; not even one of the half-dressed women I had seen on my previous visit was inside. I closed the door and continued towards Grunhelda's place.

"A bowl, please!" I said as I was standing in front of Grunhelda.
"Where did you spring from?" she asked me without handing me a bowl. "Your uncle wondered where you've gone. I said you jumped on to a ship."
"Why did you say that for?"
"I wanted to make him worry. I thought he deserved to."
"Where is he now?"
"Still sleeping!"
"Let him! I'll have my breakfast while waiting for him. So, may I have a bowl, please."
"Not until you tell me where you've been."
"I spent the night inside a Christian church."
I could see that Grunhelda was quite surprised, almost shocked.
"Whatever for?" She asked.
"To keep away from the rain! Now, may I have my bowl?"
She shook with laughter and threw a bowl at me.
I had nearly finished my breakfast when my uncle made his appearance, still half-asleep. He stopped when he saw me. I thought he was going to say something to me but he must have changed his mind as, instead, he moved on towards Grunhelda. I needed to speak to him, so I shouted:
"Uncle, come and sit by me!"
He did not reply but I saw him and Grunhelda talking to each other. I could but wait. At last, she gave him a bowl and he made his way to the cauldron before coming to the table and sitting across it from me.
"I'm hearing all kinds of stories about you," he said.

"What do you expect? You're never with me," I replied and I added, "I have made a decision: I want to go back home. I don't care whether you come with me or not, I want you to arrange for me to get on a boat home as soon as possible."

"What of your training to become a warrior? Don't you want to be one any more?"

"I can train anywhere. So, will you arrange a passage on a boat?"

"Give me a few days and I'll come with you. In the meantime, could you explain to me how you got yourself into a Christian church?"

"I met with that monk that stands outside the gates and we had a chat at his place last night."

"Did he not try to convert you?"

"He spoke a lot about his beliefs. I listened. I can make my own mind up, you know."

"Sure, you can! But remember this: how can people trust anyone who betrays his own Gods?"

# CHAPTER 8

It was the beginning of May. We had been marching for a week. The Prince of Gwynedd was leading the army into enemy territory along the border between the Kingdoms of Northumbria and Mercia. Many Welshmen from Gwynedd were following their Prince. However, the Prince of Powys had decided to remain neutral and had forbidden any of his men to join our army. On the other hand, the Prince of Penrith had sent a contingent under the leadership of his son, Ulls. Ulls had no experience of war. He had been sent by his father who thought it was time for him to acquire some. He was a very arrogant young man who kept refusing to take orders from anyone except from the Prince of Gwynedd himself. And, of course, there were us, Vikings, led by my uncle Elgar. A few had come over from Ireland but most were our neighbours from Helsby.

I had been training all through the winter after my return from Ireland, sometimes with my father and sometimes with my uncle. A couple of weeks before I left home, my father helped me to cast a brand new sword. He also made a reinforced shield for me. He was good at this kind of thing. He had resigned himself to seeing me become a warrior but, in spite of his misgivings that I was still too young, he did his very best to ensure that I was well prepared. My mother said nothing until the very last day.

"Son," she told me, "remember that you are not only a Viking hiring your sword but also a Welshman defending your own country."

So far, I had only been shadowing my uncle, even accompanying him to meetings with the Prince of Gwynedd, Ulls and other commanders. I would not speak but would listen carefully to what was being discussed. I had no trouble at all understanding what was being said since they all spoke Welsh and I did too. It was not so for my uncle whose knowledge of Welsh was limited and who would hardly make any comments at such meetings. As no enemy had been seen yet, the question was whether to go any further into enemy territory. Some at the meeting were for advancing further, others were for staying put for the time being. Neither my uncle nor the Prince had given an opinion when Ulls spoke:
"I have come to make war. That is why my father sent me. So war it is."
"We don't know the enemy's tactics," replied my uncle in broken Welsh. "They may be laying a trap for us."
This answer irritated Ulls.
"Who asked for your opinion? Do we have to listen to this clown who cannot even speak properly? He should not be at this meeting. Prince! Dismiss him!"
I could see that my uncle did not quite understand what had been said and I strongly felt that I could not let it rest and that it was my duty to answer him:
"Whether he can speak properly or not is irrelevant. What matters is his experience and of that he has plenty."
There was surprise on everyone's face, not only because I spoke in fluent Welsh but also because I had dared to answer Ulls. The latter drew his sword partially from its scabbard and spat out:

"I should kill you!"

"I'm afraid of no man," I said. "If you want a fight, I'll give you one."

"Please!" the Prince of Gwynedd intervened. "Let's keep all fighting for when we meet with the enemy."

"Fine with me!" I answered.

"Well said, young man! What is your name?" enquired the Prince.

"Ap Thor!"

"I'll remember that name," hissed Ulls.

"Well! Ap Thor!" the Prince continued, ignoring the interruption. "What are your thoughts: should we advance further or stay put?"

"I do not have enough experience to answer your question, but I could do with a day of rest from marching."

There was general laughter at my answer. Even the Prince smiled as he said:

"It's not a bad suggestion. Shall we adjourn until tomorrow night for a decision?"

Everyone nodded except Ulls who growled:

"I hate those Vikings."

A couple of days later, we sighted the enemy, or rather two enemies. There was a fairly large army inside Northumbria and a far smaller one in Mercia. We, Vikings, were sent to deal with the latter. This was a move that the enemy did not seem to have anticipated. They stopped and stared at us. For a moment, we thought they were going to make a stand but they withdrew instead. We pursued them. It was late afternoon when they turned around and faced us just outside a village whose inhabitants had joined them. My uncle, realising it would be dark soon, decided upon an immediate attack. We formed two rows, checked our shields were well attached to our arms and drew our swords. I was in the second row. We charged. There was a mighty clash of swords and shields. The Saxons were no match for us. Half of them lay dead on the battlefield and the other half took refuge inside the village. Elgar gave order to burn it but not before he had positioned us all around it with orders not to let anybody escape. Many surrendered. A few tried to run past us. One such made for me. It was my chance to show what I could do. I gave such a strong blow with my sword that his broke. That surprised him long enough for me to lunge forward into his neck. Blood spurted out on to me and he fell to the ground. He was my first kill. I should have been elated and proud, instead I stood rooted to the spot unable to move. I was feeling sick. The village was all ablaze by now. I heard my name called:

"Ap Thor! Ap Thor!"

"Who wants me?" I asked.

One of the older Vikings who had come from Ireland answered back.

"We need your help over here."

He was standing over a group of prisoners, crouched on the ground. In spite of my nausea, I moved over. I saw the prisoners recoil at my sight. I then realised I was still holding my sword which was dripping with blood.

"One of them," the old Viking said while looking at me strangely, "keeps repeating he's no Saxon. Check whether he's Welsh. You speak their language, don't you?"

I put my sword back in its scabbard. There was a stench of blood and urine and I was feeling sweat pouring down my forehead. For one moment, I thought I was going to faint. I controlled myself and asked in Welsh:

"Who speaks my language?"

"I do!" replied one of the prisoners while the others wondered what I said.

"What is your name?" I asked.

"Gwendwr!"

"What are you doing amongst the Saxons?"

"I was taken prisoner some twenty years ago. I was made a slave and I've lived as a slave ever since."

"Well, you're free now. Come!"

As he got up, the old Viking asked me in Norse, "what have you said to him?"

"He's no Saxon. I've set him free. I'm taking him to my uncle."

I spoke those words in Norse. Then, addressing Gwendwr in Welsh, I said:

"Follow me!"

As we moved away, we heard screams: the other prisoners were being put to the sword.

"Who are those people you're with?" asked Gwendwr. "They speak neither Saxon nor Welsh."

"They're Vikings!"

"And you?"

"I'm a Viking too."

"But you speak perfect Welsh."

"My mother's Welsh. Oh! Here's my uncle! He's our commander."

Elgar looked at me in the same strange way that the old Viking had done. I looked down and saw that I was covered in blood.

"I'm all right! Here's a Welshman I've rescued from slavery."

"Appie! Have you been hurt?"

"Enemy blood! Uncle, did you know that the Saxons have slaves?"

"It would not surprise me. Why do you ask?"

"This is Gwendwr. He has spent the last twenty years as a slave. I have told him he is now free."

"You deal with him! I have other matters to attend to."

As Elgar walked away, I turned to Gwendwr:

"Tell me where you're from."

"From Gwynedd!"

"Where about?"

"I doubt you would know: I'm from the Land-between-the-two-rivers. But tell me what is this army of yours doing in those parts?"

"War! Actually, we've been pursuing those Saxons. Now that we've killed them, I don't know what my uncle will decide to do next. I suppose we'll retrace our steps and rejoin the main army."

"Are there more of you?"

"I mean the Prince of Gwynedd's army. He's fighting the Northumbrians."

"But, we're in Mercia. Wait! Do you know there are many more slaves around here?"

"No, I know very little. Are they Welsh too?"

"Yes, they should be rescued. I have not heard of this country preparing for war. Just organise a raid and liberate them!"

"I'll speak to my uncle."

My uncle agreed to Gwendwr's suggestion and, for the next few days, we followed his directions from village to village, liberating one or two of his compatriots in each of them. What we failed to realise was that, as we did so, we were encroaching more and more into enemy territory. Elgar was beginning to feel anxious but most of the Vikings seemed to enjoy the jaunt. At last, we reached a small town. A group of men had been tied down just outside the gates. They were the

Welsh slaves. The Vikings did not like this. They made me ask them whether there was an army inside the town. The answer was negative. In spite of this, Elgar decided not to attack. Instead, we retraced our steps straight away. We did not go far before we noticed an army barring the way. We changed tack and headed due West. The enemy shadowed us, keeping to the North of us. Now, Elgar was making us walk as fast as we could. We all followed him in silence but I could see that the rescued slaves were fearful of recapture. On the third day, I could not hold my tongue any longer. I went to Elgar and asked him:

"Uncle, what are we doing?"

Before he could answer me, one of the Vikings told him to look to the South. We saw another army. Elgar remained undisturbed and barked an order:

"Quick march! No stragglers!"

I translated to the Welsh. A few Vikings formed a rearguard to ensure no one was falling behind. Gwendwr came up to me:

"What is he up to?"

"I don't know," I replied.

"Can't you ask him?"

I shook my head. I trusted my uncle Elgar completely. Based on all the stories he had told me of his life as a warrior, I did not for a moment doubt he would know what the best course of action was. However, I was still surprised that, when night fell, he did not give the order to stop. The night was nearly black as there only was a small crescent moon. We came to a small river.

"Have a quick drink," said Elgar, "before we carry on."

"Are we not stopping for the night?" I asked him.

"Better not!" was his brief answer.

When dawn came, we were all very tired, but we could not see our enemy. Still, we walked on all morning. Then, we saw it: a huge ditch was in front of us, followed by a man-made mount, stretching as far as the eye could see both to our right and to our left. It was Offa's Dyke, the acknowledged border between Saxons and Welsh. Once on the other side, we would be safe. It looked easy enough and we all perked up until we noticed that there were soldiers on the dyke. At about the same time, we could see movement at some distance behind us. The two armies which had been shadowing us and we had outdistanced with our night march were doing their best to catch up with us. Elgar ordered us to sit in a circle around him.

"Ap Thor, I need you to translate for me. I want everybody to agree on our next course of action. We could surrender or we could do the unexpected and attack the soldiers on the dyke. If we surrender, we shall all end up slaves. If we attack, we have the disadvantage of having to climb first but, once we have fought our way through, we can run down the other side and into freedom. Now, tell me which you prefer."

The Vikings' answer was immediate: attack! The Welsh, on the other hand, looked at each other but said nothing. I pressed them for an answer. They did not give me any. Elgar was looking at me. I had to do something. I spoke to them again:

"We, Vikings, are too proud to be slaves. We'd rather die fighting, our swords in our hands. Our decision is made. We attack. Whether you want to join or not is up to you. We move now."

I turned to my uncle and said:

"Lead the way!"

Everybody followed him. We stopped at the bottom of the ditch, formed a battle line and started climbing. The Saxons at the top were mere sentries. They offered little resistance. The main armies were still too far behind to stop us. Soon, we were running down on the other side, tired but elated at having at last reached Powys and what we thought was freedom.

# CHAPTER 9

Gwendwr and I were going home. It had been an eventful past month. After we managed to go over Offa's Dyke, we frightened the Welsh people on the other side. All the more so when the Saxon army, that had been pursuing us, paraded on top of the Dyke. The men of Powys were fearing an invasion. We had compromised their wish to remain neutral and they kept us prisoners while negotiations were taking place. Most of the slaves we had freed were from Powys and were allowed home. When this happened, I talked to Gwendwr:

"Why are you not leaving with the others? Surely, you should have been treated the same, eh?"

"After so many years away from home, a few days won't make any difference."

"We could make the journey together since both our families live in the land between the two rivers."

"That's a good idea. It's always best not to travel alone. The others are from the mountains to the West, so I could not have gone with them."

"I wonder how far you are from us. Do you remember the town of Helsby?"

"I've never heard of it."

"That's where most of the Vikings settled."

"There were no Vikings in our part of the world."

"Well, my mother's name's Gwendwlyn. I remember her mother, my grandmother, but she died when I was still a child."

"My sister's name's Gwendwlyn too. I also had a brother. I used to live in a very big house."

"Oh! My mother had two brothers. One of them died of his injuries incurred in battle, but I don't remember him. Nor do I remember her father, who died during a subsequent war when I was very young."

"What of her other brother?"

"She never speaks of him. Apparently, he disappeared."

"How?"

"Well! Her father and her two brothers went to war together. During some fighting he disappeared. He could have been taken prisoner but no one knew for sure."

Gwendwr said nothing and remained in deep thought for a while. I did not want to interrupt. I was going to move away when he asked me:

"Do you think your mother could be my sister?"

I was taken aback. I had been so keen to be a Viking and Gwendwr is such a common name among the Welsh that it had never occurred to me there could be a link between us, that we could be related, even at the mention of his sister's name. I did not know what to answer. I felt such a fool.

"Say something," he continued, "I described the house. There is none like it for miles around. Don't tell me you do not know of such a house! Have I got no family left?"

"Was it originally a Roman villa?"

"Yes!"

"Then, I feel sure you're my uncle."

We remained silent for a while, looking at each other. I did not know what his thoughts were at that time but mine were about my mother and how pleased she would be when she saw him.

Early the following morning, I spoke to my other uncle, Elgar, with much excitement.

"Uncle!" I said, "I've just discovered that Gwendwr is also my uncle."

"What do you mean?"

"My mother is his sister."

"Has he been telling you stories?"

"I don't think so. It all fits in. You may not know but she once told me that one of her brothers was a prisoner of the Saxons."

"So, what are you going to do about it?"

"It's given me an idea. I'll insist on being Welsh and ask to be allowed to go home with my uncle."

"Hmm!" Elgar thought for a minute before he added: "It might work but, if it does, remember to go and see the Prince of Gwynedd in order to secure my freedom as well as that of the other Vikings."

"Of course, uncle."

The idea worked and that is why Gwendwr and I were walking together. I told him all about me and my father. How good he was as a blacksmith, and how he taught me the trade. I proudly told Gwendwr that I had cast my own sword. I also told him about the dilapidated state of the house and I asked him to tell me about his life as a slave of the Saxons but this, he refused. At last, after nearly a week, we reached home. My mother came running towards me and embraced me.

"You're home and safe," she said and then whispered: "Who is this man with you? He keeps looking at me in a strange way."

"Guess! You know him," I replied. "His name is Gwendwr."

"My brother! Gwendwr! My brother! Is that really you? I knew I would see you again."

They fell into each other's arms. Tears were pouring down my mother's face and Gwendwr was looking slightly embarrassed by this open display of affection. I crept away to give them some privacy and went to the forge. The welcome from my father could not have been more different. It was perhaps because a customer was present.

"Dad! I'm home," I shouted with excitement, looking at the familiar surroundings.

"Should you not be with the army fighting instead of coming home?" my father replied, shocked at my light-heartedness.

"What do you mean?"

We had exchanged those words in Norse. To my surprise, my father then turned to his customer and spoke to him in Welsh:

"This is my son. Tell him the news you've just told me."

"A Saxon army is invading us!"

"Where is the Prince of Gwynedd?" I asked.

"He's not been heard of for weeks," said the customer.

"Weren't you with him?" added my father.

"Only at the beginning. We were faced with two armies, so we split. Elgar, myself and all the Vikings were ordered to attack one of the armies, which we defeated and pursued into Mercia. We raided part of that country, liberating Welsh slaves on the way, and ended up in Powys, where my uncle still is."

"That's typical of my brother."

"I don't know what you mean. All the Vikings are being held by the Prince of Powys in exchange for his country not to be attacked. I managed to leave by claiming to be Welsh."

"Is that so?" asked the customer. "Then, we're lost. We have no one to defend us."

"Don't say that!" I objected. "I can fight and so can my father. I'm sure you can fight too and there must be others who would be prepared to answer a call to arms."

"But who would make that call?" queried my father. "There is no one to lead us."

"Yes, there is," I answered.

"Who?"

"Me!"

"You're not even twenty. Who will obey someone so young?"

"Dad! Do you prefer us to be killed and our homes burnt?" I asked and, turning towards the customer, I added, "and you, would you not rather fight?"

"Possibly."

"Me and my father will cast swords for the next three days. Please go round the farmsteads and villages and come back here on the morning of the fourth day with as many willing men as possible. When the work is done, I shall go to Helsby and recruit as many Vikings as I can and you, father, will join us and fight alongside me."

Gwendwr and my father agreed to come with me. On the first day of the campaign, a dozen or so Welshmen turned up at our farm. That was the start of my army. We marched to Helsby and were joined by every Viking able to bear arms. I had just given the order to continue marching when I noticed a ship coming up the river. I gave the order for Gwendwr and the Welsh to go forward passing through as many villages as possible in order to recruit a lot more men and to meet us again at a ford a fair distance to the South. Meanwhile, I would wait for that boat with my father and the Viking contingent in the hope to increase my army. I was not disappointed. It brought thirty Vikings ready to fight. However, their leader, Rurik, objected to my leadership. I had to convince him:

"My father and my uncle both fought alongside Eldred the Avenger. My father is here, my uncle is not. If you will not have me as your leader, then accept my father."

They agreed and we marched south. As we did so, even more and more Welshmen joined the Welsh contingent. I had put Gwendwr in charge of it. I was the only one to speak both Welsh and Norse and, because of that, I managed to remain in overall control. Both my father and Welsh uncle had not been fighting for twenty years nor had they ever commanded a group of men. They were therefore quite happy to leave the decisions to me and were content relaying them to the men.

We had been marching for over a week when we finally caught sight of the enemy. It was towards the end of the day. We had just sighted a hillock in the distance and were making our way towards it, with the intention to camp there for the night when we discovered the Saxons were marching close by. I decided we should attack forthwith. I divided the Welsh contingent into two groups. I would command one in the centre. Gwendwr, with the other half, would stand on my left. My father, with the Viking contingent, would fight on my right. I also ordered some space between the three groups to make our army appear bigger. I straightaway ran into trouble: the Vikings wanted the centre position.

"I can't allow that," I told my father.

"It makes sense," he replied. "The stronger troops are always at the centre."

"I know that but it is also why I don't want you in the centre."

"That's madness, lad! We know the Vikings are experienced. What can be said of the Welsh? They're a totally unknown quantity."

"They may be but I shall have to trust them. In the meantime, your experience should ensure success on your side. I am relying on you."

"Let's hope Rurik sees it that way."

"Be strong, father, tell him to obey you. Now, let's advance and not argue!"

And with those words, I took my position in front of the entire army, drew my sword, beat my shield with it and advanced forward. I felt so proud. The whole army behind me was marching to my beat. The enemy, in front, hastily drew themselves up in battle formation but did not move forward. It was then, and only then, that I truly realised the enormity of what I was doing and I panicked. I could not advance one more step. As I stopped, so did the men behind me. There was an eerie silence. I looked up at the sky. The sun was close to the horizon. There was little time left for a battle. I could not decide. Suddenly, it was out of my hands: a loud shout was heard from the enemy, followed by the thud of dozens of running feet. I raised my sword and moved forward, slowly gathering speed. My men followed. They were shouting too. Soon, there was the clash of swords on shields.

The Saxons put up a strong resistance and it was nearly dark when the Vikings began making any advance on their side of the field. The Welsh stood firm. In the twilight, the Saxons withdrew towards the hillock. We did not pursue but let them camp on the top. At the same time, I gave the order to retreat. I did not want to camp too close to the enemy. Gwendwr approached me.

"That was harder than I thought," he said.

"Did you expect a walk over?" I answered back. "It's just a first battle, a taster. Tomorrow will be the real one."

"You don't plan an attack, do you?"

"Of course, I do. What else do you suggest?"

"We should go on a march and let them follow us. We did that in Mercia."

"Mercia was different. There, we were the invaders. Now, we are the defenders. If anyone should march, it's them."

I did not want an argument so I moved away. I was still excited from the battle and I knew I would not be able to sleep. I went looking for my father. He was sitting among the Vikings. I joined him.

"You showed courage today," Rurik said to me. "I was not expecting it."

"Why so?"

"You're so young!"

'My son has always wanted to be a warrior. I'm proud of him," my father said to all the company.

"What are your plans for tomorrow?" Rurik asked.

"We must be ready at first light," I replied. "Not because I plan an early attack, but in case the enemy moves first."

"Vikings should fight together," Rurik insisted. "I should be beside you, not pushed to one side like I was today."

"I did not mean to offend you, Rurik. There are nearly three times more Welsh. If I divide them, who will lead the right wing? No, it has worked rather well today, so let us not change our strategy."

Rurik did not reply and my only hope was that he would see my point of view and agree. I laid down and fell asleep.

By the middle of the following morning, we had taken our position at the bottom of the hillock. The Saxons had made no move. I was not keen on going uphill to attack. So, we just waited. There were enough clouds in the sky to stop the sun's rays from bearing down on us for too long. However, the men were growing impatient and, by midday, I decided to move forward but no further than halfway up. Soon after we stopped, the enemy started to move, very slowly but with a great deal of noise. I gave the signal to advance. There was no rush from either side. It was a very deliberate advance. Suddenly, the Saxons stopped and moved back up. I ordered my men to stop. I had the feeling that something was not right. I turned round and saw an army coming towards us on the plain below. They were too far from us to be recognised as either friends or foes. I gave the order for my men to spread out and be ready to move fast if the enemy wanted to run down on the other side. I did not want the Saxons to escape without a fight. Then a joyful cry went up from the Welsh ranks and I knew it was the Prince of Gwynedd's army advancing towards us. I gave renewed orders to Gwendwr and my father to maintain the blockade before walking down to meet the Prince. As I came closer, I saw it was no army but a bedraggled band of men.

"Ap Thor, at your service, my Prince," I said.

At the sight of a Viking in full battle gear standing there in front of him, the Prince of Gwynedd stood speechless.

"I am Ap Thor," I said again. "Surely, you remember me. I need your help. I cannot defeat the Saxons on my own."

"Ap Thor!" the Prince repeated, "Ap Thor! Yes! You're that young fellow who prefers a day's rest to a day's march."

"The very same, my Lord! As I have said, I need your help."

"What help can I give you? We are being pursued. We need to take refuge in the mountains to the West."

"Are you telling me there's a Saxon army following you?"

"Yes! And we've suffered defeat after defeat."

"That stops here, Prince. I have an army of Welsh and Vikings ready to help you but, before they do, your men must join mine in attacking the other Saxon army on top of that hillock."

I saw the look of panic on the Prince's face. One of his counsellors spoke:

"No one here is fit to fight."

"I shall be the judge of that. Time is of the essence. Tell the men to follow me."

"Where to?" asked the same counsellor.

I was losing my patience. I addressed the men directly:

"Welshmen are waiting for you up that hill. Follow me and join them."

"You have no right to give my men any order," said the Prince, angrily.

"Then, walk alongside me and let them follow you," I replied as I took hold of his arm.

There was little that he could do. I was young and strong. He was old and defeated.

# CHAPTER 10

By joining the two armies together, mine and the Prince of Gwynedd's, I could manage a full circle round the hillock. It was only a thin line. I ordered the men to advance. The Saxons remained on the top. I could not fathom their tactic but I needed to wait for their next move. Suddenly, they rushed down on one side, broke through our lines almost immediately before I could order any reinforcements. When I did so, only the Vikings were quick enough to move round and catch the back of them and pursue them. I was disappointed. For the third time, victory had eluded me. I had decided to try to rally the Welsh for a pursuit when I caught sight of an army in the distance. I realised it must be the Saxon army that had been pursuing the Prince of Gwynedd. I rushed down to recall the Vikings. I needed to keep as many men as possible alive. Rurik interrupted me:

"You should give us the chance of pursuit."

"Not with another Saxon army coming!"

He looked in the direction I was pointing and recalled his men. He vented his disappointment by killing every Saxon still breathing on his way up the hill. I did not interfere. Meanwhile, the Welsh had moved to the top of the hillock. I had to go all the way up to find Gwendwr.

"Why did you not pursue?" I asked him.

"The Prince gave the order to go to the top."

"You're in my army not his. You take orders from me not him."

"I dare not disobey the Prince."

"It seems to me to be an excuse to avoid fighting. Now, call your men and be ready to follow me. We are not staying up here."

Before he could answer, I went looking for the Prince. I found him resting on a rock and looking miserable. When he saw me, he turned his head away.

"Prince!" I said. "We need to talk. My army is undefeated As I said before, I need your help. Alone, I cannot achieve victory."

"Can't you see that my men can fight no more?"

"I don't believe it is so. Maybe, you have had enough. Let them choose between making a stand here with me or following you into the mountains and be called cowards ever after."

He turned towards his counsellors. None of them dared to speak. I continued:

"I am not staying up here. My camp is down below. This is what I suggest: you spend the night here and tomorrow we attack the Saxons."

"They are too strong for us," said one of the counsellors.

"Nonsense!" I replied. "Not if you follow my plan. It is simple. You attack them from the front and I attack them from the rear."

"When, tomorrow?" the Prince asked.

"I'll wait until you're ready to come down and that will be the signal for us to move."

As we woke up the following morning, it was raining heavily. I sighed with relief when I noticed the Prince's army was still on top of the hillock. I had feared he might have fled under cover of darkness. Gwendwr came to me. I feared what he was going to tell me.

"I don't think there will be any battle today," he said, "the ground is too wet and slippery. Look! The enemy is still in camp."

"Why have you always got to be so negative?" I asked him.

"I'm not negative. I simply state the facts."

"As my uncle, I would expect a bit more support from you."

"I follow your orders but, at times, you are too impetuous, you take too many risks. I don't want to be taken prisoner and end up a slave again."

"Oh! Is that what is the matter with you? By Odin, what am I to do? You don't succeed if you don't take risks and I want to succeed. Gwendwr! If you fight hard, you won't be taken prisoner. I need victory, total victory. I won't achieve it without your help."

"You have my help but not when you're reckless."

By the end of the morning, the rain had stopped and at the same time, the two Saxon armies had lined up as one at the bottom of the hillock. I ordered my men to be ready to advance as soon as the Prince's army came down the hillock as planned. It never happened. The clouds dispersed, the sun came out and still no one had moved. It seemed that another day would be wasted in stalemate when, towards the beginning of the evening, half the Saxon army started to climb the hillock.

"Shall we go in?" asked Rurik.

"Not yet!" I answered.

I was right to hold my men back as the enemy stopped half way up and the Prince did not move. I looked at the sky: the sun was close to the horizon. There was not much time left for battle. I could fight one army but not two. Neither could I be sure the Prince would go on the offensive if I were the first to make a move. Then, to my surprise, both Saxon armies moved at the same time, in the same direction, upwards. There was no time to lose. I also decided to go up hill and catch the enemy sideways. When we were level with the second army, I ordered my men to turn and attack. The enemy was not prepared for such a move. We had the advantage and the Vikings amongst us made the best of it, killing and breaking their ranks. Soon, the enemy was running back down, with us in hot pursuit. As we reached the bottom, I turned round and I could not see anything of the other army. I grew anxious as it would soon be dark. I ordered my men to stop, regroup and march back to the camp. When we nearly reached it, we caught sight of two armies moving away from us. It was easy to realise what had happened. The Prince of Gwynedd, instead of fighting, had simply ordered his men down the other side of the hillock and were being pursued by the Saxon army. Once more, he was in full retreat.

My father was walking alongside me. After a while, he spoke:
"Son, you must be disappointed."
"Father! What would you do?"
"You ordered us back to camp and it will be dark very shortly. It is too late to change your mind now but you must have a plan for tomorrow."
"We can't expect the Prince to come back, can we?"
"Quite!"
"Question: will the Saxons keep on pursuing him?"
"Very likely!"
"But not for sure! Thanks, father! I now know what to do."

At first light, we were up and ready to march. We went back to the battlefield of the evening before. The Saxons had camped not far from it and they seemed to be still asleep. I gave the order to attack. It was carnage. Soon, they were in full flight and we had captured many prisoners. We learnt from them that their other army had not returned. As victors, we took their swords, their shields, their armlets and some of their clothes. I asked Gwendwr to translate for me. This is what I said:

"Saxons! I am Ap Thor! Remember my name! Today, I let you live. Go back to your country! If I catch any of you on our soil again, I'll put you to the sword."

We did not tarry. I wanted to catch up with the other Saxon army and, at the same time, rescue the Prince. Towards evening, my father exclaimed:

"They're making for the mines."

"The ones you buy your ore from?" I enquired.

"Yes! It's obvious from the direction they're going, but, when I go there, I take a different road."

"Is there more than one way to the mines?"

"The other road is narrow, along a river. It's fine for a single traveller."

This gave me an idea. The weather was fine and I could expect the moon to shine during the night. I told my father to lead the way. I asked Rurik and his men to form the rearguard and not to tolerate any stragglers. We walked for most of the night and it was still dark when we reached the mines. I ordered my men to rest while we waited for the miners to wake up. When they saw us, they were surprised and frightened. My father was known to the elder in charge and appraised him of the situation. I joined them.

"I'd greatly appreciate it if you would join my army," I said.

"What help could I be?" asked the elder.

"Not just you, every miner!"

"We don't have any arms."

"That's not a problem. We've got spare ones we captured from the Saxons. But the bigger my army looks the better to strike fear into their hearts."

"I'll call the men."

As he went away, I asked my father: "Do you think they'll join us?"

"Let's hope so. In the meantime, follow me."

We climbed past the entrance to the mines to some kind of look-out that gave us a good view of the countryside around. From it, we were able to see the two armies: one was already on the march and approaching. I estimated it would reach us by mid-morning. The other appeared to be motionless. We climbed down and heard the good news: The men would not be working the mines but joining us. I ordered an immediate march. Not long after, I was standing in front of the Prince of Gwynedd.

"Prince," I said, "we meet again."

"Where did you spring from?"

"I told you I would not let you retreat. Shall we join our forces? Are you prepared to lead your men now?"

"If I must."

"Then turn round and we all march and face the Saxons."

The Prince agreed and soon both armies were facing each other. I felt that this would be the final battle and would bring the war to an end. Someone had to give the order to attack. I wished the Prince would do it. I advanced a few steps. No one followed me. I walked to the Prince and said to him: "We're all behind you. Now is the time to attack."

"I know," he replied, "but I am afraid."

"Don't be! I'll stand by your side and so will my uncle Gwendwr."

I beat my sword on my shield. The men did the same. There was no turning back. As we advanced, so did the enemy. Soon, the two armies clashed. The Prince fell. I killed the man in front of me. No side was giving way. Men were falling everywhere, some just hurt, some dying. After a while, there was no longer a continuous line. Men had to fight in small groups, climbing over the dead. I was nearly surrounded but stepped back just in time to avoid capture. I had no idea which side was winning. I prayed to Odin that it was us. As more bodies fell, the fighting had to stop. Both sides retreated behind the piles of corpses and dying men. No one side could claim victory. I needed to do something to re-start the fighting. I called to the men on my left to re-group and, with them following me, I moved to the right and linked up with the Viking wing. The Saxons cheered. I wondered why. My father enlightened me:

"You are making us leave the battlefield. We are giving them victory. That's what they are shouting about."

"Not for long!" was my answer as I indicated to the men to follow me. My plan was simple: to go round the dead and attack the remnant of the enemy from the side. It worked all the more brilliantly because the Saxons were not expecting it. In fact, they had begun to strip the dead and were completely taken by surprise when we attacked. Some managed to escape but most surrendered and begged for their lives. I ordered them to throw down their swords, their shields, to remove their armlets and their clothes and then I told them to go back to their own country. They did not wait around to be told twice. Some just immediately ran away, others helped their wounded comrades to walk away. The victory was mine at last!

I still had a few things to do. I asked my father to supervise the gathering of spoils, which would be shared on the following day. I told Rurik to gather the bodies of any dead Vikings, making sure they were still holding their swords in their hands and to build a funeral pyre so that they may enter Valhalla on that very night. Then, I went looking for the Prince. I found him some distance at the back of the army. He was not alone. As I came closer, I recognised the person with him as Gwendwr. I looked at both of them. The Prince had some dried blood on one side of his face. He was also the first to speak:

"Ap Thor! Your uncle saved my life!"

I looked at Gwendwr. There was no trace of blood, sweat or dust on him. I had to ask:

"Gwendwr! Did you fight at all?"

"I saved the Prince's life," he replied.

"Uncle! How could you stay away, when so many good men lost their lives?"

"Don't be angry, Ap Thor!" said the Prince. "You won us a victory and I shall reward you for it. I appoint you as counsellor."

"Thank you!" I said. "May I ask a question? When we started the campaign into Northumbria all those weeks ago, I remember a young man called Ulls. Where is he now? I have not seen him."

"Let me bring you up to date," answered the Prince. "After Elgar, you and the Vikings went your way into Mercia, we received a messenger from Penrith. They were being attacked from the North. The Prince was asking for the return of his son and his men. We had to oblige but, then, we were left with too few men to fight the Northumbrians with any kind of success. We were expecting you to return. When we realised you would not, and having lost a few skirmishes, we had no choice but to retreat."

"We liberated a few Welshmen in our foray but, perhaps, their freedom was not worth so many dead."

"You cannot say that," Gwendwr interrupted. "Being a slave and treated as such was horrible."

"Prince," I continued, "Elgar and his men would have returned to you if we had not been stopped by the Prince of

Powys from doing so. You must consort with him to obtain their release and thus their freedom."

"There are many things to discuss," the Prince of Gwynned answered. "It is late. It has been a long day. Night will soon fall. Let's leave the discussion until the morning. I shall call a meeting with my counsellors. You will both attend."

The Prince got up and moved away, leaving me facing my uncle.

"Why did he ask you to come?" I questioned.

"Because I, too, am a counsellor. He appointed me as such for saving his life. You should be happy for me."

I could not. I was feeling disgust and repugnance for the man that was my uncle.

"When you start a fight, you finish it," I told him. "This is the Viking way. You don't look for excuses to run away."

"This is not Viking country," he replied. "We have different ways. If you want to live among us, you should accept them and certainly not try to impose your ways on us."

If I had not been so tired, I would have drawn my sword there and then. Instead, I walked down to the funeral pyre of my dead fellow Vikings that Rurik had prepared. Next to those lucky few who would wake up in Valhalla, I prayed to Odin.

# CHAPTER 11

For the past month, I had been patrolling the border between Gwynedd and Northumbria. It was very quiet. There was no military activity of any kind on the other side. After the victory over the Saxons, the Prince of Gwynedd had not only appointed me a counsellor but also Commander of the Border Patrol. He only assigned to me some forty Welshmen and Rurik and his band of Vikings, who were now down to twenty-two. What would have been their use had the Saxons raised another army, I could not imagine. The Prince wanted a lasting peace like the one that the Prince of Powys had succeeded in arranging between himself and the King of Mercia. So, he went to Powys with his counsellors, Gwendwr among them. He hoped that the Prince of Powys would agree to act as intermediary between himself and the Saxons. I would have liked to go with him in order to see my uncle Elgar again. Now that the fighting was over, I was missing him. The Prince of Gwynedd thought otherwise but he did promise to do his utmost to ensure Elgar's return, possibly with further instructions for me once peace had been agreed.

My father had gone home the day after the battle. So had many of the surviving men. We all had a great deal of booty. I now sported three armlets on each arm and a heavy belt, which I made myself out of my share. Each evening, after my arrival at the border, I used the camp fire to work on the belt. The result was magnificent. When the work was done, Rurik asked me to do the same for him. I obliged. Afterwards, with nothing to do in the evening, I felt empty. I was missing my father's forge and my work as a blacksmith. The excitement that I had felt when leading men into battle had long died. If I had not given my word to my Prince, I would probably have returned home. Under the circumstances, to do so would have been desertion. I had to wait for an order but I was growing impatient. When it finally came, to my surprise, it was brought by Gwendwr. My first question was: "Gwendwr! Where is Elgar?"

"Ap Thor! Good news!" he replied, ignoring my question completely. "Peace has been agreed. The Prince of Powys has been a true friend to our Prince of Gwynedd. The King of Mercia helped. Offa's Dyke remains the official border between Saxons and Welsh. No one is to cross it. We don't need the Vikings' hired swords any more. They've been told to leave. This last army of yours is to be disbanded. You are free to go home."

"Gwendwr! You did not answer my question: Where is Elgar?"

"Gone!"

"Where?"

"I don't know. I don't speak Norse. I never spoke to him. One day he was there with the other Vikings, the next day they were all gone. Orders from both Princes, I believe. It's not for me to question their actions. Neither should you."

"Let's hope he's gone home to his brother. I'll go there too once I've said my goodbyes."

"Before you do so, hear me out please. I know you feel drawn to the Viking way of life but our Prince of Gwynedd does not want any more Vikings to settle on his lands. The message I carry for you from him is to tell Rurik that he and his men must move out of Gwynedd."

"Just like that? What about any reward for their help?"

"They have had their share of the booty. That's ample enough. However, the Prince of Penrith might need their help and I've heard the Vikings have a settlement, called Odin's Town, to the North of his land."

"Any more orders I should know about?"

"No!"

"What about you? What are your orders?"

"I have none. I shall go home to my sister. I hope we shall be travelling together."

"I'll let you know tomorrow. I will spend tonight with Rurik. You're welcome to stay in our camp."

I knew that Gwendwr was my uncle but my feelings for him were not the same as those for my other uncle, Elgar. Somehow, Gwendwr was more of a stranger to me than a relative and the more time I spent with him, the more I thought of him as a stranger I did not want to make friends with. On the other hand, a mutual respect had developed between me and Rurik. If, at the beginning, he had some resentment against me due to my youth, it had gone now. During the fighting, I had been able to rely on him more than on anybody else bar my father. Afterwards, as we walked to the border, we developed some comradeship that turned into friendship, especially after I made that belt for him. Now, I had to tell him he was not welcome to stay in Gwynedd and I was not relishing the task.

That evening, as we were all sitting round the camp fire eating our dinner, I had little appetite. Gwendwr had chosen to sit among the Welsh and must have been telling them funny stories or cracking jokes as they were regularly bursting into laughter. As usual, Rurik was sittting beside me.

"Ap Thor," he said, "if you'd prefer to sit with your uncle, I won't take offence."

"I'm all right where I am," I muttered.

"Then, what's the matter with you? Are you ill or something? You've not touched your food."

"So, you've noticed. "

"Something's troubling you, isn't it?"

"It's what I've heard from the Prince, conveyed by Gwendwr."

"Bad news?"

"Sort of! I'd better tell you now: you and your men are being dismissed and you have to leave Gwynedd."

I could see it was a shock to Rurik. He did not answer me straight away. I threw my food away in disgust and said:

"I'm sorry."

"Don't be! You asked me to fight, not the Prince. I'm on his land. If he does not want me here, I shall have to move. Where to? I don't know."

"You could go North and see whether the Prince of Penrith needs help."

"Another Welsh Prince?"

"Yes! I met his son at the beginning of the campaign. Very arrogant, he was. Sent by his father to gain experience, he refused to obey anyone."

Rurik laughed.

"He was recalled by his father when the latter's land got attacked," I said. "If you decide to go, I shall walk with you part of the way. Otherwise, you can always come with me to my home until you're ready to take a boat to some foreign shore."

"I shall have to discuss it with my men. I won't do it tonight though. Don't worry about it. Instead, just tell me your own plans."

"Gwendwr wants me to go home with him. I'd like to see my father again, take some rest. I can't however see myself as a blacksmith for the rest of my life. A time will come when I shall crave excitement and adventure again. Then, like you, I shall be roaming the earth, offering my sword to whom may need it."

"Spoken like a true Viking!"

The following morning, the Welsh left for home with the exception of Gwendwr while Rurik and his men were discussing their future plans. They did not seem to be able to agree. Gwendwr grew impatient.

"What's going on?" he asked me.

"Let them decide what they do next," I said

"Just come with me! They're not your concern any more."

"You're wrong. They are my concern for two reasons: one, I asked them to follow me all those weeks ago and two, I have to ensure the Prince's orders are followed."

"The problem with you, Ap Thor, is that you worry too much. You should let go."

"And the problem with you, Gwendwr, is that you could not give a damn."

After a while, I walked over to Rurik and said:

"You may not want to decide now. Whichever way you choose, the road is the same for the next couple of days. Let's march now and think about it."

"What do you think we should do?" asked Rurik.

"I told you last night what your options are. It's not up to me to decide for you. If your men are prepared to follow you, Rurik, you decide for them. Otherwise, you may have to split and let some follow you and some go their own way. As for me, I shall go home first to see my father and possibly my other uncle or at least to get news of him."

"I doubt we will want to split. We've been together for a few years now and a strong bond has developed between all of us. I don't think any single one of us would want to break it but, before I decide for us all, do you really think there is fighting to be done in the North?"

"I could not tell you for sure. Gwendwr says there is. I might be tempted to go and check it out for myself at some later date. For now, I want a rest from fighting."

"We do not have that luxury as we are not allowed to settle here. So, let's go!"

Two days later, no decision had been taken. The Vikings had agreed to follow Rurik whatever his choice would be. Gwendwr was sulking. He had insisted on staying with me but, as I was talking to Rurik in Norse all the time, he could not understand a word of it. So, when we were setting up camp for the night, Gwendwr bluntly asked me:

"Are you going to join them and let me walk home alone?"

"Don't be stupid!" I replied. "I like Rurik. He reminds me of my uncle Elgar in a way, but I want to see my father again. I suppose you want to see your sister again too. There's going to be a whole new life for you helping her on the farm."

"Who says I want to work on my sister's farm?"

"What else could you do? When at home, I've always helped in the forge."

"Good for you! But just think for a minute. For the past twenty years, I have toiled as a slave on Saxon farms. Should I be reminded of it every day of my life?"

"If you feel that way, I suppose no one can force you but my mother will be disappointed."

"Why don't you help her?"

"I do sometimes."

The following morning, Rurik came to me and simply said:
"We're going North."

"Best of luck!" I replied and we embraced. Then, he and his men walked away without looking back. I watched them until they disappeared from sight. Only then, did I turn West and started to make my way home with Gwendwr. The journey lasted over a week during which time I hardly spoke, answering my uncle with either a nod or a grunt. I was angry with him, I was angry with myself, I was angry with the world. Why? I did not know.

At last, we reached home. It was late in the day and my parents were already eating dinner when we arrived. We joined them after they greeted us warmly. Later on, my mother looked at me and pointing to my armlets and belt asked:

"Are these spoils of war?"

"They are," I answered.

"Where did you get the belt from?" asked my father. "I don't remember you wearing it when you left."

"I made it myself. Do you like it?"

My father fingered it. I took it off and gave it to him for closer inspection. After a thorough examination, he exclaimed:

"Excellent workmanship! I taught you well."

"I know, dad. Tell me, has life changed around here?"

"It's the same as it always was. It's as if there has never been a war."

"But we know otherwise, don't we?"

"I prefer to forget."

"Why?"

"War is not my calling. I can fight as well as the next man if needs be but I would not make it my life. How about you, son?"

"I like it. I like leading men into battle. I like the din and brute force. I like the move and counter move when two armies vie for advantage on the battlefield."

"So, you'll leave us again."

"One day, yes! Tell me, did Elgar call?"

"I have not seen your uncle since you left with him. What is he doing nowadays?"

"When he was allowed to leave Powys, he did not tell Gwendwr what his plans were. He has not called upon me. I thought he might have visited you."

"No, he didn't. I'm not surprised, though. If you remember, when you were a child, there were years between his visits. He could be anywhere now. One day, he'll surprise us all by his return."

I settled into a routine. I needed to keep fit and practice but my father refused to partner me so, twice a week, I would go to Helsby and do so with other Vikings. After half a day of exercise, we would adjourn to the local inn and spend the rest of the day drinking and reminiscing about past deeds real or exaggerated. Most other days I would spend at the forge in the company of my father. We had little to say to each other so, like before, we worked in silence. My mother continued to toil on the farm on her own. Gwendwr, as he had told me, refused to do any work. He spent his days in total idleness. I suggested he accompanies me to Helsby on one of my jaunts. He refused. My mother was feeling angry and embarrassed about his behaviour. The atmosphere at dinner time became very strained. Nobody hardly ever spoke.

# CHAPTER 12

About two months after my return home, at the beginning of winter, on one of those days I would spent in Helsby, I drank too much. I realised I was in no state to walk back home, especially in the dark. I therefore decided to spend the night at the inn. Late the following morning, when I awoke, all the worse for wear, I forced myself to make my way home straight away. It was a cold, crisp day with hazy sunshine and I thought that a brisk walk would help my fragile state. My head was still aching and I felt better looking at the ground in front of me. Suddenly, I became aware of being watched by two men who were standing by the side of the road. They were dressed in white robes, which indicated they were Druids. As I came level with them, the older of the two spoke:

"Do you know where Ap Thor lives?"

I stopped and looked at both of them with eyes wide open. I, of course, wondered why they were looking for me. I thought best not to reveal myself. I therefore answered with a question:

"Why do you want to know and what is your business with him?"

"I'm Rhys ap Rhys, Bard," answered the other Druid.

"I'm not interested in your name but why you want to see him."

"I'm a Bard. I sing of the deeds of heroes. I want to hear from him the true story of his exploits. How, single-handedly, he saved Gwynedd from the Saxons. How he rescued the Prince from a pursuing army. Then, I shall travel the length of the

Welsh lands and, stopping in the evening, around a glowing fire, with drinks flowing, I shall tell of the heroic actions of a true Welshman."

"He's a Viking, actually," I said.

"His mother is Welsh," stated the older Druid. "That makes him a Welshman. Who his father is does not matter. More to the point, we need to talk to him. Can you please tell us where we can find him?"

"I'm a Viking and proud of it. I fought the way Vikings fight. Will you say that?"

The two druids looked at each other. They seemed afraid to speak.

"Come!" I said, "I'll show you the way."

"Thanks!" answered the older Druid. "Did you fight under Ap Thor?"

"I was on the battlefield," I replied, still unwilling to reveal myself.

"Tell me all you know about him," said Rhys ap Rhys.

"He's a blacksmith, like his father."

"Who taught him to fight?" asked Rhys ap Rhys. "How did he learn to command armies? What feats did he accomplish? This is what I need to know to speak true."

"As I said before, he is a Viking. He learnt from Vikings and trained among Vikings."

"You're proud to be a Viking, aren't you?" said the older Druid.

"Very."

"I suppose," he continued, "you consider him as one of your own. I don't blame you. However, please do not take offence. What is important to us is his Welshness. This young man with me has a talent as a bard which needs developing. To sing the right story could make his name famous. He must sing about a Welsh hero so, Ap Thor has to be a Welsh hero."

"And you could not have a Viking as a Welsh hero, could you?" I interrupted.

"That would never do," said Rhys ap Rhys. "I'll speak to Ap Thor. I'm sure he would have a different attitude from yours. Who would not in exchange for fame?"

"We have our sagas and our heroes but his mother might be more forthcoming about his Welshness. She has a great respect for you, Druids."

By this time, we had reached the mount where I would climb and use as a look-out when waiting for my father to return from his trips to the mines. The two Druids stopped, faced the mount and bowed. As they walked on, I asked them:

"Why did you do that?"

"This is a sacred place," answered the older Druid. "This is how we show our respect."

"How do you know it's a sacred place?"

"The stone circle on the top tells us. Long, long ago, our ancestors created those places to bring the people together in the worship of the New Year."

"We must part," I said. "The house you can see on your right is the place you are looking for. I walk further on. We shall meet again."

Those last words puzzled the two Druids. I could see it on their faces. I moved on without turning back. I was making my way directly to the forge. I needed to warn my father about our visitors. I had a suspicion he would not be too pleased. He had never warmed to my mother's religion, maintaining that Odin was the only God worth knowing.

"Good night was it, last night?" was my father's greeting as I walked through the forge doorway. "Came straight to me, eh! Afraid to face your mother?"

"Dad! Don't be ridiculous! Yes, it was a good night but we have visitors at the farm."

"Visitors?"

"Yes, a couple of Druids. I met them on my way here. They are looking for me."

"Whatever for?"

"Ap Thor is a great Welsh hero and they want to sing about him. I did not tell them who I was."

"Best lie low here for a while, shouldn't you?"

I worked the rest of the day with my father. Then, at our usual time, we closed shop and walked home. As we entered the house, my mother said:

"Here he is."

"Ap Thor, it is a great honour to meet you." Rhys ap Rhys greeted my father.

I burst out laughing. My mother looked embarrassed while Gwendwr smiled. The Druids looked astounded to see me again.

"I am Thor," my father said, a twinkle in his eye. "This is Ap Thor, my son."

"These strangers are Druids," stated my mother. "They've come to see you."

"I know, we met before," I answered. "Now that we are all here, perhaps we could sit down to a meal."

"Excellent idea!" said Gwendwr.

The two druids looked slightly puzzled.

"Forget this morning," I said, "and ask me any question you want answering."

The older of the two was the first to regain his composure and thus to speak:

"You had both Welsh and Vikings under your command, hadn't you? How did you manage to be obeyed?"

"Simple!" I replied. "Gwendwr, here, as my Welsh uncle, led the Welsh. My father, Thor, who once fought alongside Eldred the Avenger, led the Vikings. I don't suppose you have heard of Eldred."

"No, we have not."

"He's well respected among us. However, if it's only the Welsh side of the story you want to hear, I suggest you speak to Gwendwr."

"I shall be delighted," broke in Gwendwr. "In the final battle, I even saved the Prince of Gwynedd's life for which he rewarded me by appointing me one of his counsellors."

"We are deeply honoured," said Rhys ap Rhys. "I would be forever grateful if you would speak to a poor, humble bard like myself."

"I'm also one of the Prince's counsellors," I said. "You are both welcome to stay here as long as you need. Isn't that so, mother?"

"Absolutely!" said Gwendwlyn. "It is not often that Druids come this way. My house is truly blessed with your presence."

My mother was overjoyed with the Druids' presence. For once, my father did not make any barbed remarks to her. We presented to our visitors a truly united family. Gwendwr never stopped talking to them for the first few days. A couple of times, they came up to the forge and were quite impressed with my skills. I was reluctant to say anything. Perhaps, if they had been more ready to accept my Viking heritage, I might have been more willing to open up to them. After about a week, their daily patterns changed. They would leave early in the morning and return just in time for the evening meal when they would ask a question or two. Those questions were always precise as if Rhys ap Rhys needed to clarify some point for his story. I was in no doubt it was he who was composing it. Where would they go? I could not tell. I also began to wonder how he would describe me, how he would present my deeds. I had never met a bard before and therefore never heard any of their recitations. One evening, becoming impatient, I asked:

"Rhys, how is the story progressing."

"It will soon be done," he replied.

"In a few days' time," said the other Druid, "we would like to invite you to one of our ceremonies."

"I would be delighted to come," said my mother straight away.

"Where would that be?" I asked

"Count me in," chipped in Gwendwr.

"I'd like you all to come. It will happen at dawn on that sacred place nearby."

"Which is?" asked my father.

"The mount with the stones on the top," I replied, then I added: "I shall come, and you should too, dad."

"What for?"

"To celebrate the completion of my song about your son," said Rhys ap Rhys.

"And to say our goodbyes and thanks!" added the other Druid. "We'll choose a clear night when the stars will guide us to the mount, for we need to reach it before dawn."

The ceremony happened a few days afterwards when we walked at the dead of night and reached the sacred place before the sun came up. Rhys ap Rhys took his position with his back against one of the standing stones and faced East. He remained standing while the other Druid sat down in front of him also facing East. We were asked to sit down in front of them with our back to them and told to wait. As the first ray of the rising sun burst on us, Rhys ap Rhys started to recite the story of Ap Thor. His voice was clear and the magic of his words recreated the events of the past. As the sun rose over the horizon and blinded us, it became easier just to listen and what a story it was! I was not Ap Thor any more but the embodiment of Welsh resistance. The men who joined me had risen to the defence of their land. The Prince of Gwynedd had in me the most faithful and courageous of his subjects. The battles were not battles but the extermination of an unworthy enemy and the peace that followed was allowing the Welsh people to enjoy undisturbed their green valleys and bubbling mountain streams.

When Rhys ap Rhys stopped, I did not move. I needed time to think. His story was not the reality I had known, yet it was a story I could entirely approve of. I regretted not to have cooperated better with the author for I realised his worth as a storyteller. It was too late now for he had told us that the two of them would be on their way as soon as the ceremony was over. As I got up and looked around, I saw them walking away side by side. I ran after them.

"Please wait!" I shouted.

"It's time for us to move on," said the older Druid.

"I know but I have something for you."

From my pocket, I took a small armlet and handed it to Rhys ap Rhys. He hesitated.

"Please take it," I said. "I have made it specially for you."

"It's really beautiful. I had no idea you were such a good craftsman. Thank you!"

I, again, put my hand in my pocket and took out another armlet which I gave to the other Druid.

"You should not have," said the latter. "We don't know how to thank you."

"Just wear them, that'll be thanks enough for me."

The Druids moved on and I turned back towards my home. My father, mother and uncle were already on their way. I caught up with them. As I did so, I thought aloud:

"I wonder how many people will now know about me."

"It makes us all very proud of you," said my mother. "Don't you agree, Gwendwr?"

"I told them the story because I was there," Gwendwr replied. "You should be proud of me too."

"We are," my mother answered, "but my son gave you leadership and that's why they are going to sing his praises and not yours."

Before Gwendwr could answer, my father spoke to me in Norse so that only I could understand:

"The quiet life you now have among us must feel strange. Are you happy just to help me at the forge? If you want more adventures, don't let me stop you, I will understand. I remember, not so long ago, when you were pestering me to let you go to war. I don't believe anything has changed, has it?"

"No, father, but one does not go to war in winter. When spring comes, it will be different."

# CHAPTER 13

Spring came late that year. I had already told my father that I was planning to leave when the winter was over. Meanwhile, after the Druids' departure, Gwendwr returned to his lethargic state, refusing to help in any way either on the farm or in the house but expecting to be fed day in day out. I used some of my free time to repair and embellish my shield as well as to recast my sword in readiness for any fighting that I might find. Thus, of an evening, at the end of the meal, I spoke about my decision:

"Mother, I need to tell you something. You may have guessed, I am going to leave home again. Gwendwr, I'd like you to come with me."

"I never thought you would remain here for ever." Gwendwlyn replied. "What exactly are your plans?"

"I shall go North."

"Why are you asking me to come with you?" Gwendwr enquired. "And why go North?"

"You've said it many times before: it's better not to travel alone. As to the direction we'll take, if you come, I guess there may be some fighting under the Prince of Penrith this summer. That's why I plan to go North but tell me, Gwendwr, would you not like to fight again."

"No! Certainly not as an ordinary foot soldier, especially as I am still a counsellor to the Prince of Gwynedd."

"So am I! As such, we should be well received wherever we go."

"I'll think about it."

I gave him a week to decide. My mother, in the meantime, felt sad but said nothing. My father was proud of me and hoping I would do all the things he never did. My own feelings were mixed. I knew I wouldn't achieve anything if I stayed. I said goodbye to my Viking buddies in Helsby. None of them wanted to come with me. They had their own women and children, I was still single and therefore free. One late afternoon, I went back to the top of the mount and watched the sun go down as I used to while waiting for my father in years gone by but it somehow looked different. I do not know what I was expecting but, instead of remembering my innocence as a child, I could not help thinking of Rhys ap Rhys reciting my deeds. On my way back, the sight of the river reminded me of my first boat trip when I sailed to Ireland with Elgar. A lot had happened since then. For one thing, I was no more the wide-eyed boy I had been and I still had my dreams that had been imparted to me by Elgar's recounting of his life exploits. I still wanted to be a Viking warrior, on a par with Eldred. Yet, so far, I had only made my mark as a Welshman. I could not deny it and, if I were to do that, it would upset my mother who had remained faithful to her Welsh heritage. It was not enough for me however; I needed more. This is why I had decided to move on. I had asked Gwendwr to join me as a way of getting him away from my parents' home where he had outstayed his welcome. I did not relish his company that much, especially as he did not appreciate my Viking enthusiasm. Of course, I had no idea whether he would come but eventually he did. The day after he made his decision known to me, we were on our way.

The nights were still chilly but the days were pleasantly warm and sunny. We had a long way to go. At the beginning of the journey, the land was flat and walking was easy. Then, we reached a forest which took us two days to cross. Afterwards, it was hilly country, criss-crossed with rivers and lakes. Progress was slow. Information was hard to come by. Gwendwr was beginning to complain. The few people we met took little notice of him. They were more impressed with me on account of my shield, my armlets and my belt. So far as we could make out from our brief encounters with the locals, there had been war before the winter. No one could or would say if war had restarted. Only the Prince of Penrith would know and he lived further North, always further North.

We were sheltering for the night where we could. More often than not, it was in some abandoned, half-derelict hut. Then, the weather changed. Mist was a common occurrence with drizzle and the occasional heavy rain shower. We pressed on. I was beginning to grow impatient: the journey seemed to be never ending. Gwendwr discovered a cave by the shore of one of the lakes and decided we should stop there for a while. I disagreed but, in the morning after a night spent inside, he refused to budge. The rain had stopped so I decided to look around, leaving him behind. I walked uphill with the intention of reaching the top when, close to my goal, I heard the sound of swords clashing. I stopped, listened and then made my way towards the source of the noise. I could not see anything on account of the hedges that were dividing the fields. After crossing a few, I saw them: two people who, from the way they were handling their swords, could only be practicing. As I came closer, I noticed that one was quite elderly, while the other was fairly young and definitively still learning. When they saw me, they stopped. I came closer and addressed the younger of the two:

"You'll never learn if your partner does not act more aggressively towards you and make you sweat."

"Stranger," the older one said, "we don't need your advice. I suggest you go on your way and let us be."

"Excuse my friend," said the other one, "he is overprotective. Perhaps you would care to show me what you mean."

"Why not?" I replied as I drew my sword.

"Stop!" said the older fellow, putting himself between me and his student. "I can't allow it."

"I shall be the judge of that," the younger one answered him and, in a tone of command, added: "Gryff, remember your place! Move away and let me fight!"

"I'm ready," I said. "Strike first!"

In the beginning, I just parried the blows. After a dozen or so, I started to attack. My opponent could hardly respond. I increased the speed of my moves and it was not long before my adversary's sword flew in the air. As it touched the ground, I put my foot on it.

"You are very good. Now, could you hand me back my sword?"

"You lost it," I said. "It's mine now."

"What kind of person are you? Is that your game: to offer to teach me so you can acquire my sword?"

Gryff advanced towards me, sword in front.

"Stop!" I said. "I don't want to hurt you."

"You will return the sword or I'll fight you for it," he replied. "I'm a veteran of many battles and I am afraid of no one."

As I neither answered nor moved, he lunged at me but missed. A new fight was on. He was better than the younger fighter but still no threat to me. As we moved around the field, my previous opponent picked up the sword and rushed towards me. I was so furious about this cowardly act that I aimed a blow with such speed and strength that my adversary's sword broke. At the same time, the point of my sword was on my young opponent's throat. I could see into the eyes that faced me, first there was fear, then hatred. Gryff, in the meantime, dropped his sword and shouted:

"Do not hurt us. You can have whatever you want, just spare us."

I laughed.

"Could you move your sword away, please?" the younger one begged. "I'm sorry if I have offended you."

I did as I was asked but kept my sword in my hand in readiness. I did not want any more surprises. I also needed to tell them a few home truths:

"You both have a lot to learn if you want to become real fighters. You should also have better arms. Those swords of yours are of very poor workmanship. And as for you, young fellow, never, I repeat, never attack someone from the back."

"I said I'm sorry. Now, will you let us go?"

I smiled before answering:

"Of course, you are free to go but, before you do so, please tell me where I can find the Prince of Penrith, if you know of his whereabouts."

They looked at each other before the younger one spoke again:

"Who are you and what do you want with him?"

"My name is Ap Thor and my business is my own."

"Go down to the lake, follow the shore to your right and go up the second valley. From the top, you will see the town of Penrith, where Penrith, our Prince of Penrith, lives."

"Thank you! I've heard you call your friend Gryff but I don't know your name."

"You don't need to. The next time we meet, perhaps someone will tell you."

I put my sword back into its scabbard and started walking down the hill back to the cave. I found Gwendwr sitting just outside.

"I knew you would come back," he said when he saw me.

"I met some people. I now know which way to go."

"Thanks for coming back for me!"

"Don't flatter yourself! The way is alongside the shore of this lake."

"Ah! Ah! Very funny!"

"Are you coming?"

"I may as well, I suppose."

It was the begining of the afternoon when we reached the entrance to the second valley that was going upwards pretty steeply. I wanted to reach the top before dark but Gwendwr was moving ever so slowly. He soon ran out of breath and had to stop. I left him behind and made my way to the top on my own. As I reached the summit, I could see nothing. For a moment, I wondered whether I had been duped and, instinctively, I put my hand on the hilt of my sword. Then, I saw smoke coming from behind the next hill. I relaxed and waited for Gwendwr. He took ages to catch up with me and, when he eventually did, I could see his disappointment at seeing nothing.

"What now?" he asked.

"We've got to go to the other side of the next hill."

"More climbing!"

"I'm afraid so."

"I'm too old for so much climbing. Go ahead!"

"I don't want to leave you behind. Also, don't you think it would look better if we were to arrive together?"

"Let's wait till tomorrow!"

"No, I would not like to spend the night here. There's no shelter whatsoever."

Gwendwr sighed deeply before saying in a resigned tone: "Let's go on!"

It was nearly night when we reached the summit of the next hill. We could see many fires in a hollow below us. This time, Gwendwr rushed forward and I followed him. As soon as he came across somebody, he asked him:
"Is the Prince of Penrith here?"
"Who wants to know?"
"I'm Gwendwr, counsellor to the Prince of Gwynedd."
These words had the immediate effect of having us being led to a smoky hall at the end of which were sitting several people, one of whom I recognised as Ulls.

An elderly man, with a large amount of grey hair, stood up and introduced himself:
"I'm Penrith, Prince of Penrith. This is my son, Ulls, and my daughter, Penrose, along with my usual entourage. Please be seated. I believe you have come from Gwynedd. Do you have a message for me?"

"No message, Prince!" Gwendwr replied. "Now that Gwynedd is at peace with the Saxons, myself and my young nephew here have decided to travel. As we are both counsellors to the Prince of Gwynedd, we thought it only polite to introduce ourselves to you while travelling through your lands."

"You are most welcome. Dinner will be served soon. I hope you will partake of it with us. In the meantime, let us drink!"

I did not mind letting Gwendwr do all the talking. I did not mind either that he had never mentioned my name. While he was drinking and emptying his cup rather quickly, I looked around. I had already noticed Ulls. He looked just the same as I remembered him: young and arrogant. His sister, who was sitting on the other side of her father from her brother, was beautifully dressed with ornaments in her hair. Behind her, stood an elderly man who looked strangely familiar. I was still racking my brains to try and remember where I had seen him before when they brought the meat in. We all tucked in. I was enjoying my dinner, all the more so after all those days spent travelling, sometimes with very little food to eat. Also, it was good to rest. Suddenly, I became aware of being stared at. I looked around and saw it was Penrose as well as the old man behind her who were both looking at me. That is when I remembered: it was Gryff. He must have recognised me from our encounter earlier that day. I looked beyond him but could not see his young companion I had crossed swords with. As he was continuing to stare at me, I smiled. Ulls was watching and misinterpreted the exchange. He got up and shouted:

"How dare you, a stranger, sharing our food, smile at my sister? I shall not let this insult pass. You will answer me with your sword tomorrow morning!"

"Prince!" I said. "I am sorry if I have caused offence but I cannot fight your son without your permission."

"Granted!" the Prince of Penrith replied.

I was surprised at such a brief and quick response. Gwendwr moved away from me and I caught sight of the briefest of smiles illuminate Penrose's face. At the same time, I could not but help remembering a previous challenge from Ulls which the Prince of Gwynedd forbade me to answer. This time, the fight would happen. After a good night's sleep, I should be ready for him.

# CHAPTER 14

The word must have gone round that there was going to be a fight as a fairly large crowd had gathered on a field just on the outside of the settlement. It was mid-morning when I got the call and I followed the Prince of Penrith and Ulls. Behind me came Penrose and other members of the household. Gwendwr had made himself scarce and I could not see him anywhere. This did not surprise me. Soon, we reached the field where the fight was to take place. Ulls was glaring at me but I stayed cool. The Prince made a gesture and there was immediate silence. He then spoke:

"The first one to draw blood is declared the winner and the fighting stops."

Ulls bowed to his father. I did the same. We took our positions. The Prince gave the signal and our swords clashed. I soon realised that Ulls was just lunging at me as if he did not really seem interested in the fight. I guessed that he only wanted to draw blood and win as quickly as possible and have done with it. I would not let that happen. I also wanted to put on a good show for the people who had bothered to come and watch. By moving continuously to one side or the other, I was forcing him to adopt a defensive position. The more I did this, the more he got annoyed with my tactics and the less in control he became. His moves were getting more erratic, sometimes even missing completely. After a while, I saw my chance and took it: a heavy blow on his sword made him drop it, a quick move back up with mine and I cut him on the arm. I had won.

There was total silence from the crowd. Ulls was so surprised as to be unable to move. Penrose moved towards me and, in a voice loud enough to ensure that everyone could hear her, asked me:

"Are you Ap Thor, the one whom the bard Rhys ap Rhys sings about?"

"I am."

Turning to her brother, she told him:

"You were a fool to fight him."

"Thank you for that word of advice," he replied with utter contempt in his voice. "You seem to forget that I was fighting for you."

"I didn't ask you to."

"Children!" their father interrupted. "Not in public! Ulls! Get that cut attended to! Penrose, if you knew who this man was, you should never have allowed the fight to take place. Ap Thor, I'm sorry. Such a hero as you are should have been treated with more respect. Please stay with us for a few days. I'd like to make amends."

"I shall be delighted. I could do with a few days rest after the long journey we have had. Prince, I am no hero, just a man who did his duty whatever the bard may say. So, please, no special treatment, it is an honour to stay with you."

Ulls rejoined us, with Gwendwr at his side.

"I know you from somewhere," the former said. "Have we met before?"

"When you served under the Prince of Gwynedd," I replied.

"Excellent!" said the Prince of Penrith. "Now, you can be friends."

"Father! He's no Welshman. He's a Viking. I remember him now, serving with the Viking contingent."

"Is this true?" asked the Prince. "The bard did not mention it."

"Rhys ap Rhys got his story from my uncle Gwendwr. My other uncle, Elgar, is a Viking, like my father. My mother is Welsh and I had been a good fighter for my Prince."

"I do not doubt it. We have the testimony of the bard for it," said the Prince of Penrith as he continued: "What I do not understand, however, is why nothing of your Viking origin is spoken of."

"It would not have done," Gwendwr answered on my behalf. "I told Rhys ap Rhys what he needed to know and no more. Now, Ulls, if ever I witness any heroic deeds from you, I will tell the bard and you too can be sung about."

"I'd like that very much, Gwendwr. Let's drink to that!"

The two of them went their way. The crowd had dispersed some time before. I found myself alone with the Prince of Penrith.

"Will there be any fighting this summer?" I asked him.

"Who knows! I have had no reports of any Saxon movements. Why do you ask?"

"I'd like to put my sword at your service if needed, Lord."

"I prefer peace any time. It's what my country needs. When fighting starts, you never know how it will end. But you, youngsters, always want to prove yourselves. Even my daughter thinks she can fight. She went with me to war last year but I made sure she kept well back from the battlefield. She's very competitive, especially against her brother. Whatever he gets, she wants too."

I took leave of the Prince. As I was staying as his guest, there was something I had to do. I had not yet seen the youth I had fought with the day before but I knew Gryff was around. I would first get a new sword, to replace the one I broke, and then look for them. I therefore needed to enquire where to find a blacksmith, and was told there was a forge round the hill by the river. I made my way there and came upon a ramshackle building that was being used as a forge. Inside, were two people. One, obviously, was the blacksmith. The other seemed strangely familiar. As I got closer, I recognised Penrose. She looked surprised to see me. We did not speak. I looked around and saw that the blacksmith was going to pour some hot metal on a broken sword.

"What are you doing?" I asked.

"He's repairing the sword that you broke," Penrose replied.

I was taken aback by her words as much as by the lack of competence of the man.

"You cannot solder a sword back together. It would be totally useless to anyone," I said.

"I have repaired dozens of swords and no one has ever complained," replied the blacksmith rather angrily.

"Probably because they're dead! Did you originally make this one as well?"

"Of course! I'm the only blacksmith around here. Everybody has a sword cast by me, be he Prince or soldier, and I'm very proud of the fact."

I drew my sword. Penrose moved back a couple of steps and the blacksmith lifted his hammer.

"I only want to show you what a well made sword looks like," I said as I let its end rest on my left arm and supported the hilt with my right hand.

Nobody moved.

"Come on! Don't be afraid! Have a closer look!"

"May I hold it?" Penrose asked.

"Of course!"

She took it gingerly, weighed it and then started to swing it around. She stopped, looked puzzled, swung it again, this time faster before stopping with its point close to my face. I did not move. I was thinking back to her father's words and wondered what she actually knew about fighting. She surely could handle a sword, I had just seen proof of it. I needed to break an awkward silence:

"That's what a good sword does: it follows your hand."

The blacksmith came closer, still holding the hammer.

"Have a good look!" I said.

"This has been done by a master craftsman," was his reply after a short inspection. "You are very lucky to have acquired it. It would give you an edge in any fight. I'm not surprised you won this morning."

"Are you saying," Penrose asked, "that it is better than any of the ones you cast?"

"Definitely!"

"In that case, I'll keep it."

As she said so, she moved her cloak aside and put my sword into a scabbard on her belt. I was surprised she was so dressed. I could not help asking her:

"Do you always carry a sword?"

"Most of the time, yes!"

"Whatever for?"

"My brother and father both carry swords, why not me? I can do anything my brother does. I've always tried to emulate him, ever since I was little. He does not like it but I don't care. It will come in useful one day. My father indulges me because he believes that eventually I'll grow out of it. However, I exercise every day and, last year, I joined my father on the battlefield. Now, I have a good sword. I'll be afraid of no one. Thank you for it."

"A good sword does not make a good soldier. Until I see you fight, I reserve my judgement."

"Blacksmith! Tell him whose sword it is you are repairing."

"Yours, Princess!"

I looked at her astounded. She laughed and, as she did so, her face became radiant and beautiful in a way I had not noticed before. She removed her cloak and tied back her hair. There now could be no doubt in my mind: she was the youth I had crossed swords with in that field the morning before.

"I had no idea," I said. "Why did you not make yourself known to me?"

"It was more fun that way," she answered.

I came closer to her while talking:

"As I have told you, you have a lot to learn. At the present, you are not so good as your brother. Gryff is not teaching you correctly. He's too respectful of you. I could not understand why then, but I know now."

"And I suppose the great Ap Thor would not care to teach a woman!" she said, mockingly, still unaware of my intention. All I had to do was to move another step forward, extend my arm and grab my sword out of her scabbard. I did just that and regained my property. She looked confounded while the blacksmith's jaw dropped.

"No, Penrose, I'd be delighted to teach you if you're prepared to make the effort but, first, you need a sword."

"Let me finish repairing your sword, then, Ma'am," said the blacksmith as he gave it a few hammer blows.

"You're wasting your time. Penrose, you deserve better. If I am to teach you, you will use a sword as good as mine. One that would not break, not even if it strikes a stone."

"That's impossible," the blacksmith answered.

"Where would I get such a sword?" asked Penrose. "Or is this an excuse to go back on your word?"

"You did not ask who made my sword."

"Why should I? He's probably living miles away."

"You are wrong. He stands before you. I cast my own sword because I learnt this skill from the best: my father."

Nobody answered me. After a while, I spoke again:

"Blacksmith, if you allow me the use of your forge, I'll show you how it's done and Penrose will have a sword as good as mine."

"Are you for real?" Penrose asked. "Can you really cast me a sword like your own?"

"I also cast this belt I'm wearing, out of the spoils from my last campaign, the one that Rhys ap Rhys speaks about."

"He did not mention the belt."

"Neither did he mention the fact that my father is a Viking."

"The same Viking who taught you this trade?" asked the blacksmith.

"Yes!"

"So, is it all Viking workmanship?"

"Of course!"

"Lady, you cannot accept his sword. As a Welsh Princess, you can only accept Welsh artefacts."

"Who says?" asked Penrose. "I should have the best and if the best is Viking workmanship, so be it. Blacksmith, let him do the job! That's an order!"

I set to work. I threw the old sword into the fire to get a good melt down. I looked at the cast, cleaned it, picked some of the dust mixed with iron shavings from the floor of the forge and spread the mixture onto the mould. I worked the bellows to increase the heat from the fire, stirred the melting iron, poured it out, sprinkled some earth on the top, let it cool a bit, used the hammer to flatten the edges and, when satisfied, dipped it into cold water. All that time, both Penrose and the blacksmith had been watching me with intense curiosity but without saying a word. However, I was far from finished. Now was the most crucial part: to turn it into an effective weapon. I dipped it into the fire many times, hammered at it to thin it on the sides first, then on the point. I washed it many times, let it dry, heated it up, gave it more gentle taps with the hammer, inspected it and repeated the process time and again. At last, it was nearly done. I only needed to do the finishing touches. I looked around but could not see what I needed.

"Blacksmith!" I asked. "Where is your sharpening stone?"

"I don't have one."

I had been sweating for over two hours and still could not hand Penrose a finished product. I felt frustrated but I controlled myself.

"I'm sorry, Princess, you will have to wait a bit longer for your sword," I said. "I'll have to take it with me and finish it in my quarters."

Without saying goodbye to any one, I turned on my heels and left the forge. Penrose ran after me.

"What's wrong with you?" she asked.

I continued walking in silence as fast as I could. She was making an effort to keep up with me. I started to run. She ran too. We soon found ourselves close to the settlement. I stopped.

"I'll give you this sword tomorrow when we meet for your lesson. I suppose there is a quicker way to reach that field where I first met you. You will need to show me."

"No!" she interrupted me. "Gryff will. Just wait for him to come for you."

She then left me.

# CHAPTER 15

That evening, I wanted to be by myself. I always found it relaxing to rub the sharpening stone up and down the sides of a weapon. I also needed to make sure that the sword I would be giving to Penrose on the following morning was as sharp as could be. At the same time, I had to decide whether I was going to stay on until she was proficient or leave in a few days as originally intended. I was so deeply absorbed in both my thoughts and my work that I did not notice Gwendwr coming in. He was now standing in the middle of the room looking at me.

"Do you plan to kill someone?" he asked.

"Pardon?"

"Joke!"

"Do you want anything?"

"I need to talk. I made good friends with Ulls today. We actually spent the day together. He told me so much about himself. I'm sure he has lots more to tell me. He also wants me to find Rhys ap Rhys. He's determined that the Bard should sing about him rather than about you. I hope you don't mind."

"You're free to do as you please. I don't think this has anything to do with me."

"On the contrary, I need to stay at least two weeks here before looking for the Bard. How does this fit in with your plans."

"I don't mind staying a while longer. Do you know where Rhys ap Rhys has gone to?"

"No, not exactly, people think he's gone North."

"Fine! I understand Odin's Town is North too."

"What the hell do you want to go to Odin's Town for?"

"That's always been an ultimate purpose of mine. I hope to find my uncle Elgar there."

"But I can't go to a Viking town."

"Not really, no! So, I'll go looking for Elgar and you go in search of the Bard."

"Charming! I thought we would always stick together."

"Gwendwr! Go back to Ulls. I'm not in the mood to be sociable. I'll have a bite to eat here and an early night. Convey my apologies to the Prince of Penrith for my absence, will you?"

"Sure!"

I was again alone with my thoughts. Having finished Penrose's sword to my satisfaction, I had a short rest before I sharpened my own. When I had finished with that task, I lay down to rest for the night but I could not sleep. I kept tossing and turning and asking myself the same question: why did I agree to teach Penrose? I could not find the answer. I must have dozed off for, when I woke up, the sun was already up in the sky. It promised to be a beautiful day. Soon, Gryff appeared as if from nowhere.

"Are you ready?" he asked.

"Yes!" I answered, grabbing the spare sword.

"May I have a look?"

"Certainly!" I replied and handed the weapon to him.

"Exquisite! And very sharp! Where did you acquire it?"

"Are we on our way?" I said angrily.

"You cannot take that sword with you. It won't do to teach the Princess."

"What sword I use is no concern of yours. Just take me to her and keep silent."

I grabbed the sword back from him. Gryff looked at me, shrugged his shoulders, turned round and, without saying a word, walked away. I followed him. Soon, I saw Penrose waiting for us by some huge boulders. As I came closer, I noticed a narrow passage between them. She went through it with me behind her. As we emerged on the other side, I handed the sword to Penrose. She admired it but Gryff, who had followed us, was unhappy.

"Be careful!" he said. "I don't think you should handle it. You might hurt yourself."

"Send him away, please. What we do is none of his business," I told Penrose.

"Quite!" she replied as she looked at Gryff in such a way that he just walked away, mumbling something to himself that I could not understand. She then added:

"Come! Let us begin!"

I followed her and we soon found ourselves in the field where we had first met two days before. She was very keen to start but I held her back. I wanted to make her fully aware of the risks she was taking by advising her:

"Both swords, yours and mine, are made to cut, maim and kill. We need to practise with them because, on the battlefield, we'll be using these and the more we use them the better."

"Do you think I shall fight on a battlefield one day?"

"Who knows? If it happens, you have to be ready. Two things you need to possess: proper handling of the sword and stamina. I could add you also need a shield. Have you got one?"

"Not with me! Should I bring one tomorrow?"

"We'll talk about it later. For now, I want you to follow my instructions."

We spent the rest of the morning practising moves. After a brief rest, I made her run with me round the field. She soon fell behind. I called it a day. She was unhappy and made it known to me:

"Why stop now? When I was exercising with Gryff, we would do it the whole day long."

"Remember what I said about stamina. On a battlefield, you must be prepared to walk, charge, run and move fast when ordered. Just now, you could not keep up with me, that won't do."

"So, you're giving up on me."

"I never said that. I'll turn you into a soldier but you have to trust me. Anyway, it is not as if I'm leaving tomorrow."

"Will you stay to teach me then?"

"Of course, until you're ready!"

As soon as I had said those words, I regretted it. I had no intention of staying in Penrith forever but, somehow, I was doing things and saying words that I thought I did not really mean. Penrose seemed to have that effect on me and I could not understand why. I sat down and we chatted. She explained to me how her passion for fighting started:

"My father could not get my brother to start learning how to fight. He had appointed Gryff to teach him. My father and Gryff were the veterans of many campaigns as they had fought side by side. One day, I was listening to my brother's reluctance to learn. I must have been eight or nine years old. In a tantrum, he had thrown his sword on the floor. I picked it up and said I would learn how to fight instead of my brother. Nobody took me seriously until I ran towards Gryff, sword in front. He gently pushed my sword away with his own but I attacked him again. My father then told Gryff to give me a lesson, hoping to keep me quiet and to put his son to shame. This was to no avail. As a result, Ulls has been resenting me and Gryff has been training me ever since."

She stopped talking. I remained silent, waiting for her to continue. She did not. Instead, she suggested we had another clash of arms. I agreed, against my better judgement. There were times when it was impossible to say no to Penrose. Not that I minded because she was no beginner and, also, she was showing a great willingness to improve. I did not try to beat her but kept on suggesting better moves, some of which were new to her. When we stopped, at the end of the day, she asked me:

"Why has Gryff not shown me as much as you have? I've learnt more in one day with you than in all those years with him."

"Don't blame him! He probably doesn't even know some of the moves I taught you and, anyway, he's too soft with you."

"Don't say that. Gryff was a great warrior once."

"I would not dispute that but some of the moves are typically Viking ones and he probably would never have learnt about them."

"Are you trying to turn me into a Viking?"

"Vikings make the best fighters."

"That's a matter of opinion. As the daughter of the Prince of Penrith, I cannot agree with you. I must remain Welsh but you can teach me Viking tricks."

As she said it, a large smile lit up her face and there was a twinkle in her eyes.

That evening, I sat at the Prince of Penrith's table. Ulls came in late. Gwendwr was following him like a shadow. Penrose was sitting next to me. Gryff was whispering into the Prince's ear and had been doing so for a while. Suddenly, the Prince addressed me:

"Ap Thor! What do you think of my daughter? Gryff, here, tells me you have been crossing swords with her today."

"Only in a friendly way!"

"I'm sure you would prefer to exercise with someone more worthy of your experience."

"Your daughter has been well taught. It reflects well on her teacher, Gryff, I believe."

I saw Gryff look at me and raise his eyebrows but he said nothing.

"It's time for me to have a different teacher," Penrose stated. "Ap Thor will do just fine."

"How long do you plan to stay here?" asked Ulls in a rather unfriendly tone of voice.

"I shall help Gwendwr on his quest to find the Bard when you let him go," I replied.

"Ap Thor!" the Prince of Penrith said. "You must not feel obliged to teach my daughter. Don't hesitate to say no to her if she pesters you."

"Penrose could never pester me, my Lord," I replied.

"Tell me," the Prince of Penrith continued, "do you think women should learn to fight?"

"Your daughter is not just any woman."

A great deal of laughter resounded through the hall. I felt embarassed. Penrose turned towards me and smiled. I smiled back. Ulls rose and threw his cup to the ground, spilling the drink inside, then shouted:

"I won't stand for this!"

"Ulls, sit down!" Penrose said in a quiet but firm voice. "Don't show me up in front of the whole court! I'll smile to whomever I please but certainly not at you. Stop throwing your weight around and wanting to fight all and sundry, using me as a paltry excuse."

"Someone needs to defend your honour if our father won't do it," replied Ulls. "Ap Thor! Don't you think it's time for a re-match?"

"Ulls! That's enough! Sit down and behave yourself!" the Prince of Penrith said and, turning to me, he added: "I feel so ashamed of my son's behaviour. I'm really sorry."

"You need not be," I replied. "I have not taken offence."

"Good! Let's forget about this then. Let's refill those cups and drink!"

"One moment!" Penrose shouted as she got up. "Brother, as you have thrown out a challenge and as nobody else will take it up, I shall fight you tomorrow."

"Don't!" I whispered to her. "You're not ready."

There was total silence as well as consternation on the face of everyone present. Ulls, still standing, was looking at his sister, his mouth wide open, hardly believing what he had just heard. The Prince choked on his drink and could not control his coughing. Gwendwr looked at me with accusing eyes as if he held me responsible for the whole incident. After a while, the first person to speak was Gryff:

"Penrose and Ulls, you're not children any more. This rivalry between you must stop. We have honoured guests among us tonight."

"Old man! Shut up!" Ulls interrupted. "Sister, I won't accept your challenge, you're not a worthy opponent for me."

"You only say that because you're afraid I'll beat you and you could not live it down," Penrose replied before walking out of the hall.

I followed her and, as I caught up with her outside, I asked her:

"Did you not hear what I whispered to you in there?"

"It's a beautiful night," she replied. "Look at all those stars!"

"You can't fight your brother. Not now, anyway. You're not good enough. You need more practice, otherwise you'll lose."

"I believe you care for me. That's sweet."

She went on her way and I went on mine. Soon Gwendwr joined me. He looked troubled.

"What was all that about?" he asked.

"How should I know?" I replied.

"Surely you must know something, you've spent the whole day with Penrose."

"And you with Ulls!"

"Come on, nephew! It's not the same. You're teaching her how to fight and she challenges her brother. I'm only listening to what Ulls is saying."

"I don't think it will happen. You need not worry about it."

"I value my friendship with Ulls and he likes me."

"Good for you, uncle. Now, if you don't mind, I shall retire for the night."

"And spend tomorrow with Penrose?"

"That's the plan."

But, deep inside, I was not so sure. However, early the following day, I made my way towards the boulders and passageway. As I was hesitating to get through it, I saw Penrose approaching from behind me.

"I'm glad you came," I said.

"You said many unkind words to me last night. I'm not prepared to talk to you today."

She kept her word. We trained in silence. We rested without exchanging a word. When, at last, I called it a day and told her how much she had improved, her only answer was:

"You don't have to lie. Go back to Penrith. I shall stay here for a while longer."

"Whatever for?"

"The stillness of the countryside as the sun sets," she said wistfully.

It did not make any sense to me but I did not wish to argue. I made my way back on my own. The next few days turned out to be similar. I guessed it was time for a change. I told her to meet me at the forge with her shield. As she asked me why, I refused to answer and when I turned up at the forge the following morning, the blacksmith was surprised to see me again.

"What brings you here today?" he asked when he saw me.

"Have you ever reinforced a shield?" I questioned him.

"What are you talking about?"

"You'll soon see and hopefully learn if Penrose comes."

She did but only after having made me wait nearly half the day. She brought her own shield with her as I had asked her to. I set to work. I made a very thin sheet of metal as a lining on the inside and a more ornate cover for the outside. It was painstaking work requiring a great deal of hammering. The blacksmith was hovering over me all the time. I assumed he wanted to learn a few tricks from me. I was not giving anything away. I was not speaking either. Penrose had sat on a three-legged stool by the door. She occasionally looked at me but, most of the time, she was looking away. Ever since the evening when she challenged her brother and I whispered to her that she was not good enough to beat him, she had never behaved the same towards me. She was distant, keeping talk to a minimum, but always pushing herself to the limit in order to improve. I could not make out what the matter was. However, once or twice, I asked her whether I had offended her but her answer was always the same:

"It's not up to me to explain, it's up to you to guess."

At last, I had finished. I handed the shield to her without speaking.

"Can you explain to me why you added all that covering to my shield?" she asked without taking the shield from my hand.

"There are several reasons: as the daughter of the Prince of Penrith, your shield should reflect your status. It's personal to you. The embossing on the front spells out your name. And there's the safety aspect from a purely military point of view."

She looked at it and seemed pleased when she deciphered her name. A hint of a smile came upon her lips. She took it from me and, as she slipped it over her left arm, she remarked:

"It's quite light. I would have thought that all that metal would have made it very heavy."

"It's strong enough so that no sword is able to pierce it. A real advantage in battle!"

"How's that?"

"Sometimes, a sword can penetrate an ordinary shield and you might get a cut on your arm. If you kill your opponent or seriously injure him and he lets go of his sword stuck on your shield, what can you do? It hinders its use. Why do you think that we Vikings are so good in battle?"

"Another of your Viking tricks?"

I laughed. She did too. We walked back to Penrith side by side.

For the next two days, I trained her in the use of the shield. She was more relaxed than she had been for a while and it made the day pass more quickly and more pleasantly. I felt happier too. At the end of the second day, I said:

"Do you remember my words when I recast your sword?"

"You said many things."

"True! I also said you could cut a stone with it."

"A likely story!"

"I think you are ready now. You should be able to do it. I'll show you how."

She laughed. At the top of the field there was a rather large stone. Pointing to it, I said:

"If you don't try, you'll never know."

She looked at me, undecided as to what to do next. I walked towards the stone. She followed me.

"This is how you do it. You hold your sword with both hands, raise it to above your head, and strike the stone as fast and as hard as you can."

She glanced towards me before trying. The sword cut into the stone but she could not remove it.

"Look! I've lost my sword or is it another of your tricks?" she asked.

"Sometimes, your sword can get wedged in your opponent's shield. There's a way to remove it. The very same knowledge you need to recover your sword from this stone. Grab the hilt with both hands and let me show you."

I stood close behind her and put my hands over hers and started a rocking movement. I tried to concentrate on what I was doing but I found it difficult with Penrose's body so close to mine.

"When I tell you to, you must pull as hard as you can," I whispered into her ear. "Are you ready? Pull!"

I pulled too. As I did so, I fell backwards and so did she on top of me.

"I've done it!" she shouted as she dropped the sword and turned over.

She was still half on top of me. What she did next took me completely by surprise: She kissed me. Before I could say anything, she kissed me again... and again... and again...

# CHAPTER 16

We forgot time. The sun set. The stars appeared in the sky. We were still lying on the grass where we had fallen, still in each other's arms, still kissing.

"I wish this day would never end," Penrose said as she looked up and, noticing a thin crescent of a moon just above the horizon, she added: "This will be our moon. Whenever we see it like that, if we are not together, we shall think of each other. Promise?"

"Anything you say! And congratulations!"

"Whatever for?"

"You know as much as I do about fighting."

"How can you say that at a time like this?"

She was annoyed. She got up, picked her sword and shield and walked away. I followed and caught up with her.

"What's wrong?" I asked.

"You always say the wrong thing at the wrong time."

I thought best not to answer. As we reached Penrith, we saw something was afoot. There was a different feel to the place. We soon found out why. News had come during the day that a Saxon army was on the march.

"That means war," Penrose stated. "We must see my father at once."

We made our way to the big hall. There was a hive of activity. However, the sight of Penrose fully armed momentarily caught everyone's attention. Gwendwr, who had been standing next to Ulls, ran towards me as soon as he saw me.

"Where have you been?" he asked. "Do you know what's happening? We're marching tomorrow. You're coming with us."

"Not so fast, uncle! Who are we?"

"You and me, of course!"

"Who else is marching?"

"Ulls is leading the first contingent and he has asked me to be his second in command."

"Congratulations! Who else is going?"

"No one else. That's it for now. Him, you and me and the men from Penrith."

"Are you mad? I would never serve under Ulls. Whatever possessed you? You go with him if you want but don't expect me to be by your side."

"What will you do?"

"I don't know and, actually, that's none of your business."

I made my way to the Prince of Penrith. Penrose was talking to him. I had to wait and stood at some distance to be polite as I did not want to give the impression I was eavesdropping. Gwendwr had rejoined Ulls. I do not know what he said to him but the latter exclaimed loudly enough for everyone to hear:

"I don't want him. You're here to serve me. I choose who fights for me not you."

I could not help smiling upon hearing this outburst. There was no love lost between him and me.

A little later, the Prince of Penrith walked over to me and, taking me to one side, asked me:

"Some days ago, you offered your services in case of war. War has arrived. Does your offer still stand?"

"Of course, Prince," I replied. "But I understand that Ulls is going and I don't think I could serve under him. What I could do, however, is to try and recruit some Vikings to fight for you. I understand they have settled around Odin's Town. Is it very far?"

"The truth is I am poor. I cannot afford to pay mercenaries. Ulls is going first, mostly to find out as much as he can about the enemy's intentions. I have sent Gryff to call up more men from every corner of my lands. When they arrive, will you join them?"

"You seem to forget, Prince, that I once commanded an army. I am not really prepared to fight as an ordinary soldier."

"I see. Mmm. You want a command. Then you will have to wait."

He walked away and Penrose approached me. She was still fully armed.

"Ulls is leading an advance party," she said. "I told my father I wanted to be fully active during this war and not just an observer like last year. He disagrees because he thinks that no one would want to fight alongside me. You would, wouldn't you?"

"He's not keen to give me a command either."

"Oh! You're so irritating at times. Can't you for once answer my question?"

"Of course, I'll fight alongside you. I know you can fight. I've trained you."

"Tell this to my father, then,"

"Some other time, perhaps. Just now, I think he has other things on his mind."

The following morning, Ulls, Gwendwr and some hundred men marched away to war. After their departure, the settlement looked deserted. I caught sight of Penrose, again fully armed, making her way towards the boulders. I ran to catch up with her.

"Where are you going?" I asked, a little out of breath. "Surely, you don't expect to do more training with me, today of all days?"

"What's special about today?"

"War has started. Training is over."

"Just like that? What about last evening? Did I dream it? Did it mean nothing to you?"

I did not answer. How could I? I did not want to be alone with her because of what happened last evening. Or was it because I could not trust myself? I was flattered, I admit, but how was I supposed to react? If she had been anybody else, it would have been different but she was the daughter of the Prince of Penrith whose hospitality I was a recipient of.

"I'm waiting for your answer," she said after a little while. "Or have you nothing to say?"

I grabbed her and planted a kiss on her lips. She responded at once with more kisses. That day, we did go to the usual field but we did not train. In the warmth of early summer, we became lovers.

Men were arriving by the day in answer to their Prince's call to arms. Gryff had not yet returned when a message was received from Ulls: the Saxon army was huge and he needed reinforcements at once in case of attack. Otherwise, he would have to retreat. The Prince of Penrith called a meeting of his counsellors to which he invited me. Penrose was there too. She looked beautiful. She had taken care of her hair, letting it flow over her shoulders and put on her best cloak but, underneath, she wore tight fitting clothes and a belt from which hung her sword. She was sitting on her father's right, a place usually occupied by Ulls. When I came in, she smiled at me and I smiled back. This was observed by some of the counsellors present who quickly glanced from her to me and back. I ignored them and addressed the Prince of Penrith:

"You called for me?"

The Prince barely acknowledged me. Instead, he spoke to the gathering:

"This is the situation: Gryff has not returned yet but there are plenty of men ready to march. My son is asking for reinforcements. Shall I send them?"

Everybody looked at everybody else but nobody spoke. After a short while, the Prince continued:

"As more men are due to arrive, I cannot leave Penrith. The choice is simple: either we wait for Gryff and he can take them all to my son or we appoint someone else. And this time, I need an answer."

"Who else but Gryff could do it?" asked one of the counsellors.

"How dangerous is the situation?" another one enquired.

"Very, according to my son," the Prince replied. "Of course, there is Ap Thor. We have all heard of his deeds when the Bard Rhys ap Rhys visited us. Will our men agree to march under him and accept his orders? Many might resent a foreigner. You are my counsellors, say something!"

Again the counsellors remained silent. I could not figure out why. I ventured an opinion:

"I think they should march tomorrow. As to who should lead them, may I suggest your daughter, Penrose."

There was uproar. Everyone was talking. Penrose looked surprised at first. She soon recovered, rose to her feet and told her father:

"I'm ready to lead your men."

The Prince of Penrith turned towards me. He could hardly contain his anger:

"Whatever possessed you to suggest this? You're playing into her hands. What good would she be on the battlefield? Playing at soldier is different from being one."

"I beg to disagree," I replied. "Your daughter is as good as your son. If she wants to make herself useful, give her the chance. I can vouch for her readiness."

All eyes were turned to the Prince and it was evident that all the counsellors were expecting him to speak. Instead, Penrose did:

"Father, why don't you appoint Ap Thor joint commander with me. As your daughter, I would command respect from the men but I shall defer to him on tactics."

"That's a silly idea. I won't entertain it," replied the Prince. "I think it's time you grow up, Penrose, and stop those childish games."

"One moment, please!" I said. "It would be an honour for me to serve alongside Penrose."

"I don't think you quite understand," the Prince said. "My daughter likes to have her own way. She's totally irresponsible. Because we humour her and let her train with a sword does not mean we can put her in charge of an army."

"You forget she's your daughter, Prince," I answered. "She will neither let you down nor your people. I'll trust her to do a good job. Spread the word: we're marching tomorrow at first light."

"Just a moment!" said one of the counsellors who had not spoken before. "Nothing has been decided. I'm sure you will all agree when I say the matter needs further discussion."

"Your Prince's son has asked for reinforcements," I said. "What discussion do you need when there are men ready to march?"

"Ap Thor is right," Penrose said. "And you know it, Father."

We had been marching at a brisk pace for most of the day. It was now the middle of the afternoon and I called a halt. That morning, as we left Penrith, it had been rather chaotic. Nobody was expecting Penrose to be there so early and therefore were not ready for an immediate departure. She and I did not wait. We just started and everybody had to follow as best they could and, for most of the day, our contingent of men did not look like an army at all. That is why I decided to stop.

"We're not setting up camp yet," I shouted. "We are doing some training. Line up in two lines facing each other with shields on and swords out."

I moved to the centre of one line and indicated to Penrose to face me. Like everyone else, she had tied her shield to her left arm and was holding her sword in her right hand. Most of the men were puzzled. They had not expected their Prince's daughter to be ready to fight or even to obey any command of mine. They were even more surprised when I and Penrose started exercising. I shouted:

"Come on! Exercise time!"

They did as they were told. The clash of swords by so many people made such a noise that one could have believed that an actual battle was taking place. I was pleased with the result because it showed the men were bonding. However, I was not prepared to let them off lightly. After about an hour, I told them to stop, be ready to move on, and I made them run. I kept them running until it was almost dark and we stopped to camp for the night. Penrose was completely worn out but she neither fell behind nor complained and I was proud of her.

Three days of forced marching later, we reached Ulls' army. He had not expected to be reinforced so soon. Penrose insisted on the two armies remaining separate while camping close by. To my surprise, her brother agreed. Gwendwr barely acknowledged my presence. I gave my men a morning's rest but insisted on one to one training in the afternoon with me and Penrose leading by example. The noise attracted Ulls who could not believe his eyes at the sight of his sister exercising like any of the men.

"What are you doing, sister?" he asked. "Surely, this is not necessary."

"I'm making sure," she replied, "that I shall be ready when the fighting starts. Don't you train?"

"I don't need to," he answered with his usual arrogance.

"Tell me," I said, "what are the Saxons doing."

"They're over there. I'm waiting for them to make the first move."

"How many are they?'

"No idea!"

"Have you not been spying on them?"

"Whatever for? There's an army there. If they come, we withdraw or fight them. I don't know which yet."

Without waiting for an answer, he left. Penrose saw that I was disconcerted.

"Don't worry," she told me, "he's like that most of the time but if he has to, he'll fight."

"I hope so but I'll have to go and spy tomorrow morning. I want to see for myself what we are up against."

"May I come?"

"Why not?"

The weather had changed. We woke up to a light drizzle. This would make it unlikely for any battle to start today. It would also help to hide me on my spying trip and let me approach the enemy closer. Penrose was coming along and I chose two soldiers to accompany us. The ground was uneven and I was looking for a good spot to spy on the enemy without being seen when I noticed a small mount some distance in front of me. I made for it, followed by the other three. As we were going to climb it, we saw some movement at the top. It was occupied by the enemy. They must have seen us coming for they stood side by side with shields overlapping. I counted six of them.

"Penrose to my right!" I said. "One each on either side of us. Lock shields and draw swords."

"You're not going to attack, are you?" asked the soldier on Penrose's right side.

"We have no choice," I replied. "Forward!"

The enemy responded by rushing down the side. There was a mighty clash as we met. Penrose could not quite hold her ground, leaving a gap between me and her. It gave me the chance to put my sword through her opponent's neck. He fell to the ground. I turned round and the fight started in earnest. Keen to avenge their comrade, two of them were attacking me. I was too busy defending myself to see how the others were doing. I decided to fall back a little bit then lunge forward. It worked: I hit one of them in the leg. I turned my attention to the other but he fled. I turned round and finished off the first. As I did so, one of my men fell. I rushed to his defence and killed his opponent. I was now free to help Penrose. She was giving her all to defend herself. With me joining her, the enemy stood no chance and was soon killed. At about the same time, the remaining enemy was being disposed off and we were victorious. I made my way to the top. As I did so, I heard the sound of someone vomiting. It was Penrose.

By now, the rain had stopped and the sun was making an appearance giving me a good view of the countryside around me. I could now see both the enemy's camp and our camp and then, turning towards the South, I saw the unmistakable sign of an army on the march. From the direction they were coming, it could not be Gryff: the Saxons were getting reinforcements. They must have been expecting them. This would explain why they had not attacked us yet. Action was needed and fast. No one had followed me up to the top of this mount and, as I turned back and down, I could see why: Penrose was as white as a sheet and unsure whether she was going to be sick or not. The fallen man had a nasty wound in his side and his comrade was trying to stop the bleeding by closing it with clumps of grass.

"No time to waste!" I said. "Back to camp! Penrose, move! And you too! Can you amble along?"

"I think he can if I help him," replied the soldier who like me was unscathed, "but we won't be able to walk very fast."

"Try your best. Penrose and I need to hurry back."

"What for?" she asked me as she took hold of my arm.

"We need a council of war with Ulls."

"Is it that serious?"

"Yes, it is."

The quick march did Penrose some good. As soon as we reached camp, we made our way to Ulls' quarters. He was taken aback by the livid expression on Penrose's face.

"What happened?" he asked, seeming to show real concern for his sister.

"The Saxons are getting reinforcements," I said, "we need to move."

"Gwendwr!" Ulls shouted. "Did you hear it? The Saxon army is getting bigger."

"We have to retreat." Gwendwr said. "We cannot stay here."

"That's what Ap Thor has just been saying," Ulls answered.

"I did not say that, only that we need to move. I've spied on them and I know they've spied on us. They know our positions and that won't do."

"You also said they were getting reinforcements," Ulls added.

"They have not reached their camp yet. That gives us some advantage if we move now."

"Retreat is what I said," repeated Gwendwr.

"My intention would be to move further North," I said. "If they follow us, as I expect they will, they are bound to find themselves between us and the army that Gryff is bringing if he comes soon enough."

"It's risky, but it might work," Ulls admitted.

"It worked in Gwynedd," stated Gwendwr. "Ap Thor is quite good at this kind of tactic. It might work again."

"Agreed then?" I asked. "We strike camp now?"

They all nodded. Penrose and I went back to our men. She was still fragile and hung on to my arm and that was the way we led the march to a new camp.

# CHAPTER 17

After half a day's march, Ulls wanted to stop.

"I think we've gone far enough," he said, "any further and Gryff might not find us."

"You may be right," I agreed. "Let's stop here. It's as good a spot as any. Penrose, how do you feel?"

"Better!" she replied. "I think the march did me good. I'm sorry for the way I behaved. I could not help it."

"You did very well, keeping on fighting to the end," I praised her. "Forget about your weak stomach. It happens to most people after their first kill."

"What are you talking about?" Ulls enquired. "I was not aware of any fighting. How did you get involved, sister? Ap Thor, could my sister have been hurt?"

"She was not," I said. "So, let us say no more about it."

That evening the fact that Penrose fought and then marched arm in arm with me was the men's talk. They were not too surprised about the fighting. They all knew that she liked to sport arms and that Gryff had been training her. Few knew about my involvement and many speculated as to whether there was anything going on between us. However, after the events of the morning, she needed comfort and reassurance. Ignoring what the men might conclude, she insisted on spending the night close to me, even to the extent that she fell asleep in my arms.

I woke up early, carefully disengaged myself from Penrose so as not to wake her and walked about the camp. Everything seemed in order and no enemy activity had been spotted. I came back and sat by Penrose, still asleep. I closed my eyes and dozed off. Gwendwr woke me up:

"Ulls is looking for you," he said.

"Can't he come to me?"

"He's watching the enemy."

These words made me jump up. Penrose was still asleep. I woke her up and the three of us made our way to where Ulls was standing looking at the Saxon army taking position. It was an impressive sight. I reckoned they outnumbered us three to one. They did not seem to be in a hurry. Our own men were lining up of their own accord. I told them to stand down. I did not want any confrontation. Instead, I gave the order to strike camp and be ready to march. Ulls then realised I had taken control and he made his discontent known:

"What are you trying to do? Giving orders without consulting me?"

"Surely," I said, "you are not thinking of engaging the enemy. There are too many of them."

"They want a battle."

"We don't! We move East. Marching is all we can do until Gryff arrives with reinforcements. Then, you will have your battle."

"Sounds reasonable!" Penrose commented. "Don't you agree?"

I waited until the Saxon army was all set, facing us and ready to attack. I then gave the order to march as planned. To follow us, they needed to change from facing North to facing East, not an easy task for an army that is ready to attack with shields interlocked. I told our men to quick march so that we could have a head start. A couple of hours later, I spotted a fairly large mount slightly to the right of us. I ordered the men to run so that we could secure it before the Saxons realised what we were after. We succeeded. Ulls, of course, was unhappy and so was Gwendwr. The former because he was unable to give any orders to the troops and the latter because he was fearing I intended to fight after all. Penrose, on the other hand, was beginning to panic. She had just realised the real meaning of war: how close she was to an enemy who wanted to kill us. How her thought of it as a game was not a game any more. How she was trapped, together with a couple of hundred men, in relying on the decision of one man for their survival. I worried because I knew that if the men were noticing Penrose's panic, they would panic too. I therefore called her to my side as I was watching the enemy's moves down below.

"Penrose!" I said. "Do you trust me?"

"Of course! Why would I sleep with you otherwise?"

"That's not what I mean at all. I was referring to the conduct of the war."

"Oh! Well! To tell you the truth, I am afraid."

"Afraid to die or afraid because you don't know what's going to happen next?"

"A bit of both, I suppose."

"Now, I ask you again: do you trust me to get you through this?"

"Honestly?"

"Honestly!"

"I don't know. We seem to be going from crisis to crisis."

"You're supposed to be a commander. What would you do?"

"I've no idea. Fight? Retreat? I just don't know."

"So, I ask you again: do you trust me to give the right commands?"

"You have the experience and the reputation so, I suppose, in a way, I do trust you."

"Good! Don't spoil your dreams with fear! You wanted to go to war, to command like your brother. You have the chance today, don't let it pass or you will regret it."

"I don't know what to say. What should we do now?"

"What do you think the Saxons are doing?"

"Are they setting up camp?"

"Well spotted! What do you conclude?"

"They won't attack us?"

"Perfect! So, what do we do?"

"What can we do?"

"I'll tell you. We retire early. Set up double sentry and be ready to get up at first light."

"Are you expecting fighting tomorrow then?"

I did not reply. Instead, I took her in my arms and kissed her. I heard a few cheers. I realised we had been seen.

By the middle of the next morning, the Saxon army had been standing in full battle array for about two hours. I had used the same tactic as the day before by ordering the men to be ready but not to stand. The four of us, Ulls, Gwendwr, Penrose and myself, were closely watching the enemy.

"Do you notice anything peculiar about them today?" I asked.

"No!" said Gwendwr.

"What are we supposed to notice?" Ulls enquired. "It's still the same army as yesterday."

"There seems to be fewer of them." Penrose said. "Or am I mistaken?"

"You are not," I said.

"I'm damned!" Ulls exclaimed. "Where are the rest of them?"

As we pondered that question, we saw three men move forward from the Saxon ranks with a flag of truce. I straight away gave the order for the men to stand in full battle order right behind us. I asked one of them to hold a flag of truce next to us.

"Gwendwr!" I said. "You remember your Saxon, don't you? I want you to translate what I shall be saying."

"Don't you think I should be the one to negotiate?" Ulls interrupted. "After all, my father is the Prince of Penrith."

"I defeated two of their armies a couple of years ago," I replied. "I need to reveal myself so I shall speak. You may afterwards."

"Brother!" Penrose said. "Let Ap Thor speaks! We need to show a united front."

Ulls frowned but kept quiet. The three Saxons were advancing cautiously, stopping now and then to see whether we would come down towards them. I refused to move in spite of entreaties from Gwendwr. I could now have a closer look at them and was surprised to see that the one in the middle was a Christian monk. He was wearing a dirty robe and had a large wooden cross hanging on a rope from his neck. The other two were tall and stocky and wearing the garb of ordinary soldiers. One of them was carrying the flag of truce and the other, when he thought he was within hearing distance from us, shouted:

"I have been sent by Bewulf, the son of the King of Northumbria, to offer you terms for your surrender."

I walked towards them. I had no intention to shout. Gwendwr had no choice but to follow me since he was to be my interpreter. Penrose kept close to me. She wanted to be part of the negotiations if there were to be any. Ulls followed behind, sulking. When I considered we were close enough, I spoke:

"Know that I am Ap Thor who defeated you in Gwynedd. Tell Bewulf that I shall talk peace but not surrender. And you, monk with the wooden cross, know that my God is Odin."

Upon hearing those words, the monk crossed himself, whispered something to the other two and all three turned their back on us without giving a reply. Ulls was furious and vented his anger on me:

"Is it the way to conclude negotiations? We are too few in numbers. We have no chance to win. We followed you and we're trapped. I say, we send a delegation to them and we agree terms of surrender."

"Is it as bad as that?" Penrose asked me, visibly shaken.

"Not in the least!" I replied, putting on a brave face. "We have to wait for their next move. Who knows? They might come back and agree to peace. In the meantime, let's order the men to stand down. I don't want any of them to be unduly tired when action will be required as fresh troops always have the advantage."

We did not have to wait long. We soon saw a Saxon contingent leaves the main army and march to the North of us when they turned round and faced us in full battle formation.

"What now?" Asked Ulls.

"We wait," I said.

"Should we not move?" Penrose questioned me.

"We could," I replied. "But I think it's too soon. Gwendwr! Do you remember the enemy tactics in Mercia?"

"When they shadowed us but never attacked?"

"That's the one, Gwendwr. Do you think they're planning something similar here?"

"You mean, they want to force us out, don't you?"

"Something like that."

By the middle of the afternoon, we saw further movement in the enemy ranks. They were sending another contingent to the North of us. However, it did not stop but marched past the one already stationed there and moved on to the back of us where it stopped. We were now surrounded on three sides. I looked at the position of the sun. There was still plenty of time before nightfall. I could feel everybody looking at me waiting for an order. I did not give any. The silence became almost unbearable. Penrose was the first to break it:

"What are we to do now?"

"Wait," was my brief answer and, to show I was not worried, I sat down next to Penrose. She took hold of my hand. I turned my head towards her and smiled. She smiled back. It was the kind of smile that made her look radiant and beautiful and that had attracted me to her when I first saw it.

"I love you," I whispered.

"I love you too," she whispered back.

Before I could say anything else, one of the men came running towards us.

"The enemy is moving," he shouted.

"Where?" I asked as I could see no movement.

"On the other side," he answered.

I got up and ran to the other side. Everyone was perking up. I could feel expectation in the air but what I saw surprised me: The enemy contingent had split into two and one half of it was making its way to close the gap on the fourth side. To me, it was a mistake on their part and I was going to exploit it to the full. I called Gwendwr and told him to pick thirty men and have them stand ready facing the main army. I then ordered everyone else to stand ready facing in the opposite direction. I walked to Gwendwr and gave him his order:

"You stay where you are until we've reached the bottom of the hill on the side behind you and we've engaged the enemy. Then, you follow us. Kill as many as you can but don't stop. Your aim is to break through and reform with us on their other side."

"What happens afterwards?" he enquired.

"You don't need to know but make sure you time it right."

I rejoined Ulls and Penrose at the front of the other troops and gave the signal to advance. When we reached half way down the side, I gave the order to charge. Our impetus was no match for the enemy who broke rank and was cut down. Gwendwr and his men followed soon afterwards and, as they reached us, I ordered to disengage and reform. We had now crossed the enemy ranks and were looking towards the mount we had just run down from. The enemy contingent we had attacked was in full disarray and made no effort to attack us. My next order then was to turn round and march away from that hill. Penrose's sword had blood on it and Ulls' arm had a small cut. Gwendwr and I were unscathed and we only lost six men. Also, we were free and there was enough daylight left for us to put some distance between us and the Saxons who, I assumed, would eventually be following us. However, we did not know the lay of the land and soon reached a river. There was consternation. No one likes to fight with his back to water.

I ordered a halt. We could not see the enemy behind us. We only assumed they were in pursuit of us. I asked for volunteers to check whether we could cross the river as it was not fast flowing. They succeeded in reaching the opposite bank but had been up to their chest in water. When I gave the order to cross, the men hesitated. I turned to Penrose:

"Come on! We go first! And shout to the men to follow you."

As she hesitated, I added:

"This is your first command of the campaign, don't mess it up."

She took her sword out of its scabbard, raised it high above her head, shouted "Follow me!" and plunged into the water. This had the desired effect. As she came out on the other side, dripping wet, she asked me:

"Did we have to cross?"

"You have much to learn," I replied.

"Teach me!" she said with a twinkle in her eye.

As the last man came out of the river, I noticed the unmistakable sign of an army on the march. I ordered the men to line up along the riverbank ready for battle. Then, I asked Ulls, Gwendwr and Penrose to stand with me in front of them and, thus, we waited for the Saxons to approach. Of course, before they could attack us, they would have to cross the river. I doubted they would do so but I wanted to show them we were not a defeated army on the run. As they came nearer to the water's edge, there appeared to be some confusion in their ranks. Then, they retreated some distance and set up camp. I ordered our men to stand down and settle for the night. I ordered sentries to be posted all around us just in case the enemy would, under cover of darkness, cross the river either upstream or downstream and attack us from behind. One could never be too careful.

The following morning, the enemy was nowhere to be seen. It unnerved the men, no more so than Gwendwr. In times of crisis, I did not like to have him around. Even Penrose noticed that something was wrong with him and asked me:

"Is anything the matter with your uncle, today?"

"As usual, he's afraid he may have to fight," I replied and, seeing the look of surprise on her face, I added: "I've seen it many times before. I don't take any notice any more. We need to move soon however, where is your brother?"

We found him at the south end of the camp.

"Here you are!" he said as soon as he saw us. "Time to move. We follow the river."

"No way!" I interrupted him. "We don't know the country around here. Let's play safe and retrace our steps."

"Do you mean crossing the river again?" Penrose asked, visibly unhappy at the thought.

"Yes!" I replied. "And then, we walk back all the way to the first camp."

"Whatever for?" Ulls said. "For all we know the enemy might be waiting for us out of sight."

"That is a chance we will have to take," I answered. "I'll be ready for them if they show up and, if they don't, Gryff will more easily find us."

"Good point," Ulls assented. "Let's do it!"

We re-crossed the river and marched forward. It soon became evident the enemy was not lying in wait for us. Everybody felt relieved but a horrible thought crossed my mind: what if the Saxons had turned round and decided to invade the lands of Penrith instead of dealing with us. If that were the case, we needed to hurry.

# CHAPTER 18

It was almost night when we reached our destination without having sighted the enemy and I gave the order to stop. Everybody was exhausted. After we had crossed the river, we marched back to where we had broken through the Saxon ranks but, instead of again taking position on the hilltop, we by-passed it and continued towards the lands of Penrith. I had told no one, not even Penrose, of my fears but pressed on just in case I was right. When, at last, we reached the original camp where Penrose's contingent had joined up with Ulls' and therefore had covered two days' march in one very long day, I still insisted on setting up the camp round that little mount where we had had our first skirmish. I knew that, come the morning, I would be able, from the top of it, to have a good view of the countryside around and be able to ascertain what our next move should be. Penrose who, for the last couple of miles, had walked like an automaton, collapsed at my feet as soon as we reached the top of the mount as I, at last, gave the signal to stop for the night. The men remained on the plain below but half of them lay down straight away. I did not know where Ulls and Gwendwr were. They did not bother to join me and I did not look for them. I just sat down, put my head in my hands, tried to think but instead drifted off into sleep.

The loud, cracking noise of thunder woke me suddenly and, but for the dark clouds in the sky, it would probably had been broad daylight. I thanked Odin for this timely reminder that I should get up. I looked around: nobody was moving. Lighning lit up the sky for a couple of seconds and then it started to rain. At first, just a few heavy drops but, soon, they were followed by such an outburst that everybody got soaked in no time. People huddled together. Lightning and thunder followed in quick succession. I was standing up, straining my eyes, hoping to see where the enemy was. Penrose soon joined me, pressed against me and I could feel she was shivering. The rain was relentless. As I was looking East a lightning bolt went all the way from the sky to a solitary tree followed by the loudest clap of thunder. I saw the tree split into two, one half of which fell to the ground. I understood the sign and shouted:

"Thank you, Odin!"

"What did you say?" Penrose asked. "And who is Odin?"

I realised I had spoken in my father's language and that Penrose did not understand me. I turned towards her. The rain had played havoc with her hair. I moved some of it away from her face. She smiled. I held her tight in my arms and kissed her. I was feeling such love for her at that moment that I became oblivious to anything else. We only separated when the rain stopped. Soon afterwards, the clouds dispersed and a bright sun appeared. Its warmth helped us to dry but the ground remained wet and muddy.

"Odin is my God," I said. "He manifests himself in the thunder. It was good to hear from him."

"You did not look afraid at all."

"Why should I be afraid of my God? On the contrary, he has given me reassurance. I know that I do not have to fear the future. That's why I said thank you."

We smiled at each other and were still smiling when a very subdued Ulls climbed up to us.

"What are you so cheerful about?" he said. "This has been a frightening morning."

"Ap Thor does not think so," Penrose replied. "And where is your shadow, Gwendwr?"

"Gwendwr is cowering under a bush somewhere," Ulls answered. "He can be such a coward at times."

"Oh! you've noticed," I said. "Anyway, let's decide what we do next. This is a good spot and we should wait until we spy something."

"Like what?" Ulls enquired.

"Sight of the enemy or sight of Gryff and our reinforcements."

"I'll wait with you."

Penrose and I would have preferred to be left alone but we did not want to antagonise her brother. So far, he had said nothing about our budding relationship and, in a way, we were grateful for it.

It was early afternoon before I noticed some movement in the distance. Unfortunately, it was in the South-East. Seeing the puzzlement on my face, Ulls looked in the same direction and exclaimed:

"More Saxons?"

"A second army?" I echoed.

"What makes you say that?" Penrose asked.

"That side is Northumbria," I said and, turning towards the South-West, I added, "and this side is Penrith."

"We know there are Saxons around, don't we?" she stated.

"You don't understand," her brother explained. "The ones we fought are somewhere in the North. There is no way it can be them, coming from the South as they are. We have to assume these are reinforcements."

"Let's get the men ready," I suggested. "An attack on them might be worthwhile."

"I agree with you," he assented then added angrily, "where is Gwendwr?"

Ulls and I went down among the men and gave orders. Some were pleased at the possibility of action. Others grumbled because of the state of the ground. I could not care one way or the other. What mattered to me was winning. After a while, I made my way back to the mount where I had left Penrose. As I approached, she was waving to me. I waved back to the amusement of some of the men.

"Hurry up!" she shouted when she thought I was within hearing distance, "there's something you should see."

I was intrigued and ran up to her. She pointed in the direction of the North-East. I looked up. What I saw changed everything. Another army was marching Southwards, most probably the Saxon army we had been avoiding. An attack was now out of the question. Retreat seemed the sensible thing to do. We were too few to stand up to two armies. Yet, I remembered Odin's message and wondered whether I had misinterpreted it. I looked around when something caught my eye. It was far away to the South-West. I kept looking, hoping against hope it was a third army, a Welsh army. I sent Penrose to look for her brother while I stayed and tried to calculate which army would arrive first.

"Reinforcements at last!" Ulls said as soon as he arrived, accompanied by Gwendwr this time, and after he had looked in the direction I was pointing to.

"I suggest we line up the men facing East and hope the Saxons won't attack today." I replied.

"Why?" Gwendwr asked. "Would it not be better to go and meet our own men?"

Penrose looked at me. I shook my head. She spoke:

"Gwendwr, no one is asking for your opinion."

"I agree with Ap Thor," Ulls stated.

We all fell silent and waited. After a while, we sent Gwendwr to get the men into position. We could see the armies approaching. Ours would only reach us close to nightfall. What the two Saxon armies would do was anybody's guess. Suddenly, the one from the South-East stopped. Soon after, the one from the North-East changed course and made for the one that had stopped. I let out a sigh of relief. It was unlikely we would be attacked that evening. I was to be proved right. In the meantime, it was time to tell our men the good news that reinforcements were coming. However, we got a surprise when we realised that the Prince of Penrith himself, and not Gryff, was leading the men. Ulls rushed to welcome his father. Penrose and I followed at a steadier pace.

"Welcome, father!" he said. "Now, you can take charge."

Father and son embraced before the former enquired:

"Has it just been a stand-off?"

"Not in the least! We have marched and fought and counter-marched and all on Ap Thor's orders."

"But I put you in charge. It was up to you. What happened?"

"How could I stand up against both him and my sister?"

"Penrose has no idea about war. I cannot understand how you let her dictate to you."

"They were always side by side, leading the men, even into battle."

The Prince of Penrith remained speechless. As he saw us, he turned to Penrose:

"Have you gone mad? Your brother has been telling me you have been fighting."

"Nice to see you again, father!" she replied. "Yes, I fought like any of the soldiers. I marched like they did without complaining. I told you before, whatever my brother can do, I can do too. I am his equal and you should treat me as such. I have earned Ap Thor's respect and I am proud of it."

"Is that what it is all about: earning Ap Thor's respect?" the Prince said mockingly. "As my daughter, he ought to treat you with respect. Don't mistake this for an approval of your behaviour. Same with the men. Now that I am here, you will forget all ideas of command. Gryff, who came with me, will ensure your safety."

"No!" Penrose shouted. "I'm no more a little girl, but a grown woman. I know what I want and it is not Gryff following me everywhere. I can take care of myself. You can deprive me of my command if you like. I'll just fight alongside the men. I am not afraid."

"I can vouch for that," I said. "You should not belittle your daughter. She does you proud."

"Stay out of this!" the Prince ordered me. "I shall deal with my daughter the way I see fit without interference from a stranger."

"I don't think he's a stranger any more," Gwendwr broke in. "They are side by side all the time, whether it be day or night."

I looked at my uncle totally astounded and shook my head. I wondered what could have possessed him to have opened his mouth in the way he did.

"Is that so?" the Prince of Penrith asked.

"Yes, father!" Penrose answered as she took hold of my arm. "We are lovers."

The silence that followed was broken by Ulls suddenly laughing.

"You don't know what you are talking about, little sister," he said and, turning to me, he added:

"You did not, did you?"

"That's nobody's business," I said angrily. "Come, Penrose, we'll discuss things with your father in the morning."

We walked back to the mount. Nobody followed us. As darkness fell, we were able to get some privacy at last, a welcome change from the last few days.

I was woken up by the sun on my face. It was just past daybreak. I got up and looked out. It was more a habit than anything else. Penrose had woken up as well and she was calling me:

"Come and join me again. It's too early to be about."

Instead of answering her call, I squinted my eyes: there was movement in the grass at some distance from us. It was moving towards us. It could only be but a Saxon spying party. There was not enough disturbance of the vegetation that I could see for it to be anything larger. Neither could I see any other disturbance which would indicate it to be an advance or reconnaissance party. However, we had to act, and fast, if we did not want the enemy to know too much about us. I grabbed my sword and shield and told Penrose to do the same. Then, we collected some thirty men and moved out. We were walking as fast as we could, bent double to avoid being seen. My orders were clear: Penrose would lead a third of the men in a frontal attack while I would try to move to the back of the enemy and cut their retreat with another third. The remaining ten men would attack from the side. It all went according to plan. The enemy was taken by surprise. I caught the only one who tried to escape back towards his camp and cut him down. He died at my feet. The others were soon surrounded and most of them killed. Three of them threw down their arms and raised their hands in a gesture of surrender. I ordered they be spared and brought back to our camp as prisoners. We also stripped the fallen enemy of their arms and clothes, ensuring that no one was left alive to tell the tale. As we were walking back, I noticed that Penrose's shield was covered in blood.

"How did this happen?" I asked her.

"I cut his face open and he fell onto my shield before sliding down as I put my sword through him."

In our absence, the whole camp had got up and were standing ready, waiting for orders. The Prince of Penrith noticed Penrose's bloody shield and called for Gryff:

"Gryff! I told you to protect my daughter."

"Gwendwr!" I shouted. "You question the prisoners. You remember your Saxon, I hope."

"I do," he replied, "it would be my pleasure."

They refused to talk. I ordered one of them to be put to death. Two of our men forced him to kneel, raising his arms from behind and thus forcing his head down. I took my sword out, raised it with both hands and brought it down quickly and forcefully. His head rolled.

"Have you seen how it's done?" I asked Penrose. "You do the next one."

She looked at me but said nothing. Gwendwr was again asking questions of the two prisoners but no answer was forthcoming. I did notice, however, that the younger of the two was beginning to sweat. Obviously, he was fearing death. The other one was more arrogant. I therefore chose the latter to be the next one to die. As he was forced to kneel, I said to Penrose:

"Your turn."

She moved forward and took her sword out. I saw some of the men turn away. I knew what they were thinking: if you do not succeed with the first blow, it becomes very messy. They did not want to see that happen and the resulting butchery. Both Ulls and the Prince of Penrith were staring ahead. Their jaws had dropped. Gryff was looking at me. His face was expressing dismay. Penrose raised her sword and brought it down in one swift movement. The head rolled. Some of the men applauded, which I found disconcerting. I ordered the third prisoner to be made to kneel. He begged to be spared: he would talk. This is what he said as translated by Gwendwr:

"I have come with the King of Northumbria's army. We only arrived yesterday. His son has been in the field for some time. The King ordered the merger of the two armies into one which, he says, is one thousand men strong. He is a strong King and very powerful. No one else could field a thousand men. He will win any battle. He wanted us to find out how many you were and how strong you are. We did not succeed because you caught us. He may send more men to spy on you or just attack. I don't think it will be today because he has ordered his men to rest after so many days' march. He says that rested men fight better. He is a good King and a good Christian. We are all Christians. The monks tell us that if we die at the hands of pagans, we are martyrs. I prefer to live that's why I've spoken. You will spare my life, won't you?"

There was silence as everyone was pondering over the information received. Penrose was the first to break it by asking:

"How many are we?"

"About four hundred," her father replied. "I don't know how anyone can fight back a thousand men."

"That is, if it's true," I said. "I would think it nearer the truth to assume they are twice as many as us and no more."

"Even so, the odds are stacked against us," the Prince stated.

"I disagree," I answered. "So far, we have won every skirmish. Your children can vouch for that. Also, I don't think they are as good soldiers as we are. It's time to make a stand. I would reinforce the camp by building a ditch all around it. This mount gives us the advantage as we can see all the enemy's moves from the top. Then, I'll just wait until they attack."

"What if they don't attack?" asked Gryff.

"Then, we would have to attack them," the Prince said. "For that, a few reinforcements would be welcome. Ap Thor, do you think you could recruit some Vikings to help us?"

"You said before, when I offered, that you have no such money to pay for their help," I replied.

"If we win, there would be plenty of booty. Surely, they would fight for that."

"They might. I won't know until I ask. If that's your wish, Prince, I must not lose time but go straight away to Odin's Town and come back as soon as possible with as many Vikings as will follow me. In the meantime, reinforce the camp and defend it with all your might. Then, when I'm back, we'll fight a final battle for total victory."

"You feel so sure of yourself, don't you?" Ulls said. "But you won't be here when they first attack us."

"You should not be afraid," I answered. "Remember that we have already defeated them in skirmishes. If you need any encouragement, let your sister fight alongside you. Penrose, do me proud, while I'm away."

I had nothing more to say. So, I embraced her and went on my way, hoping for the best.

# CHAPTER 19

It took me three days to reach Odin's Town. It had been built in a hollow between two promontories next to a river but close to the sea. During the journey, which I made alone, I had time to think. After so many months spent among the Welsh, I wondered what it would feel like being among Vikings again. Would I meet my uncle Elgar at long last or had he moved on? Would there be anyone who remembered me as their leader in Gwynedd? If not, would anyone be prepared to follow me in fighting for the Prince of Penrith? And why do I want to fight for him? Could I tell the truth? That it was because of Penrose. There was no doubt that we were attracted to each other but was it love? I was able to teach her the art of war and thereby help her to fulfil her ambition to be her brother's equal. I rather enjoyed doing so and certainly did not feel threatened by the fact she could now fight nearly as well as I. When the war was over, could we still be together, would her father allow it? And what of her brother? When I first met him, we did not get on. Indeed, we fought each other but, now, we had been able to campaign together and he had said nothing about my relationship with his sister. I could not even tell whether he approved or not. And what of Gryff? What exactly was his role? Why had the Prince of Penrith put him in charge of looking after Penrose? That he had looked after her as a child, I could understand but not now. Was there something I did not know? How could I find out? Could Gwendwr help by questioning Ulls on my behalf? Or should I just ask Penrose herself? These were the questions that plagued my mind but, as I came closer to Odin's Town, I needed to banish all these thoughts away. Soon, I could see men exercising in a field that was bordering on the path leading to its gate. As I walked past, nobody took the least bit of notice of my presence. They just continued with their training and, as I looked at the men, one face looked familiar. I went closer and, when I was sure, I called his name out:

"Rurik! It's me, Ap Thor."

The man I had so addressed stopped and turned towards me. After a moment's hesitation, he spoke:

"Ap Thor! Is that really you? Have you come at last?"

We embraced and slapped each other on the back while the men under his command surrounded us. They remembered me well enough and suggested my arrival deserved a celebration at a local inn. I did not object. I could do with a drink, a real, strong drink and something decent to eat after my long journey.

"I see you are travelling alone," Rurik said as we entered the town. "Your uncle, what was his name? He's not with you, is he?"

"Actually," I answered, "I'm on a mission to recruit men to fight for the Prince of Penrith against the Saxons. My uncle, Gwendwr, is with the Prince's son as we speak. We did travel together and were staying as the Prince's guests when news came of Saxons on the move. We had to fight for him. Now, they are facing an army which, according to a captured prisoner, is a thousand strong."

"A thousand strong!" Rurik exclaimed. "Is that possible? Have you seen this?"

"From a distance, yes. But I don't believe they are that many. Close to, possibly, however they certainly outnumber us. So, tomorrow, I'll go on a recruitment drive and I hope you will help me. But tonight, I'd like to look for my uncle, Elgar, if he ever came here. Does that name mean anything to you?"

"I'm afraid not," Rurik answered.

"I know of a drunkard by the name of Elgar," said one of the men. "You usually find him at that ramshackle inn by the river, you know, the one with a few easy girls hanging around."

"Sounds like my uncle all right," I said. "I don't know my way around. Will you take me there?"

"Wait till tomorrow," Rurik suggested.

"I'd better not," I replied. "Tomorrow, he'll be too drunk. I need to catch him while he's still half-sober."

My guide took me to the door of the inn but refused to go in. As soon as I went inside, I knew why and I did not blame him. There was shouting and drunken laughter. There was hardly any light with even darker recesses around the room. As I stood there, wondering how I would find my uncle among the crowd, a woman, older than me, with some rags by way of a cloak and nothing else, was showing me a pair of sagging breasts while asking:

"Do you like what you see?"

"I'm looking for a man by the name of Elgar," I said. "Do you know him?"

"I know many men but not their names," she answered and then laughed at her own joke.

I walked further in, trying to look at people's faces but so far I could not see Elgar anywhere. I reached one of those dark recesses and saw a woman and a man sprawled on the floor. They did not take the slightest notice of me as I stepped back and realised it was hopeless. I made my way back to the door, turned around, pulled out my sword, hit my shield with it a few times until most of the noise had subsided and shouted at the top of my voice:

"Elgar! Show yourself!"

From one of the corners of the room came a feeble answer:

"I'll fight you tomorrow."

"It's Ap Thor," I shouted again. "Come out now!"

"Appie!" Elgar replied as he got up and made his way towards me on some unsteady legs. "By Odin, where have you been?"

I put my sword back in its scabbard, grabbed Elgar by the arm and dragged him out.

"Where are you staying?" I asked him.

"Nowhere and everywhere. I'm homeless."

"What happened to you? I can't imagine you being the same person that fired my imagination when I was a boy. You know when you told me of all those deeds you accomplished in far flung lands when you were a soldier and acted like one."

"What's so different now? I'm still a soldier. I always will be a soldier."

"So, I can rely on you, then?"

"For what?"

"To fight by my side. What do you think I've come for? I'm raising a band of men. Rurik is coming, will you?"

"Of course I will, but who's Rurik and where do we fight?"

"It's been a long time since we were last together. Why did you not come and see me when the men of Powys let you go?"

"I don't know. I guess I wanted to redeem myself, especially, after the imposed rest and they were saying there was fighting up North in Penrith."

"Did you actually fight for the Prince of Penrith?"

"Of course, Ulls knew me and I had no problem joining his father's army but, once the campaign was over, I was told to move to this place here in the North, made for us Vikings and that we call Odin's Town."

"I went back to my father and spent the winter with him and with Gwendwr. You do remember Gwendwr, don't you, who turned out to be my mother's long-lost brother whom we liberated from slavery."

"Yes, that was what Gwendwr was saying. Was it true?"

"Of course, it was. He's come with me, you know, and, like you did, he's now fighting with Ulls but I'm not so fond of him as I am of you."

"Of course, you're a Viking, he's not! Now, shall we go back inside?"

"Not in there! Let's go to some decent inn, I want you sober for tomorrow."

"Appie! Don't you appreciate women and drink?"

"Uncle! I can drink when necessary. As for women, I'd rather remain faithful to the one I love. Now, come on!"

"If I must but, tell me first, have you found a woman?"

"Yes! Here's a decent inn for the night and I'll tell you all about her when we march tomorrow."

By midday, with the help of Rurik, his men, Elgar and my own exertions, I had assembled about sixty men ready to march. I did not want to wait any longer. I also made it plain that I wanted to reach the battlefield in no more than three days. I hoped that the Prince of Penrith would be able to hold that long against the Saxons and that we would tip the scales to his advantage. We therefore walked briskly for the next two days when, towards evening, we saw a lonely figure, dressed in white, walking in front of us. Rurik was the first to notice:

"I wonder who that is."

"He looks like a Druid," I replied. "Let us not frighten him."

Having heard us coming up behind him, he had stopped and was looking at us. As we came closer, I recognised him:

"Rhys ap Rhys! Well, I'll be damned! Are you on your own? Where is your elderly companion?"

"Ap Thor, the Welsh Hero!" Rhys exclaimed. "What an honour to see you again! I'm on my way to the battle of the year! Are you too?"

"I'm bringing reinforcements, all Vikings. The enemy is boasting an army of a thousand men. Something to sing about, eh, Rhys, if we beat them."

"Indeed! Are we far?"

"Another day's march if you can keep pace with us but tell me, first, where have you been?"

"My companion and I went among the Scots. One of their clans adopted us. Alpin, their Chief, wanted his own personal Druid. He chose my companion. He's now quite feeble and too old to walk much, but I did not want to miss the action, to have something new to sing about. I take my role as a bard very seriously indeed."

"I know!" I interrupted. "Travel with us and I can fill you in. Much has happened since I last saw you."

At last, we were in sight of the Prince of Penrith's camp. I thought it a good sign to see it had not moved. I decided to go all the way and join his army but we were stopped by Gryff who must have seen us coming and was walking towards us.

"Stop!" he said. "It's better if you camp away from our men. The truth is, Ap Thor, we don't need your Vikings."

"What has happened?" I asked while noticing Gwendwr running towards us.

"Peace has been agreed between the Prince of Penrith and the King of Northumbria."

"And Penrose has been betrothed to Bewulf," Gwendwr added.

That last piece of news was so unexpected and shocked me so much that I turned pale and wobbled on my legs. Elgar, who had been standing by me, noticed, put his arm around my shoulders and asked:

"Appie! What's the matter?"

I could not answer, I was speechless. Rhys ap Rhys stepped forward and enquired:

"Has there been any fighting?"

"No!" Gryff replied. "The King of Northumbria offered peace to my Prince before any blows were exchanged. Bard! You will have to speak of peace instead of war and of the union of my Prince's daughter with the King's son."

I turned towards the Vikings that had followed me but not understood what had been said and simply told them:

"Let's camp here for now. Apparently, peace has been agreed. Elgar, Rurik, you come with me."

Gryff was about to say something but stopped as he had seen Penrose coming. She was still dressed as a soldier with the sword I had cast for her hanging from her side. As I saw her, my heart missed a beat and then beat faster. Ignoring everybody around me, I walked straight to her, took her in my arms and kissed her. She kissed me back.

"It's so good to see you again." I whispered.

"Have you been told the news?" she asked.

"Gryff told me about peace and Gwendwr, in his usual tactless way, about your betrothal. Is it all true?"

"Yes!" she replied. "But there are conditions. I would have liked to tell you myself."

I turned towards Elgar and Rurik, my arm linked to Penrose's arm and I made the introductions:

"This is Penrose, daughter of the Prince of Penrith. And Penrose, this is my uncle on my father's side, Elgar, and this is Rurik who commands his own band of men. Now, let's go and see your father."

"You fought for my brother, Ulls, didn't you?" she said, addressing Elgar. "I did not know you two were related."

"How is your father?" I asked her. "I hope we'll be welcome at his table."

"Of course!" she answered. "I missed you, Ap Thor."

We led the group arm in arm. Gryff looked unhappy while Gwendwr kept talking to Rhys ap Rhys and both Rurik and Elgar followed us in silence.

# CHAPTER 20

Our arrival made a stir in the camp. The fact that Rhys ap Rhys had come with us was even more of a surprise. He was treated with honour and respect as was fitting for a bard. The Prince of Penrith asked him to sit on his immediate right between himself and his son and was soon seen talking to him for most of the evening. Ulls ignored them and kept drinking cup for cup with Gwendwr, Elgar and Rurik as all three of them had decided to sit close to the Prince's son. Penrose and I chose to sit at some distance, hoping for some privacy, which was denied us as Gryff settled himself behind us. However, I decided to ignore his presence.

"Penrose!" I said. "You must tell me everything that has happened since I left."

"Where shall I sart? I missed you so much. Did you really need to go? I think that, if you had stayed, things would have turned out differently."

"How?"

"I think you would have gone for a showdown with the Saxons and not agreed peace terms at the first opportunity."

"What did happen exactly?"

"As soon as you had left, I set the men in my contingent to build the ditch as you ordered. My father had them stop. I objected. Ulls took sides against me, the main reason being that they were afraid to be surrounded and end up prisoners within their own ditch. I managed to persuade them to agree to have at least the ditch built on the side facing the enemy to slow down a frontal attack."

"Was it built?"

"Yes! But, as the day progressed, there was no sign of enemy activity and this unnerved my father who, then, started talking about withdrawing. Fortunately, Ulls agreed with me that we should hold our ground for the time being and that it was far too soon to show our backs."

I could not help laughing as I briefly thought back to the Prince of Gwynedd doing the very same thing years ago. When I had recovered, I asked:

"Was anyone else part of the discussion?"

"Yes, Gwendwr and Gryff. The former sided with my father and the latter suggested I move to a safer place."

"Why is Gryff always trying to protect you? I can't understand it."

"Don't ask!" Gryff said and I realised he had been listening to us, so I turned towards him and asked bluntly:

"Are you spying on us?"

"Far from it," he answered. "I'm only following her late mother's instructions."

"What is he talking about?" I asked.

"My father and Gryff grew up together," Penrose replied. "Whenever they would go to war, they would fight side by side. After my mother married my father, every time they went on a campaign, she would ask Gryff to protect her husband. She was also convinced that he would be the only person able to protect me after her death. So, when she developed a fever and knew she would not survive, she had him swear to dedicate his life to me as she lay dying. That is what he has done ever since."

"I suppose I should be grateful to you for this," I said, addressing Gryff. "But, now, Penrose is a grown woman and you should realise there are times when your presence is not welcome, like now."

"On the contrary," he replied, "now is not the time when you two should be seen together or have you forgotten about the betrothal?"

"I have not," Penrose answered. "As Ap Thor said, your presence tonight is unwelcome. Please go and join my father."

I looked at him. I had intended to scare him off by slightly drawing my sword but, when I saw how hurt he was by Penrose's words, I could not do it. Instead, I told him:

"I am now looking after her, betrothal or no betrothal. I'm sure she's grateful for everything you have done in the past but now it's time to let go."

Gryff got up without saying a word. He did not go and sit by the Prince of Penrith as we had asked him to do but, instead, left and disappeared into the night. I turned towards Penrose, gave her a hug and kissed her. She smiled at me that wonderful smile of hers. It was the first time she had done so since I had come back. At the same time, without saying a word, she got up, took hold of my hand and led me to that small mount in the middle of the camp. There was no one on the top.

"This is where I sleep," she said. "I have forbidden anyone to come here. We won't be disturbed."

I did not know whether I wanted to wake up or not. I was in that state when people wonder whether to turn over and close their eyes again. However, when I saw Penrose was awake, sitting next to me and looking down at me, I smiled at her and was rewarded with a kiss.

"I never told you what you wanted to know last night, did I?"

"You did not but now is not the time," I said as I grabbed her and forced her to lie alongside me.

"No, Ap Thor, don't be so greedy! Now, you listen to me. The day after you left, we woke up to the spectacle of the full Saxon army arrayed in battle. It was quite a sight and I could believe there were a thousand of them. Everyone expected to have to fight but, just as before, they sent three men with a flag of truce."

"And was one of them a monk?" I interrupted.

"Yes! As a matter of fact, I think it was the same one as before, only his robe was even dirtier."

I gave a short laugh as I slid my arm round her shoulders and asked:

"Who met them from our side?"

"My father, my brother and myself, with Gwendwr and Gryff behind us. I was expecting the Saxons to offer terms of surrender like last time. Instead, they offered peace right away. At first, I wondered why but, then, I remembered you telling them that you would discuss peace but not surrender. I must admit I was quite surprised by such an offer and, I believe, so was everyone else. We were then told that the King of Northumbria himself was at the head of his army and would conduct the peace negotiations in person if we had anyone that could match his rank among us. My father said that as Prince of Penrith and Commander-in-Chief of his army, he would be prepared to talk to the King of Northumbria but that a neutral meeting place would have to be agreed. As a sign of good faith, he sent Gryff for preliminary talks."

Penrose stopped. She looked pensive for a couple of minutes before adding:

"You know, Ap Thor, I think we were a bit hard on the old man last night."

"You're quite fond of him, aren't you?"

"He never complains and follows my father's dictates at all times. What's more, he has always been there for me even if, at times, I have been a difficult child."

"You? Never!"

"I wanted to be a boy and he never said that was wrong."

"Well! You're all woman now."

I planted a kiss on her lips and she responded right away. We were still in a close embrace when we heard someone coughing nearby. We looked up and saw Rhys ap Rhys standing there, a little unsure as to what to do next.

"Have you lost your way?" I asked.

"No!" he answered. "I was told I would find Penrose here. I need to ask a few questions of her."

"What about?" Penrose asked.

"Last night, when I was talking with your father, he asked me to sing of the peace between Saxons and Welsh and of your marriage to Bewulf. What I'd like to know are your feelings on the matter so that what I say about you will ring true."

"I have always known that my father would find a husband for me. He has now done so. If it helps to reconcile Saxons and Welsh after centuries of fighting, who am I to object? I have met Bewulf but not spoken to him. He's a Christian, you know, and he wants me to convert before he marries me."

"What?" Rhys ap Rhys exclaimed. "Surely, you have not agreed, have you? As a Druid, I must dissuade you from forsaking the religion of your ancestors."

"My father does not see it like that. I have not told Ap Thor all that has been agreed yet, so what I say to you now, Rhys ap Rhys, might surprise him."

"Is it not just peace and a wedding?" I asked.

"Far from it!" Penrose replied. "We must stay within our lands and allow monks to come in and try to convert our people, while the Saxons will be free to conquer and rule the lands to the North of us and we must let them do it."

"That's not been agreed, has it?" I asked.

"In principle, yes! We'll all meet again soon to formally agree on those terms. That's why both armies are still in camp and have not moved."

"It cannot go ahead," I said. "What of Odin's Town? We, Vikings, won't be ignored."

"Do they plan to attack the Scots as well?" Rhys ap Rhys chipped in. "If what you say is true, I'd better make my way back right away and warn Alpin."

"And I, to see the Prince. Penrose, come with me."

As we walked down the mount, we met with Rurik who was on his way to see me.

"Ap Thor!" he said. "What are we doing? You brought us here. You must not abandon us. We won't go back empty-handed."

"Not now!" I replied. "I have more pressing affairs to attend to."

"Like spending the night with her ladyship?"

"Rurik! Don't you say anything against her! Perhaps you should know. The peace agreement with the Saxons is very bad. It gives them freedom to all the lands to the North of us."

"You mean we would be isolated," said Rurik.

"Quite!" I said. "Let me deal with it. In the meantime, you and your men don't budge."

I hurried through the camp to the Prince of Penrith. I wondered how I would deal with the subject when in his presence. I decided to be bold.

"Prince!" I said. "You cannot accept those terms of peace."

"You have no right to object," he replied. "I am free to give my daughter away to whom I please."

"I was not referring to your daughter but to the fact that the Vikings are not part of it."

"The peace is only between me and the King of Northumbria."

"Precisely! But Vikings have fought for you in the past. You granted them Odin's Town. You asked me to bring some men to fight for you again but you cannot be bothered to protect our interests."

"What can I do? It's too late."

"The men I brought are spoiling for a fight. They are not afraid of you or the Saxons. They will be part of that peace deal or there will be war."

"I need to confer with my council first. Please, do not do anything rash."

"Then, invite us to your council."

The Prince reluctantly agreed and, later that day, Elgar, Rurik and myself met formally with the Prince, Ulls, Penrose, Gryff, Gwendwr and half a dozen of his counsellors who had made the journey with him. After the Prince of Penrith had explained what problems had arisen, Gwendwr was the first to speak:

"I personally would be very afraid of an angry Viking. Let's treat it as an oversight. Surely, the Saxons can offer them the same terms as they did for us and then the problem is solved."

"I cannot go back on my word," the Prince stated. "I spoke for my people only and you, Vikings, were not present at the time."

"But you had asked for our help," Elgar cut in. "You must have known that we would come. You cannot be so dismissive of us."

"If you were to go back home, there would be no problem," the Prince suggested. "Would that not be the best solution?"

Many people present assented but Penrose objected:

"I disagree. What proof have we that, once the Saxons have conquered the land to the North of us, in spite of our treaty, they will not attack us? I might be married to the King's son but would I have any say in the matter? Don't forget I have to convert to their religion so there will be an even greater divide between us."

"I think the offer is genuine," Gryff said. "Without the marriage, I might think otherwise."

"Peace is paramount," Gwendwr stated. "Would you not agree, Ulls?"

"If there were less of them, I would have relished a battle," Ulls admitted. "Now, it is too late to have one but we could ask them to include the Vikings in their offer of peace."

"To ask is not strong enough," Rurik said. "You must insist."

"I shall do no such thing," the Prince of Penrith stated, angry by now. "I shall pay you for coming here but you're on your own."

I was about to reply when I saw a Viking running towards us. He was one of Rurik's men. He went straight to him and told him in Norse:

"There's a band of armed men coming in from the West."

Forgetting that most of the men present would not have understood and having some idea of who they might be, I asked in Welsh:

"Where is Rhys ap Rhys?"

"He said his goodbyes early this morning," Gryff answered. "Why do you ask? Has anything happened?"

"I think I'd better go back to my men," Rurik said. "We need to deal with this army before they come too close to the camp."

"Wait!" I said. "Don't be too rash, they may be friends."

"What's going on?" asked the Prince, seeing both Rurik and Elgar leaving. "Ap Thor, don't you think you should inform us instead of speaking in that other language of yours?"

"I'm sorry, Prince," I said, "the news surprised me. Apparently, there's an army coming in from the West. I don't know who they are. Could be Scots or a trick from the Saxons."

"The Saxons would not dare, would they?" Gwendwr enquired. "And why would the Scots come? Were they expected?"

"Let's find out first," I suggested. "We can continue the discussion later. Rurik and Elgar have gone to get their men to intercept the newcomers but I'd like to be present."

"I don't think there is anything else to discuss," said the Prince, becoming angry again. "I won't change my position. There's no point in you coming back. Just go and get rid of the newcomers."

"I'm on my way," I muttered.

"I'm coming with you," Penrose said.

# CHAPTER 21

By the time Penrose and I reached the Viking camp, Rurik and Elgar had already positioned their men ready for battle. We were late because we had gone back to our own quarters to fetch our shields. I doubted there would be any fighting but I was not prepared to risk that possibility, especially with Penrose by my side. We had to weave our way through the men so as to rejoin Rurik and Elgar who were waiting for me at the front. Without a word, I gave the signal to advance straight away. I could feel unease among the men. Elgar came close to me and whispered in my ear:

"You should not have brought Penrose with you. There might be fighting. Tell her to stay behind the men."

"Uncle!" I replied. "Penrose can fight as well as the best of us. I trained her."

"You... what?" Elgar asked, quite surprised.

"It's a long story! For now, let's deal with those people coming towards us. Can you identify them from their round shields?"

"Scots!" Rurik answered. "Let's hope they want peace."

Seeing the road ahead blocked by us, the Scots stopped and sent a spokesperson:

"We are the Clan Alpin and our chief is on his way to see the Prince of Penrith who, we believe, is camping nearby. We intend no harm if you let us pass peacefully."

"I am Ap Thor," I said, "one of the commanders of the Prince's armies. Welcome to his camp. My uncle, Elgar, will show your men where to stay. I need to speak with your Chief."

Soon, two men came forward, an elderly looking one and a youth who could not have been more than sixteen or seventeen years of age.

"I am Alpin, Chief of Clan Alpin," said the older of the two, "and this is Alpin mac Alpin, my son. Would you kindly take us to the Prince of Penrith?"

"Have you spoken to Rhys ap Rhys?" I asked. "It would help if you had."

"We have indeed," Alpin answered while his son stared at Penrose.

"Good! So, you already know the terms of peace and I presume you are not happy with them. Therefore, I shall take you to see the Prince presently but, first, let me introduce you to Penrose, the Prince's daughter, and Rurik, a Viking leader."

"It's a pleasure to meet the beautiful daughter of such a mighty Prince," said Alpin mac Alpin, still staring at Penrose.

"Let me escort you to my father," Penrose said curtly. "Ap Thor, lead the way."

The Prince of Penrith was far from happy when he saw that the six of us were looking for him. He offered drinks while he summoned his son to attend. The latter answered his father's call accompanied by both Gwendwr and Gryff. Alpin came to the point immediately:

"Rhys ap Rhys has told me about the disgraceful terms of peace you are trying to conclude with the Saxon king that would allow his army to attack us and conquer our lands."

"It's not so dramatic as that," the Prince answered, "your bard exaggerates. The King of Northumbria wants peace. Why talk of war?"

"Then, you will not mind if we are included in your peace treaty, will you?"

"Excellent idea!" Elgar said, "The Vikings will expect the same terms too."

"Just a minute!" the Prince interrupted. "Negotiations have already been completed. Nothing else can be done. Tomorrow, we officially ratify the agreement."

"And tomorrow, I'll be there," Alpin insisted. "I'll denounce the agreement for its injustice towards us. This will reflect badly on you. Think about it."

Without waiting for an answer, he turned and, addressing his son, said:

"Come on, son, time for us to rejoin our men."

"Cannot we stay and have more drinks?" Alpin mac Alpin asked and, turning to Penrose whose side he had stood by all this time, he added:

"Won't you ask us to stay, beautiful lady?"

"A boy like you should obey his father," Penrose answered. "Ap Thor! Let us retire."

"Father!" Ulls suddenly said. "You should think this over. It is not too late. I'm sure the King of Northumbria will not take offence and, then, we'll all have peace."

We all stood still waiting for an answer. None came. The Prince of Penrith just walked away. Soon, everybody else did the same. As Penrose and I made our way back to our quarters, she spoke:

"I hate that boy. He has not stopped looking at me since we first met. Does he have no manners? And daring to speak to me? Why did you not tell him off?"

"He's young," I answered. "He's probably never seen a woman warrior before."

"Is that what I am: a woman warrior?"

"Many people think so. I know different, you're so much more than that."

I woke up early the following morning. From the top of the mount, I could observe the Saxon army preparing for the day ahead. By the look of things, I concluded they were planning to have their full army present. We should be doing the same, I thought, but I had no idea what the Prince of Penrith's plans were or anybody else's for that matter. Penrose was still asleep. I slipped away. I went to see the men of our contingent and told them to prepare for inspection by Penrose. That way I knew they would be ready to accompany us even if no other order was given. I then went on to the Viking camp and told Elgar and Rurik to bring all their men with them.

"Why?" Elgar asked. "Is there something I should know, Appie?"

"The Saxons are getting all their men ready," I replied. "We should not be seen to be wanting and, uncle, stop calling me 'Appie', I'm not a little boy any more."

Rurik laughed and I moved on to the Scots encampment. As I approached, I was challenged.

"Message for your Chief," I answered.

I was led to him.

"Is it time to go?" he asked. "Has the Prince decided on anything yet?"

"That's not why I am here," I answered. "The Saxons are getting all their men ready. You should bring all your men with you. We must make a show of strength and unity. I also have a message for your son from Penrose: tell the lad to stop staring at her, his behaviour is not welcome."

I left without waiting for an answer but I saw Alpin mac Alpin looking embarrassed and turning red.

"Where have you been?" Penrose asked as soon as I rejoined her. "Have a look! What do you think of that?"

The Saxons had formed a giant U-shape in the centre of which stood a few people. Who were they? I could not tell from the distance where I stood. However, I thought it was about time we made a move.

"Come!" I said. "I have been out giving a few orders. Our men are waiting. We go to the meeting with them at our back."

"Is that my father's order?"

"I don't think he has given any yet. I know that the Vikings and the Scots are all coming too. That's why I want us to do the same with our own contingent."

"Let's see my father first."

We found him in an animated discussion with his son. Gwendwr and Gryff were standing at some distance from them and, when they saw us, gestured for us not to come any closer. Seeing the Viking contingent approaching at about the same time, the Prince of Penrith exploded:

"Have your own way, all of you, but don't blame me if we all end up dead."

"I think we should move on," I said. "I'll get the men while you, Penrose, get your father to attend."

This was easier said than done. Yes, my contingent advanced and so did the Vikings and the Scots but in front of them, there were just me, Elgar, Rurik, Alpin and his son. The Prince of Penrith remained behind with his family and his counsellors. The sight of the Saxon army forming a half circle around the King of Northumbria, his son and a bevy of monks, was quite impressive. You could indeed believe there were a thousand men, every single one of them ready for battle. I kept advancing. My heart was pounding but I did not want to show my fear. We wanted to renegotiate the treaty but, instead, we might be falling into a trap. I thought it best to stop. I was quite close but not close enough for a parley. The enemy would have to advance before they could speak. The monks did so while the King and his son remained where they stood.

"In the name of the true God, welcome," one of the monks said. "I don't think I know any of you."

"I am Ap Thor," I introduced myself. "Those who fought in Gwynedd might remember me. You have agreed peace terms with the Prince of Penrith but not with us, Vikings and Scots. We are the Prince's allies and ask you to let us join him in a general peace with you under the same terms."

The monks looked at each other, briefly conferred between themselves and, without giving a reply, walked back to their king. We could but wait. This was the moment the Prince of Penrith chose to appear with Ulls to his right and Penrose to his left. Gwendwr and Gryff followed behind but the Prince had no soldiers in attendance. The King of Northumbria advanced and stood facing the Prince of Penrith and asked a simple question:

"Do we have peace or not?"

"I shall keep my word," the Prince answered. "The Vikings and Scots also want peace. Will you grant it to them?"

"Never!" was the King's unequivocal answer.

"Then!" I shouted for I wanted everyone to hear me. "We shall fight you. It's peace with all or no peace at all."

The King turned away but Bewulf stopped him, also wanting to give the Prince an answer:

"I am betrothed to your daughter Penrose. This should unite our two houses and bring peace to our two nations. Do not compromise it by bowing to your allies' wishes."

"I shall not marry you," Penrose said. "For there cannot be any partial peace."

"Then, it's war," Bewulf concluded. "But as you're not ready, let's have the battle tomorrow so that you cannot accuse the Saxons of breaking the safe-conduct of a parley."

"The true God will grant us victory," said one of the monks. "Be sure of it!"

"And Odin will protect us," I answered. "As will all the Gods of our forefathers."

We returned to camp in silence. The Prince of Penrith was crestfallen. He did not believe we could win. Ulls seemed rather pleased, he was about to get the fight he had been longing for. Penrose was pensive. Gwendwr looked unhappy. Gryff was the first to break the silence:

"Ap Thor! You did not try very hard to obtain peace. As for you, Penrose, you should never have given your husband-to-be an ultimatum. Both of you should have left the Prince of Penrith to speak at all times."

"You forget that the Prince was not willing to speak," I answered. "This is not the time for recriminations. We should plan for tomorrow's battle."

"I agree with you," Ulls said. "What do you propose?"

"Do I have no say in the matter?" the Prince of Penrith asked. "Since we cannot avoid a battle, I should lead the men and you all follow."

"Yes!" I agreed. "You and Gryff should be in the centre with the men you brought. Ulls with Gwendwr and his contingent should be to your left and to his left Alpin and the Scots. To your right, Prince, Penrose and I would lead our contingent with my Uncle, Rurik and the Vikings on my right. I hope you are all happy with my suggested plan."

Alpin and Rurik nodded but Ulls objected:

"My rightful place is to the right of my father. What gives you the right to put yourself there?"

"It's very likely that Bewulf will fight on the right of his father," I replied. "The position I've given you, Ulls, gives you the opportunity to fight him, son to son so to speak. Also, would you want your sister to face him on the battlefield?"

"Of course not!" Ulls answered. "You're right, Ap Thor, I should face Bewulf. Are we all agreed on our positions, then?"

"Further discussion would be useless," the Prince of Penrith said. "Ap Thor has positioned us and seems to go for a full frontal attack. Let him bear the responsibility for the battle outcome."

A deep silence ensued. All eyes were on me. I could feel that everyone present was expecting me to say something. I wondered whether anyone was doubting the wisdom of a full frontal attack against an enemy twice our size. I had some reservations myself and I knew I had to refine my plan somehow but I did not want anyone to know. However, I was forced to speak, it was expected of me but I had to choose my words carefully:

"Your Prince has given the orders for tomorrow. There's no more we can do tonight."

I took Penrose by the arm and led her away. When we were out of earshot, I whispered:

"I'm going to spend some time with my uncle Elgar in the Viking camp. You're welcome to come as well."

"Why should I?" she replied. "There are times when I don't understand you."

"I need to see him. If you come, you'll understand."

"All I understand is that we are on the eve of a battle when we can all be killed and you prefer to spend your last moments with your uncle rather than with me."

"Don't be like that. I have my reasons but I cannot tell you now."

"Then, go! I can see that Viking blood is stronger than love."

"That's not true."

It was our first argument as lovers and I felt bad. I could not tell her what was on my mind lest somebody would overhear us. She went her way and I went mine.

Elgar was surprised when he saw me and could not help asking:

"Is there anything wrong? Why aren't you with Penrose?"

"I need to talk to you and Rurik. Where is he?"

"Sharpening his sword over there. Come, let's join him. Tell me, nephew, are you afraid for tomorrow?"

I did not answer. We both sat next to Rurik, drew our swords and joined him in sharpening the blades. We kept silent for a while. Rurik was the first to speak:

"I was surprised you decided on a frontal attack for tomorrow. From what I remember of your tactics in Gwynedd, it does not seem like you."

"You're right," I said. "I don't trust the Prince of Penrith and I know nothing of Alpin and his Scots. You, I can trust and that's why I'm here."

"What do you mean?" Elgar asked. "You can't change a battle plan at the last minute. Who would agree to it?"

"What exactly have you in mind?" Rurik enquired. "Do you think we stand a chance to win tomorrow?"

"I don't think one can field a thousand good soldiers," I replied. "I believe we can play havoc if we manage to attack those that are only making up the numbers. They will probably stand behind the first two ranks. What we need to do is to attack them from behind."

"You want us to go round and create a diversion in the enemy rear," Rurik exclaimed and added: "That's suicide. I cannot agree to it."

"You don't have to," I said. "It is not my plan. We'll start as agreed. We'll move forward. Only you won't move forward but sideways to the right until you are able to attack their flank. At the same time, Penrose's contingent that I am commanding with her will do the same and merge the two ranks into a single, elongated row with no back up but linking you to the rest of the army."

"It's very risky," stated Elgar. "How well can you be sure your men will make that move?"

"It might work," Rurik said. "At the very least, it will create confusion at one end of the enemy front. I'm for it."

"Thank you!" I answered. "Elgar?"

"Why not?" he replied.

"Then, be as early as you can tomorrow," I asked of them. "Now, I must return to Penrose."

# CHAPTER 22

It was a beautiful summer night, warm but not sultry. The sky was full of stars. I stopped to look at them. Close to the horizon was a small crescent moon. When I saw it, I thought of Penrose and of the first time we looked at it together when she said it was to be our moon. It was still spring then and the start of a wonderful time for both of us. I felt strange that, when it reappeared, we had just had an argument. I needed to make it up to her now. So, I hurried back for tomorrow might be too late for reconciliation. When I reached the top of the mount, I could see her lying down on her side already.

"I'm back," I said.
"I'm not talking to you," she replied.
"Our moon is up in the sky."
"I know, but I'm still not speaking to you."
"I needed to discuss some tactics for tomorrow."
She did not answer. I continued:
"You know, tomorrow, when there's going to be a deciding battle. I could not just leave it unplanned."
"I thought it was all arranged."
"Yes, but only everybody's position. Your father was in no mood to discuss any tactics. Do you want to know more?"
"Yes. No! Do what you please, I'm still not talking to you."
"Stop saying that! I never meant to upset you."
"Good-night!"
"That's better!"

She did not say another word that night and I did not want to force the issue.

As soon as the first rays of the sun broke through, I got up. Penrose was still asleep. I woke her up.

"We have plenty to do. Come!" I said.

She neither spoke nor moved.

"Penrose, you can give me the silent treatment if you wish but there are others to consider."

Reluctantly, she got up, put on her sword, picked up her shield and followed me. As soon as we reached our contingent, I told the men to march and follow us. We were the first to arrive on what was to be the battlefield.

"Now, listen to me! We are going to rehearse a move we shall be making. Upon my signal, you will extend the first row to your right with everyone from the second row filling in."

It was a simple manoeuvre but we had to repeat it a few times to ensure that the men became familiar with it. After I had told them to rest while waiting for other contingents to arrive, Penrose asked me:

"How is this going to work? The Vikings will be to our right."

"Not for long!" I replied. "Their order is to move even further to the right and to outflank the enemy."

"Whose idea was it?"

"Mine, but I had to make sure they agreed to it. Anyway, here they come."

The Vikings were soon followed by the Scots and Ulls and his men. We took position as agreed the day before. This left a big gap in the middle as we waited for the Prince of Penrith and his own contingent to make an appearance. Meanwhile, the Saxons made their advance all together in one massive square.

For a moment, I thought they were set to attack us straight away, even before all our men had arrived. However, they paused at some distance from us. I still do not know to this day why this was so; whether it was because there was a gap in the middle of our formation and they could not understand why or because they had already decided they would not be the first to attack.

At last, the Prince of Penrith arrived. As soon as his men had lined up, I pulled out my sword, hit my shield with it and started to advance. My men followed and so did the Vikings. The Prince sent Gryff running to me with the order to stop. He was too late. Ulls had followed my example. His men were advancing and so were the Scots.

"The Prince has not given the signal to advance," Gryff said to me while trying to recover his breath.

"Gryff!" I replied. "Last night, the Prince said I was responsible for what happens today. Therefore, I decide when to attack and the time is now. Go back and tell him if he does not follow, he's a coward!"

Gryff was going to answer when he realised that the Prince's men had taken the initiative to advance and to beat their own shields like everyone else. The Saxons, on the other hand, were not moving. I made the men go a bit faster, ready to charge when closer to the enemy. I gave the signal to Rurik. He moved away as pre-arranged. My second signal was to my own men. They deployed as previously instructed. Soon after, the enemy was engaged and the battle had started. By then, the Vikings had turned round and were attacking the Saxons on their flank, creating disarray. I had been right, many of the Saxons soldiers were no match for the Vikings or even for our own Welsh soldiers. As their left wing was crumbling, Rurik started attacking their rear, creating even more havoc. I got my men to follow the Vikings and together we created a second front at the rear of the Saxon army. Unfortunately, The Prince of Penrith could not hold his own against the King of Northumbria and was beginning to fall back. Seeing this, Bewulf disengaged some of his best fighters and brought them against us. This was serious business now. My body began to ache from the blows and cuts I was receiving. Penrose got a nasty cut on her right shoulder close to her neck. Elgar managed to reach me and told me to fall back along the rear of the Saxon army. It was a daring plan but one that worked. As we emerged at the other end, the Scots, while surprised to see us, did not hesitate to push forward and thus gave us the support we needed. It was more than welcome. Ulls, also, moved to help in our rescue, leaving his father to be pushed back even further. Bewulf, for some reason, did not push his advantage but decided to disengage giving us a chance to regroup. I had lost most of my men, less than thirty were still fit for fighting while only about twice that number had reached safety but needed to tend their wounds. I told Penrose to look after them and to put some grass over her cut to stop the bleeding. She was worn out but acquiesced. I walked to Ulls and suggested he disengaged too.

"You're right," he said. "We could use a lull to regroup and plan our next move."

Rurik had lost half his Vikings and was standing close to us. Alpin and his Scots had fared better, only losing a few men. Ulls had lost about a third of his contingent. I had no idea what the situation was with the Saxons. I knew we had been relentless against the rear of their army but they were still able to press against the Prince of Penrith and the bulk of his army.

"Has your father suffered many losses?" I demanded of Ulls.

"I could not tell you," he answered. "But we can't leave him being pushed further and further back. We need to go to his rescue."

"No!" I said. "I have a better plan but I need to consult with Rurik and Alpin first."

"Why?"

"Come with me and I'll explain it all."

We found Elgar and Rurik talking to Alpin some distance from their men. As soon as we reached them, I asked:

"Alpin, where is your son? Has he been hurt."

"No, he's caring for the wounded. Shall I call him?"

"Please! We need to discuss our next move," I answered.

As Alpin went looking for his son, we followed him and found his son sitting next to Penrose. I felt slightly annoyed, all the more so when she said:

"This young man has been wonderful. He's dressed my wound. He also says it's pretty deep but I feel ready to rejoin the fray."

"Good!" I said. "Now, this is what I propose: Rurik and Alpin attack Bewulf while Ulls and I go to the Prince's rescue."

"It's risky," Rurik answered. "However, I realise you can't allow the Prince to carry on withdrawing. Please don't abandon us if we run into trouble."

"We don't have to fight for long," Alpin said, "just long enough to stop the Saxon advance. Then, we should disengage and rejoin you."

We all agreed. Ulls, Penrose and I walked back to our men. I asked him:

"Have you left Gwendwr in charge?"

"No!" Ulls answered. "I don't know where he is. Early on, he said he had been hurt. I have not seen him since."

"Just like him!" I said.

The plan worked. We were again a whole army, lined up to face the enemy. The Saxons, too, had regrouped and were facing us. This lull in the battle, while welcome, was unnerving. It was still morning but the heat of the sun was beginning to be felt. Our troops were exhausted but we could not withdraw: it would be granting victory to the enemy. The Prince of Penrith had called all of us to his side. When we were all assembled, he asked me:

"What now, Ap Thor? Any more of your clever ideas?"

"What we need are fresh troops," I answered.

"You know we don't have any," the Prince snapped.

"If the Saxons don't attack, we could have fresh troops in a couple of hours, couldn't we Ap Thor?" Rurik said to everyone else's surprise.

"How so?" Ulls asked. "You can't create fresh troops out of nowhere."

"Simple!" I said. "We get everyone in a close, three rows deep formation. The men at the front lock their shields and thus form a screen behind which the other troops rest without the enemy noticing. They don't need to stand. When they are refreshed, they will be ready to fight again and in better shape than the enemy."

My plan was executed. I rested at the back next to Penrose. She was not feeling so good as the bleeding had not stopped. I put some more grass over it, she smiled but I could see she was in pain. Elgar came running to me.

"We have a problem," he said. "Some of our wounded left on the battlefield are creeping towards us. It would be bad if the shield wall opens up for them."

"Sorry, Penrose, I have to attend to this problem. I'll be back as soon as I can. Elgar, let's get several groups of men together with flags of truce to go and pick up the wounded from either side. Under no circumstances must the shield wall be breached."

Luckily for us, the Saxons did not move and we sent party after party to help our fallen comrades. As the last one made its way safely back with some wounded, Ulls came to me and said:

"I'm relieved the enemy respected our flags of truce and let us bring back all our wounded."

I had wondered why they let us do it but also why they had not rescued their own. Then, I knew. The expression on my face must have surprised Ulls for he asked:

"What's wrong?"

"They can't stay here."

"Who?"

"The wounded! Can't you see? The Saxons did us no favour. If they attack now and push us back, our path is blocked by our wounded. It would be a massacre. They have to be moved and fast. Penrose, I need your help."

"I'm not well," she replied. "I don't think I shall be much help."

"On the contrary, I want you to lead all our wounded back to camp."

"Why?" she asked.

"They would be in the way if the battle starts again but, in the camp, they will be safe."

I gave her a quick kiss and we went our respective ways. As it was getting hotter and hotter, the men who had been chosen to form that screen with their shields were sweating profusely and feeling very uncomfortable. Still, the enemy was not moving. I may have panicked for nothing.

A couple of very long hours passed by. The sun rays continued to beat down on us relentlessly. I looked up at the sky but could not spot a single cloud anywhere. Then, in the relative silence, we all heard the thud of a body falling: one of the soldiers holding up the line had fainted. It was time to bring fresher troops for that duty. However, I also wanted to annoy the enemy by confusing them. So, I ordered men to go one by one to extend that front line at one end. At the same time, I ordered the men at the other end to stand down one at a time. When the exercise was over, we found ourselves not quite facing the enemy any more. It was some time before the Saxons realised what we had done and, in turn, moved to reposition themselves facing us. I sat down to take a well deserved rest. I was thinking about Penrose and wondering how she was faring when Elgar joined me:

"That was a good move, Appie! Oops! You don't want me to call you that any more, do you?"

"No, uncle!" I replied. "This time I forgive you."

We kept silent for a while before Elgar spoke again:

"Do you remember when I used to visit you at your father's and tell you about my adventures? You always said you wanted to be a Viking warrior like me. Today, your dream has come true."

"Uncle! Am I really a Viking warrior or just fighting for the Welsh?"

"Both, I would say. What you need is a victory."

"Unlikely, today. The best we can hope for is a stalemate."

"You're not planning any more attacks then, are you?"

"Later on, possibly, when it's cooler. A final push before night falls."

"What of the Saxons? You don't think they would attack us, do you?"

"Who knows? If they do, we'll be ready for them."

Again we fell silent.

Another couple of hours had gone by. I ordered the previous manoeuvre to be repeated. This time, the Saxons promptly noticed our move and repositioned themselves at once.

Still, they did not attack. Gwendwr walked towards me, saw Elgar next to me and moved away. My two uncles would never be friends. I was resigned to that. A little while later, the Prince of Penrith came and sat by me.

"Is it worth staying on?" he asked me.

"What else can we do?" I replied.

"We could withdraw back to camp."

"That would give the Saxons the victory as they would remain in possession of the battlefield."

"Quite! We could send a flag of truce."

"And say what? Surely you don't think they would now agree to grant peace guarantees to Vikings and Scots."

"Possibly not! We could attack and renew the battle."

"I was thinking about that. Now might be too early."

"Why? We could just charge and withdraw for something to do."

"What advantage to us? How many dead and wounded? What if the enemy pursues us?"

"What then?"

"Do you want action? I can give you action: we can go on a march."

"Don't joke with me!"

"I'm not. We walk towards their camp."

"What!" exclaimed Elgar who was listening to our conversation.

"Let me explain," I said, "we walk away. They think they've won. We turn sharply to the left and start running. When they realise what our goal is, they will run to try and stop us, probably by overtaking us and barring our way. What we actually do is different: when they are level with us, we stop, turn to face them and attack. It's unlikely they'd be ready for us. We may even regain the advantage."

"Brilliant!" Elgar exclaimed. "My nephew is quite the strategist, isn't he?"

The Prince of Penrith did not reply. I could see that he was thinking. Then, he just moved away. I saw him talk to his son. I decided to go and join them.

"You have a plan," Ulls said when he saw me approaching. "I quite like it. I have only one question: why did you not present it earlier?"

"I'd like to wait a bit longer before we move," I answered.

"Nonsense!" the Prince said. "We execute it now."

I had no choice but to obey.

It all went according to plan up to a point. The Saxons split into two groups. The one we attacked, while not quite ready for our men, recovered sooner than I thought. The other enemy group whose goal seemed to have been to overtake us and bar our way, purposefully turned back and tried to attack us from behind. Fortunately, Rurik had seen them coming, disengaged his men, turned them round and had them charge. Rurik recognised Bewulf at their head and rushed towards him. In the ensuing clash, the Viking leader gave such a blow and cut to the King's son's right arm that he dropped his sword and only saved his life by hiding behind his men. Of course, the Viking contingent was too small to survive the Saxon onslaught and I had to bring my own men to their rescue. Our own line was broken and there was some confusion. I decided to withdraw but was pursued. Somehow, we managed to extricate ourselves but not without heavy loss again. Elgar had been seriously cut in his left leg and was limping. Rurik was bleeding from a cut on the right side of his face. Both the Prince of Penrith and his son had superficial cuts on their arms. Alpin had a broken sword in his hand and his son was using his sword as a walking stick, not because he had been hurt but because he was so tired he could hardly stand. In addition, many of our men had been so seriously wounded that, short of abandoning them, we could not retreat. In truth, we were now at the mercy of the enemy. Fortunately for us, they did not attack but, instead, reformed at some distance from us in a position that indicated their determination to block the way to their camp if we ever tried again.

I kept my eyes on the sun willing it to go down faster but to no avail. Nobody was moving or speaking. We were just too exhausted to even think. So, when the Saxons sent three of their monks with a flag of truce, we did not respond straight away. Gwendwr was the first to notice them. He quickly got up and shouted:
"Flag of truce! Parley! Who will come with me?"
The Prince of Penrith and his son joined Gwendwr and all three went forward to meet the Saxon delegation. I ran after them because I wanted to be present. When we were close enough, the monk in the middle of the trio shouted:
"The King of Northumbria is prepared to talk of peace with you tomorrow. Do you agree?"
"You know what we want," I answered. "The peace is to be agreed with all of us."
"Then, talk tomorrow," the monk repeated. "We cannot discuss terms, only our King can."
"We will talk tomorrow," the Prince of Penrith said. "You have my word on it."

# CHAPTER 23

Penrose had developed a fever. During the night, she became delirious. When I had rejoined her at the end of the previous day, I was so tired that I just laid down and fell asleep straight away. Somehow, I could hear her moaning but I could not wake up. When I eventually did, it was morning and Alpin mac Alpin was standing by us.

"I came to see how Penrose was doing," he said, addressing me. "She does not look good and you hardly look any better yourself. What you both need is a dip in the brook."

"What are you talking about?" I asked. "How come you look so bright and cheerful this morning when last night you could hardly walk?"

"I just told you: A dip in the brook. Don't look so surprised. We, Scots, do it all the time. There's nothing like it to feel refreshed and alive again. You should try it some time. Actually, you should try it now and so should Penrose."

"I don't think she's fit enough to be moved."

"We could carry her. Don't you want her to get better? Also, my father should have a look at her wound. He would know how to deal with it. He's got the touch. It's a gift."

I did not quite understand what he was talking about but I readily agreed and got six of our men to carry Penrose on a shield. We walked through the Scottish camp where Alpin mac Alpin asked his father to join us and then on to a brook some distance away. There, we undressed and laid down in the water. Suprisingly, I felt better very quickly. Alpin had removed the grass from Penrose's wound and, using a small dagger that he was carrying, pricked the wound. A whitish liquid ran out of it. With his hands, he pressed the flesh until blood began to appear. He then pushed her shoulder under water and kept it so for a while. All this time, his son was looking at Penrose's naked body.

"Time to get out," Alpin said. "Come to the camp with us."

We followed him. Penrose was still very weak and had to be carried. We were led to a small fire. Alpin took a small twig, quickly turned it round and round in the flame and, when satisfied, applied it to Penrose's wound. She screamed.

"Don't cover the wound until tonight," he advised, "and only if it's not dry."

Soon after we returned to our quarters, Penrose fell asleep. I kept a vigil until the middle of the day when it was time to meet with the Saxons and discuss peace terms. As usual, the King of Northumbria and his son came accompanied by a few monks. One of them spoke first:

"Our God is the true God. It is our duty to make Him known to all mankind. Our King is a true Christian and his son a very devout one. There can be no peace unless you allow free entry into your lands to any of our monks. They must also be free to preach our religion and you must not stop anyone from converting and becoming a Christian."

"We already have Christian monks among us." Alpin interrupted.

The monk was taken aback. He looked at his fellow monks before asking:

"Are you sure?"

"Of course!" Alpin answered. "You probably don't know them because they are not Saxons like you but Irish. For your information, Irish, Scots and Welsh are all Celts and virtually speak the same language and also have the same Celtic culture."

"Where is Penrose?" Bewulf enquired suddenly. "I would have thought she would be present."

"She's ill," the Prince of Penrith replied, "and as she is my daughter, I shall speak on her behalf. I am still willing to have her marry you."

"She's already asked for a monk who speaks her language fluently to teach her the tenets of our faith before she converts, hasn't she?" Bewulf continued. "I think we have an answer. Alpin, would you send one of the Celtic monks to attend to Penrose."

"Of course!" Alpin answered. "Also, while any Saxon monk would be welcome, we don't really need anyone to come. I believe there have already been a few converts among my people."

"Excellent!" the King of Northumbria said and, turning to Rurik, he asked:

"Will you accept Christian monks among you."

"We won't object," Rurik replied, "we have met with Christians before but we have a strong belief in Odin and I doubt any of us, Vikings, would be willing to convert."

"The Lord moves in mysterious ways," one of the monks said. "We shall pray for this to happen."

And so, a peace was agreed between us all and I returned to Penrose in a hurry. I was glad to find her feeling better. She wanted to know what was happening so I told her. She was silent for a while, then asked me:

"What is Odin's Town like? What is it like to live the Viking way? Is it very different from the Welsh way? Will you tell me? Or even better, will you show me?"

"We have a few customs that are different from yours," I said. "We train differently for example. Surely, you remember me teaching you Viking moves when fighting. You were not so keen on it then. Why the sudden change of heart?"

"I will have to turn my back on my family and my religion when I marry Bewulf and would then have to learn of the Saxon way of life. Why can't I learn of the Viking way of life too? It would help me to remember you."

"I would not know where to start."

"Then, take me to Odin's Town. Let me see for myself."

"You're serious about it, aren't you? Yes, I'd like to do that for you. Actually, I can do even better; we can travel there with my uncle and all the Vikings who came to fight for your father and who will now be returning home."

"When will that be?"

"I'd better find out."

Rurik was surprised when I told him, not so much about Penrose's wish but because I had agreed to it. He had decided to leave that very afternoon and to travel in short stages on account of the wounded.

"I don't really want to delay our departure," he said. "I could wait until tomorrow morning because you're a good friend but, if Penrose is not ready then, I'll leave without you. Maybe, your uncle will stay behind and the three of you could journey together at a later date."

"That's a thought," I answered.

I hurried back to Penrose and was surprised to find her speaking to Alpin mac Alpin.

"I came to say my goodbyes," he said as soon as he saw me. "My father wants to leave today. I was telling Penrose the good news about having a Celtic monk help her to convert. I'm not so fond of those Saxon monks we met, they seem to be so full of themselves."

"Convey to your father our thanks for doing so," I answered, hoping he would take the hint and leave.

"Penrose!" he went on, "if you need my help at any time, do not hesitate to ask. I am forever your devotee."

"I need to rest," Penrose said.

This time, he left. However, we were not to be alone for long as, soon afterwards, Gryff paid us a visit. When he saw the wound on Penrose's shoulder, he exclaimed:

"What happened to you? I've been told you were unwell but I did not realise you had been hurt in the battle. You're always taking too many risks. Oh! I'm so sorry to see you hurt. If there's anything I can do to help, please ask me."

"There is, actually," Penrose replied, "I want you to keep a secret until later tomorrow. I'm not returning to Penrith with my father. I've decided to visit Odin's Town…"

"What on earth for?" Gryff interrupted. "Ap Thor, have you put her up to this? It's bad enough for the two of you to be seen together all the time but going away… Words fail me."

"You worry too much, Gryff," Penrose answered. "I have my reasons for going but I shall come back and then, I shall be my father's dutiful daughter who will convert to Christianity and marry a Saxon. All I want you to do is to break the news to my father after I've left. Do you promise to do that then and not before?"

"You're asking a lot of me, my lady," Gryff said. "Would it not be better for you to tell your father, and for me to go with you?"

"Certainly not!" Penrose exclaimed.

There was an awkward silence. I broke in:

"Gryff! Let us not argue! You have got to trust her. What Penrose is about to do will eventually affect us both. Do not spoil the present. Can we rely on you?"

"I won't say a word until asked."

"Good!" I said.

Penrose had a restless night. She maintained it was the excitement of going away with me. I hoped that was true. She was up at first light and raring to go. We made our way to the Viking camp where we were welcomed by my uncle Elgar:

"You're bright and early! Let's move on. An early start is always best."

"How is your leg?" I asked.

"Still sore," Elgar answered, "I shall be limping all the way. And you, Penrose, how do you feel?"

"Better than I was. Ap Thor tells me you have travelled far and wide. Is it true?"

"I've led a soldier's life. When he was a boy, Ap Thor never tired of my reliving my adventures for him. He was a good listener. His father never spoke of the past but instead taught him how to be a blacksmith. I suppose you were not aware of that."

Penrose took her sword out of its scabbard and showed it to my uncle, asking him,

"What do you think of this?"

"Fit for the daughter of a Prince!" he replied.

"Your nephew cast it for me," she said. "So, yes, I know he's a blacksmith and a fine one at that. He's also been a good teacher. I have learnt a lot from him."

"I'm sure you did," Elgar answered, "however, something is troubling me. You don't have to answer if you don't want to but why are you going to Odin's Town?"

Penrose looked up to me, expecting me to give my uncle an answer. I did not want to. I thought it was none of his business. So, we just walked on in silence, much to his chagrin.

It took us five days to reach Odin's Town. Each day, Penrose looked better than the day before but still she was tired every evening. As we drew near, she became excited and could not contain herself. She wanted us to hurry. Rurik took me aside,

"What are you going to do when you reach the town? I don't think there's anywhere suitable for Penrose to stay."

"I could not agree with you more," I answered. "I was thinking perhaps we could camp outside the gate."

"A better location would be to choose either of the two promontories that overlook the town and stay on top of one of those for the duration of your stay."

"That's a good idea. Let's hope Penrose agrees."

"Did I hear my name?" Penrose asked. "And, please, will you both stop talking in your own language. I can't understand a word you're saying."

"I'm afraid that's the only language you will hear while there," I explained, "but, actually, we were wondering where is the best place for us to camp.".

"Aren't we staying in the town?"

"I don't live here."

"But your uncle does?"

"Indeed! But I don't think he can help us. He said something to me about being homeless but we can always ask him."

"Let me find him, while you carry on walking," Rurik offered.

I sighed with relief and soon Elgar joined us. He confirmed he did not live in the town but camped just outside.

"Penrose!" I said. "May I suggest we camp on top of one of those promontories? You choose which one you prefer."

"Why not camp with your uncle?" she asked.

"He'll camp with us," I answered. "It's better that way."

We eventually chose the one on the West of the town. A cool breeze was blowing in from the sea. I just laid down on the grass, looking up at the sky. Penrose soon joined me while Elgar set himself up some distance away to give us some privacy. We hardly spoke that evening. We just enjoyed being close together. I had decided not to make any plans and to let myself be governed by Penrose. Thus, it was the middle of the following morning before she enquired:

"Are you going to show me around the town or are you hiding something from me?"

"Let me be your guide." I said.

We walked down from our camp. I showed her the exercise field before the gate but no one was practising. Any town is pretty much the same as any other town and Penrose had to admit that it looked a bit like Penrith except that she could not understand a single word that was being spoken around her.

"If that worries you, I will have to teach you Norse," I said jokingly as, having crossed the length of the town, we found ourselves on the beach. The tide was high and, it being a hot summer's day, quite a few people were bathing and swimming in the sea.

"Let's go in!" she said as she started to undress.

"Can you swim?" I asked.

"No, but you can show me how, can't you?"

"I can't. I never learnt."

I caught sight of my uncle in the water and waved to him. He waved back and, at the same time, he gestured for us to join him.

"I can understand that," Penrose said as she stepped into the water and made for Elgar.

I had to follow her and stand chest deep in the water while my uncle was instructing her.

"Won't you join us?" my uncle asked me after a while.

"I'd like to," I answered. "You will have to teach me too."

"There's nothing to it," he replied. "Just lay on my arms."

I did so, only for him to pull his arms away and for me to sink underwater. As I emerged, Penrose was laughing her head off. I tried again but with no better result. I then saw Penrose swim effortlessly. I was miffed.

We stayed there another four days. The best times for me were the evenings when we both watched the sunset and the stars rise in the sky. The days were hot and Penrose insisted on going down to the beach and spending time in the water. In spite of her encouragement, I gave up the idea of swimming very soon. I was hopeless at it while she revelled in it. I could not understand how she could have learnt so quickly. One day, she tried to teach me but to no avail. She soon gave up the idea as she did of learning Norse.

"You know I don't like to say goodbye," Elgar reminded me on the morning of our departure.
"Are you staying on?" I asked. "You could come with us. Then carry on to the land between the two rivers and see your brother again."
"Not with my leg," he answered, "I need to rest. The journey is too long."
"Look after yourself," Penrose said to him as we left.
Five minutes later, we heard someone running after us. We stopped, turned round and saw Rurik. He embraced me and, as he did so, he whispered to me in Norse:
"She's a good woman. Are you sure you know what you are doing by going back?"
I did not answer but gave him another firm embrace and then we parted.
"What did he say to you?" Penrose asked me after a while.
"It does not matter. I'm with you now."

## CHAPTER 24

We took it easy, only walking in the morning and evening and resting during the hottest part of the day. It was a leisurely journey back to Penrith as if neither of us was in a hurry to go home. We reckoned we were about another two days' walk from Penrith and had just sat down for our midday break when we saw a lonely figure coming towards us. As he came closer, we recognised Gryff.

"Here you are!" he exclaimed as soon as he saw us. "Everyone is wondering what has happened to you. The Irish monk arrived a few days ago. Fortunately, he has decided to build a church while waiting for you, Penrose, but your father is not happy. He feared you would not be coming back."

"That's silly!" Penrose replied. "I gave you my word I would return. Did you not tell my father?"

"Yes I did, but he feared that you may be led astray."

"By whom?" she asked incredulously.

"Me, I suppose," I said.

"That's ridiculous!" Penrose stated. "Of course, I like your company, Ap Thor, but I also have duties and obligations. You should never forget that, Gryff."

"Then, let's get home as quickly as possible," Gryff answered.

"Not in this heat!" Penrose said. "You can return at once, if you want to, or remain with us. It's up to you."

Gryff decided to stay with us. By the evening of the following day we reached the river that runs close to Penrith. Crossing it by the ford, we could see a structure taking shape a few feet upstream.

"It's the church that the monk is building," Gryff informed us.

"Let's have a closer look," I said.

I made my way towards it, followed by Penrose and Gryff, who tried to stop us by saying:

"Wait! Don't go so fast. I should introduce you."

I ignored him. For some reason, I was thinking back to the Christian church I had seen all those years ago on the outskirts of Dublin and I wondered how similar this one would look. The monk, seeing people coming, stood motionless next to his half-built church. He looked familiar. I could not help myself shouting:

"Aidan! Is that you?"

"Who's calling my name?" the monk asked.

"Ap Thor!" I said. "Do you remember me?"

"No!" he answered, puzzled.

"Don't you remember a young Viking who spent a rainy night at your church near to Dublin."

"And who told me about Irish people across the sea. Yes! Now, I do remember. As you can see, I followed your advice. I crossed the sea and I have been doing my ministry among the clan Alpin."

"Successfully?" I asked. "I guess you must have if you have been chosen to teach Penrose."

"This came as a total surprise to me considering that Alpin and his son are not Christian," Aidan answered.

"I am Penrose," Penrose introduced herself. "Gryff tells me you are building a church, is it anything to do with your religion?"

"It's almost completed," Aidan said. "You are welcome to look inside."

We all went in. It was almost an exact copy of the one in Ireland with one glaring exception: there was no cross on the altar and the roof was still missing.

"You've done a good job," I said.

"Not really!" Aidan replied. "I have not been able to find a flat stone for the altar."

"Why do you need a flat stone?" Penrose enquired.

"Our religion is based around the emblem of the Cross," the monk explained. "Therefore, on top of every altar, there must be a cross. My wooden one won't stand."

I looked at the stone closely. A solution was forming in my mind, so I asked him:

"Can the cross be made of iron?"

"Yes!" he replied. "So long as it is the right shape."

"Then, meet me at the forge tomorrow morning and I'll make one for you," I said. "However, we must be on our way now. Penrose, are you coming?"

It did not take us long to reach the town and go to the Prince's Hall. As we entered, Ulls was having an argument with his father. They did not notice us but Gwendwr did and he shouted:

"Ap Thor, so nice to have you back!"

Upon hearing those words, the Prince of Penrith walked straight to me and, in an ironic tone, said to me:

"So, you finally decided to bring my daughter back to me!"

"No!" Penrose intervened. "I decided to come back and Ap Thor escorted me here. Let no one assume differently."

"Then, your work is done," the Prince said to me. "There is no reason for you to stay on, here, in Penrith."

"Father!" Penrose intervened again. "Ap Thor will stay and be present at my wedding."

"There are rumours about the two of you," Ulls said. "It would be better to do as my father suggests."

"And what are those rumours?" Penrose asked.

No one answered. Penrose sat at the table and started eating. I joined her, as did Gryff. Gwendwr coughed to attract my attention and then gestured for me to come to him. I ignored him. He came over and whispered in my ear:

"They say that you and Penrose... you know."

"That's none of your business," I replied, rather angrily.

"So! It's true then," he exclaimed.

Penrose and I looked at each other. I shrugged my shoulders. She spoke:

"There are times when I hate that uncle of yours."

"I don't blame you," I answered. "We have had a long day, we'd better retire."

She agreed, got up and I followed her. No one tried to stop us, not even her father.

The following morning, true to my word, I went to the forge accompanied by Penrose. Aidan was already there waiting for me so I asked him to draw the design of the cross he wanted in the dust and sand on the floor and I set to work. Aidan was impressed with my skill while the blacksmith looked on, hoping to learn something. A couple of hours later, the job was done but Aidan was not happy and said so: I had turned the bottom of the cross into a sharp point like that of a dagger. My answer was simple:

"Shh! Let's go to the church now."

Aidan walked alongside me and Penrose followed.

"Have you given any thought to what we discussed way back then?" he asked.

"You mean in Ireland?" I enquired.

"Yes."

"No, not really. I actually remember very little."

"Would you like to learn more?"

"I might listen to you but that does not mean I want to renounce Odin or convert to the worship of your God. For Penrose, it's different, she has to; it's a prerequisite for her marriage to Bewulf."

"You should not say that. Faith is important in our Church. When Penrose is ready to believe that our God is the one and only true God, then I shall be happy to baptise her for then her conversion will come from the heart."

"What if I'm not convinced?" Penrose asked.

"It would be wrong of me to accept you into our fold," Aidan answered. "But you two seem to be good friends. Why don't I teach you together?"

"I'd like that," Penrose answered. "What do you think, Ap Thor?"

We had reached the church and, as we walked in, I asked:

"Aidan, where do you want your cross? Show me the exact spot."

He pointed to the middle of the altar two thirds towards the back. I held the cross in both hands, raised it and brought it down as fast as I could. The sharp point penetrated the stone and the cross stood erect. Aidan looked at it in astonishment. Then, he knelt down, crossed himself, said a prayer and crossed himself again before getting up. Penrose looked on, took me by the arm and asked:

"What is he doing?"

"There's a lot I don't know about the rituals of this church," I answered, "kneeling and crossing oneself is one of them that I remember seeing Aidan do. Let's ask him."

We spent the rest of the day just talking, asking questions and trying to understand this new religion. Towards evening,

Penrose suggested that Aidan come with us and eat dinner in her father's Hall. However, he refused.

"Why?" I asked.

"I'm a simple man," he answered. "I prefer my own company."

We left and on the way back, Penrose said to me:

"You obviously know him, but I find him strange."

"I would agree with you but I'd say this in his favour: he cares about people."

We developed a routine: in the morning, we would go to our field to train together, not only to remain fit, but in case any fighting should start again. I always believed in being prepared. Penrose was fully recovered by now and was enjoying the exercise as much as I was. In the afternoon, we would make our way to Aidan's church and listen to his teaching. We learnt a lot but it left us cold. Neither Penrose nor I felt attracted by that religion. Often, on the way back, we would discuss the teaching between us and compare it with our own religions. Sometimes, I would have to explain my own faith to Penrose, telling her about Odin and the other Norse Gods. She was intrigued by the idea of Valhalla, the place where Viking warriors who die in battle, sword in hand, attain immortality. She was repelled, on the other hand, by the Christian notion of Hell and could not quite comprehend the idea of eternal punishment. Aidan tried his best to convince us that his God was actually a God of love and that, if we were to become good Christians, we would have nothing to fear.

That year, winter came very early. Heavy snowfalls isolated Penrith from the countryside around. Thick snow lay on the ground for weeks. We could not exercise and we stopped visiting Aidan and his church. Like the Prince of Penrith, Ulls,

Gryff and Gwendwr, we spent most of the day huddled by the fire chatting, eating or just keeping quiet. Our intimacy had become an open secret but no one dared say anything to us. Occasionally, I wondered how I would feel when Penrose would eventually leave but I could never bring myself to talk to her about it. Eventually, the thaw came and we ventured out. Penrose led me up the hill and, as we entered the narrow passage between those massive boulders, she confided in me:

"I'm happy when I'm with you. This has been a wonderful winter for me. I never had to prove anything to you or to myself. I tried all that last summer. I think that my warrior days are over. You believed in me as much as I believed in myself. I shall always be grateful to you for that. We achieved so much, you and I but, at the end of the day, I am my father's daughter. I had dreams of one day becoming Princess of Penrith, co-ruler with my brother Ulls. Instead, I shall one day become Queen of Northumbria. This title seems rather shallow to me. I'd sooner remain your friend but treaties have to be fulfilled, especially if it brings lasting peace to my people."

She stopped as we reached the other end of the passageway and looked around. There was still snow everywhere. I felt I needed to say something but the words would not come. She was the first to speak again:

"Do you remember when you first arrived and saw me? Was that fate or were the Gods just playing with us?"

"Maybe it was just the enthusiasm of youth."

She laughed once more that beautiful laugh that had so impressed me when I first heard it.

"I like it when you laugh."

"I know."

We kissed. As we parted, she became serious again.

"I've made my decision," she said, "I am not converting to Christianity. I don't see why I should. I shall still marry Bewulf because I've already agreed to it. When this happens, what will you do, Ap Thor?"

"I try not to think about it."

"But you must! I don't want you to be broken-hearted. You must not hesitate to do your own thing and seek your own dreams."

"You mean, going home, seeing my parents again?"

"There you are! It was not so difficult to decide after all. Let's go back now, I'm getting cold."

"We should go and see Aidan to tell him of your decision."

"What for? He never came to see us. Let us wait and not a word to anyone about this."

Three weeks later, a group of Saxon monks arrived late one evening and were led to the Prince of Penrith's Hall where we were still having dinner. They were invited to join our company and did not hesitate to do so. Their leader introduced himself as the Abbot of Durham. They had been sent by the King of Northumbria with a dual purpose: two thirds of them were to remain in the Prince of Penrith's lands and try to convert his people to Christianity while the Abbot and the other third were to escort Penrose to Durham where the wedding was to take place.

"But for now," the Abbot of Durham concluded, "here's the crucial question: have you all been baptised?"

Blank faces of astonishment appeared on all those present with the exception of Penrose and myself. I thought it fit to answer:

"No one has been baptised."

It was now the turn of the Abbot to show astonishment but, before he could say anything, Ulls intervened:

"What do you mean by 'baptised'?"

"This happens to officially mark a conversion to Christianity," Penrose answered.

"Am I to understand," the Abbot asked, "that no one has yet been converted? And where is the monk who was to teach you our faith?"

"He stays all the time in the church he built," I answered.

"He never comes here," Penrose added. "We have invited him but he's always refused."

"Where is that church?" one of the monks enquired.

"Just outside the town, by a stream," I said.

"How can he expect to convert people," the Abbot asked, "when he does not live among them? I need to see him. Could you fetch him for me?"

"It's getting late," the Prince of Penrith answered. "Let's leave it till tomorrow. Also, there seems to be some misunderstanding. No one is converting to Christianity except my daughter."

"No one at all!" the Abbot exclaimed. "The treaty between yourself and my King states you will all accept our religion."

"I was present when the treaty was discussed," Ulls interjected, "and no such thing has been agreed. You are wrong to say otherwise."

"Religion is a personal thing," said Penrose, "and should not be forced on anyone. I have listened to everything that Aidan has taught me but, ultimately, I have decided that Christianity is not for me. I shall marry Bewulf because this has been agreed in the peace treaty but he will have to let me keep my own religion."

A look of horror came upon all the monks' faces and, in unison, they crossed themselves.

"This is not possible," the Abbot stated when he had recovered from the shock, "it would be a sin. Bewulf, as a devout Christian, could not accept it, nor could I authorise it."

"And it is news to me," said the Prince of Penrith. "I need some time with my daughter."

"Father!" Penrose answered. "I am not refusing to marry Bewulf."

"Silence, daughter!" the Prince interrupted angrily. "Peace between our two countries demands that you not only marry Bewulf but also convert to his religion. For once in your life, you will do as you are told. We have humoured you in the past but then, you were a child. Now, you're a grown woman!"

"And you should treat me as one."

"Tomorrow, you will tell everyone that you agree on all conditions. If you don't, I shall disown you as my daughter and expel you from my lands. I shall exile you to either Gwynedd or Powys."

Without waiting to hear any more, Penrose got up and left the hall. I followed her and so did Gryff. Once away from prying eyes and listening ears, Gryff was the first to speak:

"You must listen to me, Penrose. I have known you since you were a babe. I gave a promise to your mother that I would always be there to protect you. I am an old man now and it would be difficult for me to follow you and end my days in exile with you. Please reconsider your decision. Surely, to convert to Christianity to please your future husband is not a step too far."

"Enough!" Penrose interrupted. "For one, I could never ask you to follow me into exile. Also, going to Northumbria in order to marry Bewulf is an exile of sorts, isn't it?"

Gryff remained silent for a while before turning to me:

"Ap Thor! Don't you have anything to say?"

"What is there to say?" I answered. "Penrose has made her mind up and, I believe, so has her father. By sending his daughter away, he might save the peace. As for you following Penrose into exile, it's up to her, don't you think? My parents live in Gwynedd and I could escort her on my way to see them."

"Who says I want to go to Gwynedd?" Penrose asked. "Can't I choose my own place of exile?"

Gryff and I exchanged glances. Penrose continued:

"Ap Thor, will you come with me, wherever I choose to go?"

"Of course!" I answered. "I shall not abandon you."

"You have not told us," Gryff said, "where you intend to go."

Penrose smiled, keeping us in suspense for a little while, before she simply said:

"Odin's Town! I liked it there."

# CHAPTER 25

Early the following morning, I was summoned by the Prince of Penrith. As soon as he saw me, he asked:

"Can you help me to understand my daughter's behaviour of yesterday?"

"I'll try," I said. "Briefly, both of us attended Aidan's instructions until snow stopped us from going to his church. When the thaw began, Penrose did not want to return any more as, by then, she had decided she will not convert. As she had said, she is still prepared to marry Bewulf."

"I know what she said but I want to keep the peace with my neighbour. Is there any way you can make her change her mind?"

"Gryff came round last night and tried just that but to no effect. She understands that you need to drive her into exile to try and save the peace but she thinks it's no different from moving to Northumbria."

"I should speak to Gryff, then. Oh! here comes Gwendwr!"

"You sent for me?" asked Gwendwr.

"Yes," the Prince replied, "I want you two to escort my daughter to Gwynedd as you are both from there."

"I have no plan to go back," Gwendwr answered. "I am happy here and Ulls needs me. I would need your son's permission if I were to go."

At that moment, the Abbot of Durham arrived, followed by all the monks, including Aidan. Immediately, he spoke:

"It is my mission in life to spread the word of Christ to all who will listen. I am very disappointed that none of you wanted to listen. You must realise this is the only true religion for the whole of mankind. For us, it is imperative you convert to it. Penrose should have been the first of many."

"I don't think you can convert people by force," Aidan interrupted. "Both Penrose and Ap Thor, here, have listened to me and made up their own minds. It is the choice that God gives to his children."

"Do not contradict me," the Abbot reprimanded Aidan. "I am following the dictates of the Pope in Rome, the head of our Church."

"We have survived as Christians for generations after our links with Rome had been cut," Aidan answered back. "It was our faith that both sustained us and made converts among the Celts."

"If that is the case," the Abbot replied, "it is time for you to rejoin the fold and again obey the Pope. However, I am not here to discuss matters of faith among ourselves. I have to report back to the King of Northumbria."

He was interrupted by the arrival of Ulls and his sister.

"Daughter!" the Prince of Penrith said as soon as he saw her. "It is not possible for you to marry Bewulf if you are not a Christian. Your actions might put the fate of this land in jeopardy. Therefore, I shall exile you to Gwynedd in the hope that the Abbot of Durham will see that I want peace."

"Can't you give us a bit more time?" Ulls asked. "I have been trying to make my sister realise the implication of it all. I fully agree that she cannot live on with us."

"To show you that I am a reasonable man," the Abbot of Durham replied, "I shall wait until tomorrow morning when I want to see her either leave with me or go into exile. As for you

Aidan, you too will leave tomorrow, back to where you came from and leave this land of Penrith for us to christianise."

With those words and with his head held high, the Abbot left, followed by all his monks with the exception of Aidan. The latter addressed me:

"Ap Thor! I'd like to apologise for my fellow monks' behaviour. It is true that I would have loved to receive both of you into the arms of our Church but such conversion must come from the heart and not to fulfill some political treaty. I shall pray for both of you that you may, one day, see the light."

That evening, the atmosphere in the Prince of Penrith's Hall was strained. On the one hand, the Abbot of Durham was making his discontent felt and on the other, the Prince was making a last ditch attempt to convince his daughter to be reasonable. This led to her storming out of the hall. Gryff was going to follow her but I stopped him. I wanted everyone present as I made my farewell speech:

"Prince, I shall leave tomorrow. I shall escort your daughter away from her ancestral home and look after her in her place of exile. You suggested Gwynedd but she refuses to go there. As you know, I am partly Viking and so to Viking land we shall go."

Everyone was taken aback except for Gryff who already knew of our plans. A hush fell over the company as I continued:

"We, Vikings, are your allies, Prince. Do not forget this. If the King of Northumbria does not maintain the peace agreed among us all, you will find us at your side."

"Is that a threat?" asked the Abbot of Durham.

"No," I replied, "but if you break the treaty with one party, you break it with all, make no mistake."

It was the turn of the monks to leave but not before one of them exclaimed as a parting shot:

"Christ, in the end, will conquer all."

After a while, Ulls enquired:

"Did you say that my sister is going to live among Vikings? What could possess her to make such a decision?"

"It surprised me as much," Gryff stated, "when she told me last night."

"I'm no Viking," said Gwendwr, "and I enjoy your company. So, may I stay in your service, Ulls?"

"I don't see why not," Ulls answered.

"We shall be on our way at first light tomorrow," I said as I too took my leave.

Penrose was happy. She woke me up as she could not wait to get started. The way to Odin's Town was past Aidan's church. I decided to see whether he was still there. Penrose followed me. We found him on his knees in front of the altar. We stood by the door and I coughed. He turned round, saw us, bowed to the altar, signed himself, got up and, opening his arms in a welcoming gesture, he asked:

"Have you changed your mind?"

"No," I replied. "But we did not wish to pass by without saying goodbye."

"That's so nice of you," he said. "I hope you will be happy. Do not worry for me: I shall go back to the few converts I have made among the Clan Alpin. In my absence, they will have looked after my church there. I don't think anyone will look after this one. I like to have my churches close to water."

"Is it why," I replied, "you built one church by the sea and one by a stream? What is the attraction of water for you?"

"Water is in continuous motion like life."

"Did you build your other church in Clan Alpin's lands near water as well?" Penrose enquired.

"Indeed!" Aidan answered. "This time, it was next to a waterfall. I find the sound of water so conducive to prayer and contemplation. I don't suppose you would understand that."

"No, not really," I said.

"There's one thing I shall miss when I leave: the cross you made for me."

"Take it with you," I suggested.

"I can't. It won't dislodge from the stone."

"Let me do it for you," I said as I went round the altar, grabbed the cross moving it sideways and, when I felt a slight wobble, I just pulled it out and upwards.

Aidan was surprised but very grateful.

"I feel sorry for him," Penrose said to me as we rejoined the main road. "I don't know why."

"Perhaps it's because he has no personal ambition."

She did not answer and I kept silent. For a while, we were both absorbed in our own thoughts. Mine centred around the fact that I was now responsible for Penrose. She had been rejected by her family and her country and had chosen my Viking way of life. What else could be the reason for her deciding to go back to Odin's Town? In a sense, I was flattered but I would also have liked to see my parents again. Now, this would be impossible because, to do so, I would have to cross the Prince of Penrith's lands and it would mean leaving Penrose behind among strangers whose language she did not even speak. However, I soon cheered up and, after a week's travel, we reached Odin's Town late one evening. We made for the promontory on top of which we stayed last time and hoped to meet my uncle Elgar there. We were due for a disappointment: all trace of the camp had disappeared and it was evident my uncle had long gone.

"It's just you and me this time," Penrose said.

I was angry because I could guess where Elgar was. This was unreasonable of me for there was no way my uncle could have known we were coming back.

"What's wrong?" Penrose asked again as I did not reply previously.

"I was expecting my uncle to be here," I said. "Let's stay here for the night and tomorrow morning I'll look for him."

"We'll look for him," she answered. "From now on, we do things together."

That was me told.

As we entered the town the following morning, we met Rurik. He could not hide his surprise and exclaimed:

"Ap Thor! What happened?"

"Penrose has been exiled for refusing to convert to Christianity. It is hoped that, by doing so, peace will be maintained with the Kingdom of Northumbria. So, we've come back here. We arrived last night. Now, we're looking for Elgar."

"I've not seen him for weeks but I suppose you've guessed where he might be, haven't you? However, I would not take Penrose with you."

We had spoken in Norse but, on hearing her name mentioned, Penrose asked in Welsh:

"What are you saying about me?"

"Only good things!" I answered.

"Liar!" she replied and laughed.

I could see she was happy, perhaps even happier than she had been for the past few months. We walked on to the waterfront and to the door of the inn where I suspected I would find my uncle.

"You should wait outside," I said.

"No, I want to come in with you. Don't try to protect me. I'd like to see all things Viking."

"Fair enough! Do as I do: put your hand on the hilt of your sword and don't look surprised."

I pushed the door open. The smell of alcohol was overpowering. The floor was covered with people lying there in various states of undress, both men and women, most of whom were snoring. I tried to walk in and look for my uncle but soon gave up. Instead, I shouted at the top of my voice:

"El-gar!"

One of the women raised herself, displaying a naked body, pointed in one direction and fell back on a fellow's naked chest. I moved over and found my uncle. I gave him a few kicks but their only effect was to make him snore even louder. In desperation, I grabbed him under the arms and dragged him out. All this time, Penrose stood by the door, a look of utter astonishment on her face. As we left and found ourselves in the street outside, she asked me:

"What is this place?"

"An inn."

I tried to wake my uncle up but it was a hopeless task. However, I was not going to leave him there so I had to ask Penrose to help me carry him. I was embarrassed but she did not seem to mind. Outside the town, I decided to stop by the exercise ground where Rurik and others were practising the art of war. We needed to rest before the climb to the top of the promontory that had been our temporary abode in the past and was to be our permanent home from now on. Fortunately, some of my former comrades-in-arms offered to help us and carried Elgar, still fast asleep, up to the top of the promontory. They knew only too well what he was like when he started his drinking bouts.

They also helped me when I started to build our house. I wanted something permanent and Penrose was in full agreement. In addition, I wanted to be self-sufficient and, thanks to the knowledge of farming that I had acquired from my mother, I started a farm of my own if on a smaller scale. I put Elgar in charge of this venture as a way to keep him away from drinking. He seemed pleased that we trusted him. Then, still on top of the promontory, I started another building.

"What is that for?" Penrose asked.

"A forge!" I replied. "There is none in Odin's Town and I need something to do. You know, don't you, how good I am as a blacksmith."

"I could do with a brooch or two," she mused, "and, perhaps, some ornate cups for when we have guests."

In the days that followed, before I could complete the building, we had a surprise visitor: Alpin mac Alpin.

When he arrived, he ignored me and made for Penrose instead.

"I've heard of your father's disgraceful behaviour," he said. "Aidan told me when he returned to my clan. When I heard, I could not rest. I had to see you, to offer you my help. This is what I propose: you come with me and I promise you that everyone in my clan will be at your service."

"I am happy here," Penrose interrupted him. "Everybody has been so kind and helpful."

"Surely, you would feel better among people who speak your language. Vikings are rough and ready, not really suitable for a Prince's daughter."

"Watch what you're saying," I intervened. "You have no right to speak like that to Penrose. You are welcome here but not to tell her what to do. By the way, how is your father?"

"He's well, thanks."

Alpin mac Alpin stayed a few days. When he realised he would never convince Penrose to follow him into Scotland, he decided to leave but not without a parting speech:

"You may not want to follow me now. I am a patient man, I can wait. Remember that my clan can be a refuge for you at any time. For the moment we part, except that you will still be present in my heart anywhere I go. My devotion and love have no bounds, remember that."

Without waiting for an answer, he turned round and left. Penrose sighed with relief. I said to her:

"I think he fancies you."

"Don't mention him," she replied, "he makes my flesh crawl."

# CHAPTER 26

Two years had passed by. Penrose and I considered ourselves as husband and wife. We had settled down the way all couples do. I would exercise on a regular basis either with my uncle Elgar or with Rurik, who had become a very good friend of mine and whom I considered almost like a brother. Penrose would not join us. As a matter of fact, she had stopped wearing a sword and therefore did not train any more. Her days as a warrior were over. Soon after I had built the forge, I was kept busy as virtually everyone living in Odin's Town wanted some repairs doing but, at this time, business was very slack and I would build the fire up only once a week. I had turned one of my armlets into a variety of jewellery for Penrose: a couple of brooches, a bracelet and a ring. I never got round to making those cups she once asked for.

During the summer, when the sun was shining, she would go to the waterfront and swim. She really enjoyed it. I would usually remain on the shore. She would tease me:

"You like fire and I like water. It's a good combination."

And she would laugh in exactly the same way as she had always done and which had so attracted me to her when we first met. The promontory upon which we had set up our abode had now acquired a name: Ap Thor's Seat. It was flattering if a little embarrassing. We heard little about the world outside as no visitor ever came to Odin's Town. Despite it being on the bank of a large river with the sea not far away, no boats ever landed there or were even sighted. I did not think many Vikings would know of the existence of this town and I assumed this was the reason why. No one, either, had tried to communicate with Ireland through crossing the Scottish clans' lands. I would have liked to let my father and mother know we were all right but Penrith stood between us and the land between the two rivers where they lived. I thought of sending Elgar with a message for them but he was not keen on the idea. When I asked him why, this was his answer:

"When I was young and went to the Empire of the East and signed up for fifteen years in their army, I never thought about my parents. If I had settled over there at the end of my stint, I would never have been in touch with them again. That's your fate once you choose the life of a Viking warrior as far as I'm concerned. So you'd better get used to the idea."

And so, we carried on our daily lives. That winter had been particularly mild and spring had come with all kinds of vegetation growth and the usual wild flowers for that time of the year but it was not getting any warmer. Then, one evening, a visitor came up to Ap Thor's Seat, it was Gryff. Penrose, in spite of her surprise, made him welcome at once and wanted to hear all the news from Penrith.

"I am afraid," he said, "I have bad news. Your father was ill most of the winter. A fortnight ago, he took a turn for the worse. A few days ago, he died."

I could see she was visibly shaken in spite of her efforts to conceal it. As was typical of her, she said nothing and Gryff continued:

"I have been sent by your brother to bring you home for his funeral."

"Does it mean my exile is over?" Penrose enquired before she collapsed in tears.

"I don't know," Gryff replied, "nothing was said before I left."

"We should leave tomorrow," I stated. "But we won't go without an escort, I'll ask Rurik to arrange for one."

We travelled as fast as we could: Penrose, myself, Gryff, Elgar, Rurik and half a dozen men to escort us. Upon our arrival, we were warmly welcomed by Ulls, who now called himself Prince of Penrith. Yet, I could sense that all was not well. No preparations had been made for the late Prince's burial. When I enquired as to the reason why, Ulls answered:

"I have invited others to come. We have to wait for their arrival."

"Who are they?" I queried.

"The King of Northumbria and the Chief of Clan Alpin, for I hope they will renew the peace treaty with me."

"Good move," said Gryff.

"I don't think so," Penrose cut in. "I have lived for the past two years in exile on account of that treaty. Brother, will you let me stay on here?"

"I can't say," he replied. "It's out of my hands. I shall do whatever is necessary to maintain peace."

"Let me remind you," I said, "that we, Vikings, are your allies whatever happens. We are just as ready to make war as to abide by any peace," and, turning to both Elgar and Rurik, I added, "aren't we?"

They nodded their acquiescence.

The following day, Bewulf arrived with a large escort of monks and men-at-arms. He had been sent by his father, the King of Northumbria to represent him. His opening speech, when he met with us, was encouraging:

"My father has asked me not only to convey his condolences on the death of your father but also his wish that you will uphold the peace treaty as it stands."

"Of course, I shall," replied Ulls, very much relieved at the thought of continuous peace.

Bewulf then turned to Penrose and surprised us when he said:

"I believe I was once betrothed to you?"

"You were," Penrose answered.

"It's all in the past, now. I am happily married to a princess from East Anglia and we are expecting our first child. God has blessed us."

"Congratulations!" I said.

It was to be another three days before Alpin and his entire clan, together with his son and the bard, Rhys ap Rhys, arrived. We were all surprised by this show of strength and Bewulf felt so uncomfortable that he asked for the renewal of the peace treaty to be dealt with forthwith. As everybody was in agreement, Bewulf asked this question:

"Is Penrose ready to convert?"

"What has this to do with the treaty?" I asked.

"It was a condition of the original treaty," Bewulf stated. "As a devout Christian, I must ask this condition to be fulfilled."

"You are wrong," Penrose intervened, "it was a pre-condition to my marrying you. I cannot do so any more because you are now married. Therefore, I don't see its relevance now."

"Didn't your father exile you for refusing?"

"He did, but my brother called me back for his funeral."

"Have you converted to Christianity?" Bewulf asked of Ulls.

"No," the latter replied.

"Has anyone?" Bewulf insisted.

There was silence. Gryff broke in:

"Penrose has suffered enough. She should not have to go back into exile."

"Are you a Christian?" Bewulf asked.

"I am not," Gryff answered, "does it matter?"

"I shall only consider a request made by a Christian but from no one else. I won't renew the treaty unless you all agree that Penrose is to be exiled as soon as her father's funeral has taken place."

There was consternation. Alpin mac Alpin chose that moment to make himself heard:

"I have previously offered for Penrose to stay among our clan. The Christian monk Aidan who explained your religion to her is living among us, converting some souls. I'd like to renew my offer for her to stay with us and give Aidan another opportunity to convert her."

"Well said!" replied Bewulf. "Do you agree to it, Ulls?"

"You are forgetting two things," Penrose interrupted, "Firstly, I am married to Ap Thor and secondly, we have a home overlooking Odin's Town."

The shock of this announcement was such that neither Ulls nor Bewulf knew what to say. Gwendwr, however, thought fit to make an unwarranted remark:

"So, you threw your lot in with the Vikings!"

"I am a Viking, Gwendwr, whether you accept it or not," I said with pride. "As for Penrose, she chose a man who is prepared to care for her; his origins do not matter so much as his deeds."

"So you say," Gwendwr replied, "but I don't think your mother would be too happy to hear you speak like that."

"Leave my mother out of this," I replied, "considering you're her brother and you could not be bothered to help her run our farm!"

This silenced Gwendwr but Alpin mac Alpin insisted:

"I still think there is much to be said for you, Penrose, to move into our lands and have the opportunity to study the Christian religion again thereby helping all of us to renew the peace."

"You must excuse my son's enthusiasm," said his father and Chief of Clan Alpin. "Surely, if exile among the Vikings was good enough for her before, it should be good enough now. As long as Ulls does not object to his sister living in exile, I do not see why we can't renew the treaty."

"Of course, my sister will return to her place of exile as soon as our father is buried," said a rather subdued Ulls, who had hoped for a different outcome that would allow Penrose to stay.

"Am I to understand then," Bewulf asked, "that I should be present at the late Prince's funeral?"

"Of course, you are more than welcome," stated Ulls who had now regained his composure.

"And this would be according to pagan rites, I suppose," Bewulf continued. "But as a Christian, I could not possibly attend. Tomorrow, we shall officially renew our peace agreement and I shall then return to Northumbria. However, I shall leave behind some of my men to ensure they witness Penrose's departure soon after."

That evening, Penrose and I did not speak. We were both engrossed in our own thoughts. I was not sure whether I would have liked to settle in Penrith again. I was so happy in our home on Ap Thor's Seat near Odin's Town that I really could not wait to return. At the same time, I doubted that Penrose would be feeling the same way. Nevertheless we had to stay until after her father's funeral, which Rhys ap Rhys had offered to arrange. However, many more Druids had been arriving at Penrith and were expecting to take part in the ceremony. The presence of the Christian monks left behind by Bewulf after his departure was unwelcome to many but not to Alpin mac Alpin who was seen mingling with them.

A few hours' walk from Penrith, on top of a hill, was a stone circle sacred to the Druids. The late Prince of Penrith's body had been transferred to the centre of that stone circle while a group of workers under the direction of Rhys ap Rhys had been excavating rubble and earth on the side of the hill to create an artificial cavern. The day of the funeral was approaching. The night before it was due, by the light of torches, the whole of Penrith led by Ulls and Penrose made their way to the stone circle. Just before dawn, a hard frost descended on the countryside, covering most of the land in white, an excellent sign according to the Druids. As the sun rose over the horizon through a pink mist, the Druids started singing. They surrounded the body of their former Prince, then lifting it and still singing, took it to the cavern. Only Ulls and Penrose, as his children, were allowed to go inside. No one else could see which of the late Prince's personal effects had been carefully laid by his body to accompany him to the nether world. As soon as they came out, the Druids themselves closed the opening to the cavern with stones using their bare hands. It was all over. The hill had reclaimed its own.

On the way back to Penrith, Alpin mac Alpin made a nuisance of himself by imposing his presence on Penrose one more time.
"You should travel with us," he said, "and remain among us. We shall share your loss and make it more acceptable to you. Anything you need, we'll provide."

"I'm sure you mean well," Penrose answered. "However, my life is with Ap Thor now. Do not spoil what we have."

"You'll find me a better man than he is," Alpin mac Alpin insisted, to Penrose's repugnance.

While this exchange was taking place, she had been holding on to my arm. I now whispered:

"Shall we get away from him?"

"Yes, but how?" she whispered back.

We moved to the side of the track and stopped.

"Anything wrong?" asked Alpin mac Alpin, stopping too.

"I'm waiting for my uncle," I replied.

He, of course, had been present with the other Vikings and, as they were somewhere in the crowd of people returning to Penrith, they were bound to walk past us. When they did so, I spoke to them in Norse so that the Scot could not understand. Following my instructions, they quickly surrounded us and made it impossible for Alpin mac Alpin to annoy Penrose any longer. He was far from pleased and I heard him mutter something which I did not quite catch but which, I thought, sounded like cursing. Upon our return to Penrith, Penrose insisted on looking for Gryff. We found him quite dejected and looking suddenly old. The death of his Prince, who was also his friend, had affected him deeply. Yet, when he saw Penrose, he commiserated with her:

"I'm so sorry, not only for your loss but also because you are going back into exile."

"Do not worry for me," answered Penrose, "Ap Thor and myself are happy living over there. Even if the ban had been lifted, we might have gone back. You on the other hand are the one who needs taking care of."

Without saying a word, Gryff took her in his arms. She embraced him too and I could see tears rolling down the old man's cheeks. It was hard to watch. I walked away and went looking for my uncle Gwendwr. He and Ulls were drunk and still drinking in the main Hall. I thought better than to talk to them. I went for some of the refreshments that had been provided along one side of the Hall as part of the funeral celebration. The table was surrounded by monks who were gulping the food as fast as they could. I grabbed a swan leg and made for the door. There, I met Alpin, the Chief of Clan Alpin.

"I believe my son has been rude towards Penrose," he said. "I can but apologise for his behaviour and put it down to youthful enthusiasm."

"His attention is not welcome," I replied. "Penrose had already told him so but he takes no notice of her."

"That's my son all right!"

I returned to Penrose. She and Gryff had sat down and were quietly reminiscing. I did not interrupt. I let them talk well into the night. The following day, she thanked me for granting her that privacy before we set on our journey back to Odin's Town.

# CHAPTER 27

It was another five years before a visitor came to see us. This time, it was Rhys ap Rhys. Not knowing where we lived, he went to Odin's Town and tried to make himself understood. The only answer he got was a gesture pointing to Ap Thor's Seat which left him baffled until a helpful Viking took him by the arm and led him in the right direction. We welcomed him with open arms.

"Rhys ap Rhys," I exclaimed, "what brings you here?"

"You've done well for yourself," he replied. "I thought I would find you in the town below."

"Did you look for me there?" I asked.

"I did and I could not understand why people kept pointing to where I stand now. I also got a fright when one of them caught my arm and pulled me up here."

I could not help laughing and so did Penrose. Eventually, our guest saw the funny side of his experience too. He was also quite impressed by my forge and told me:

"It's just like your home in the land between the two rivers. Do you miss it?"

"I'm happy with Penrose," I said, "but, yes, I'd like to know how my parents are doing."

"I miss the mountains of Wales," he replied, "but fate brought me to these parts and I should not complain. Alpin was so taken with my singing of your praises all those years ago that he appointed me Chief Druid of Clan Alpin. I was so flattered I never thought for a minute of turning him down. Now, I must spend the rest of my life among them."

"Can't you resign?" I asked.

"It is unheard of," he answered, "but I should not complain, I have been well treated."

"So, what brought you here, then?" Penrose enquired.

"I have been sent by Alpin mac Alpin with a message for you, Penrose."

I could see Penrose tense up at the mention of his name and I wondered why he had sent the Druid instead of coming himself. Rhys ap Rhys continued:

"As I have just told you, many years ago while I was travelling and singing your exploits, Ap Thor, I made such an impression on Alpin, Chief of Clan Alpin that he appointed me Chief Druid to his Clan. As such, I spent most of my days in Alpin's company or as his envoy. A few months ago, he decided to extend his lands Northwards. At the time, I thought nothing of it and followed him unreservedly as did everyone in his clan. Unfortunately, the Picts, who live in those parts, did not see it that way and attacked us. They are fearless and ruthless and their tactic is a quick attack followed by a withdrawal. Two weeks ago, in one of those skirmishes which you cannot really call a battle, Alpin was killed. His son, Alpin mac Alpin, is now the new Chief of his Clan and thought it prudent to completely withdraw from those new lands. He's not happy about this situation and I do not know what his plans are for the future but, at present, he only thinks about the celebration that will confirm him as the new Clan Chief. This will happen soon and he has sent me to invite you to come."

"That's nice of him," I said.

"Who else has he invited?" asked Penrose suspiciously.

"No one else as far as I'm aware," he replied.

"Then, I won't go!" she exclaimed. "He has pestered me in the past and I am not giving him another chance."

"He won't be happy," said Rhys ap Rhys. "He has a high regard for you Penrose and was looking forward to seeing you again. He told me as much."

"Present our apologies," I said. "I cannot force Penrose to go if she does not want to."

"Are you sure you won't change your mind?" he insisted. "Can't you convince her to go, Ap Thor? Alpin mac Alpin is not a man to be trifled with. If he's really upset, he can turn quite nasty. I've seen it happen in the past when his father had to smooth things over. I would not make an enemy of him."

"Thanks for your concern," I said, "but our minds are quite made up."

Rhys ap Rhys stayed a couple of days more but we stood firm in our decision and, realising we would not go, he left.

Less than two months later, an emissary from Northumbria arrived. He had gone to Odin's Town looking for us. Rurik met him there and brought him up to Ap Thor's Seat when he told us:

"Our King is dead. His son, Bewulf, will be crowned King soon, he wants you to be present. This will happen at Durham. I am to show you the way and ensure your safe conduct."

"I won't go alone," I said. "I want my wife Penrose, my uncle Elgar, and a suitable escort led by Rurik to come along."

"Of course!" the emissary replied.

"How soon do we have to leave?" I asked.

"The sooner the better," he answered. "Bewulf expects you to stay as his guests for a while. He has much to discuss with you."

"What about?" I enquired.

"I'm not at liberty to say but you will soon find out."

"So, Durham is where I would have been living if I had married Bewulf?" Penrose mused.

"You're Penrose!" the emissary exclaimed. "The one who preferred not to convert to Christianity and miss the opportunity to be a Queen?"

"The very same," she replied. "I'm happy as I am and regret nothing."

"Are there many Christians among you?" the emissary enquired.

"None whatsoever," I answered. "Does it matter?"

"Bewulf wants to be known as the Christian King who converts all pagans. He is far more devout than his father ever was."

The following day, we started on our journey. After a few days, we crossed the border into Northumbria. We could then see the difference, there were monks everywhere and a small church in every village as our escort was quick to point out. As we walked past the fields, we saw people hard at work. At last, we reached Durham. A camp had been set up for us on the outskirts of town.

"Are we not allowed to go inside?" I enquired.

"You are free to go wherever you want as the King's esteemed guests," our guide answered and added: "I shall advise him of your arrival."

I looked at Penrose. She was pensive, I could not fathom why. Elgar, on the other hand, was quite determined to enjoy himself:

"Nephew, shall we go to town and check out the inns?"

"I think it would be better if we stayed in the camp until we meet with the King."

"I agree with you, Ap Thor," stated Rurik.

"I think we made a mistake by coming," said Penrose feeling uneasy, "nothing good will come of it. Mark my words."

The following morning, the Abbot of Durham paid us a visit.

"Introductions are not necessary," he said, "we've all met before."

"That is true," I answered.

"I suppose," he continued, "there is no change in your attitude towards my religion. You don't need to answer. I know what you're going to say. However, I would hope you are open minded enough to look at our church, speak to our priests and perhaps reconsider your decision. In the meantime, I shall take you to see our King."

We found him, playing with his two children.

"Aren't they beautiful?" he asked as we hesitated by the door. "Come forward! I'm glad you made the journey, especially you, Penrose."

"Why me?" she queried. "We could not possibly have any more to say to each other. We are both married now and you have made sure I live in exile."

"On the contrary," he answered, "there is a kind of bond between us because you were once betrothed to me."

"Should we not forget about that, Sire?"

"No, you could be betrothed to me again! My wife, God rest her soul, died giving birth to my second son. My children need a mother. Convert to Christianity and you will be my Queen."

"You forget Sire, that I am happily married and I would not desert my husband for you."

"You are not married at all in the eyes of our Church. Only a union blessed by a priest is a valid marriage. Think about it! Don't answer me now! My father's funeral mass will be held in three days' time, I'd like you all to attend. See how we bury our dead and then, we'll speak again."

The audience was at an end. We left in silence. On our way out, we saw Alpin mac Alpin, Rhys ap Rhys and Aidan going in. We barely exchanged a glance but I wondered what game the Scot was playing by bringing the Irish monk along with him.

We did not go back to the camp but instead decided to have a look at their main church. As we entered, we could hear voices. They were coming from a group of monks that were standing in a circle close to the altar. As I approached, I noticed a coffin at the centre of the circle. Quite surprised, I stopped. A monk came towards us and said something we could not understand. Penrose asked:

"Who is in that coffin?"

It was the monk's turn not to understand. Another monk came forward and, this time, spoke our language:

"Welcome! We are praying for the soul of the departed one. You may join us."

"Who is he?" I asked.

"The late King," the monk answered. "We shall be praying day and night until his burial. This is the way we do things. You are not Christians, are you? But you are free to observe."

"It seems to me," said Penrose, "that you, monks, are always praying."

"That's why we are monks. We devote ourselves totally to God and pray on behalf of others."

I was looking around and noticed various artefacts made of gold and silver. I walked towards them. The monk followed me.

"These are offerings from people who want us to pray for their souls," he said. "Bewulf, our new king, prefers the monks of Lindisfarne to pray for him, so they get the King's offerings and they are far richer than these."

"Where are those monks?" I asked.

"Quite a way from here," he answered, "Lindisfarne is an island, along the coast, North of here. It would take you a day or two to get there and you probably would not be allowed to get near, not until you become Christians anyway; then you could offer your belt or your armlet and we would pray to God that He forgives you your sins."

Penrose and I exchanged glances. Elgar and Rurik had already left and we did the same. Once outside, Penrose vented her feelings:

"Why is it always them and us? We're not good enough and they're so special. And the King's arrogance! We're not married because one of their priests have not said so."

"Don't get upset!" I said. "In a few days, everything will be over and we'll be on our way back. In the meantime, your brother may still arrive. It would surprise me if he had not been invited. You would like to see your brother again, wouldn't you?"

"Ulls? I hardly think about him nowadays, but I rather wonder how Gryff is as you may wonder about Gwendwr."

"Oh, my other uncle! No, I don't really think about him and, anyway, he and Elgar don't get on."

Eventually, the day before the funeral, Ulls, the new Prince of Penrith, with all his entourage that included Gwendwr but not Gryff, finally arrived and was made to camp next to us. That evening, brother and sister were reunited and I kept away. However, I found out from Gwendwr that Gryff had not been well enough to make the journey.

"Old age, I think," Gwendwr informed me, "his legs sometimes give way. He spends most of his time sitting in a corner of the Hall. Some say he misses Penrose."

"I might well believe it," I replied. "Any other news?"

"No, life is pretty dull in Penrith. Actually, I'm quite excited by this trip, all the old rulers dead and our fate in the hands of their sons. Do you think they will maintain the peace?"

"Hard to say! I think Bewulf will listen to his monks who want everyone to become Christians but I cannot fathom how they will go about it."

"So, there may still be fighting for you and your Vikings!"

I laughed but did not answer.

It was a long boring day. We were called to the church soon after day-break and had to listen all day long to singing and speeches in a foreign tongue. At last, towards evening, the coffin was moved a few yards to a hole in the floor in front of the altar. It was to be the last resting place of the late King. As all the monks, led by their Abbot, filed out of the church, Bewulf, the new King, addressed us:

"In seven days' time, I shall return to this church for my coronation. I want you all to be there."

He did not wait for an answer but left the church and, as we did too, Penrose whispered to me:

"Shall we never go home?"

"Let's hope the coronation will be a more cheerful affair," I answered. "I could not stand another day like today, could you?"

"No, not really!"

When the day came, we did not know what to expect. The Abbot of Durham was standing in front of the altar, surrounded by his monks, all dressed in clean, white robes. There was total silence and Bewulf was nowhere to be seen. Suddenly, a horn was sounded and in walked the King to be. He was wearing a cape. As soon as he reached the Abbot, he knelt in front of him and dropped his cape to reveal a naked chest. Singing started only to stop every time that the Abbot was making the sign of the Cross on some part of Bewulf's body. I lost count of the number of times this happened. At last, there was silence again, the Abbot shouted:

"Arise, Bewulf, King of Northumbria!"

The horn sounded again and Bewulf and the Abbot kissed, then they walked side by side to just outside the church. There, they stopped while the Abbot shouted:

"People of Northumbria, behold your new King!"

Cheering was heard from the assembled crowd as the two of them crossed the square that separated the church from the palace. We were told to follow. As we entered the palace, we saw Bewulf sitting on a throne, the Abbot standing behind him and no sign of any festivities. We were looking at one another, wondering what we were supposed to do. We kept on walking until the Abbot made a gesture for us to stop. Bewulf then spoke:

"God has anointed me King of Northumbria. As such, it is my duty to spread His word to all four corners of the earth. For many years now, I have been asking from you, Welsh, Scots and Vikings to convert. I can no longer be at peace with pagans. I shall however show you Christ's mercy by granting you a year's grace during which time I expect every one of you to become acquainted with my religion."

We were too stunned to give an answer. The Abbot then approached us and said:

"You have heard my King's wish, there is nothing else for you here. Go back to your camps and prepare to leave."

## CHAPTER 28

It was the spring equinox. A storm had been brewing for the past couple of days and gale force winds were blowing with a violence we had never seen before. Up on Ap Thor's Seat, the gale was even worse. We dared not stay indoors in case the house blew down on us. Elgar had left us and taken refuge in some inn in Odin's Town. I was in two minds whether we should follow him. I did not want to make the decision and left it to Penrose. So long as she was prepared to stay, I would stay with her. Suddenly, she exclaimed:

"What's that?"

I looked in the direction where she was pointing, somewhere on the river. Whatever it was, it was moving fast and towards us.

"They're boats!" I shouted loud enough for her to hear me over the noise of the wind. "By Odin, they're Viking boats and they are about to crash on the shore. I'd better go down and see what help I can give."

"I will come with you."

We rushed downhill and into the town. The alarm had already been raised and everyone was making for the shoreline. From there, we could see that their sails were in shreds and the boats were far too low in the water for them to be safe much longer. I caught sight of Rurik and walked over to him.

"Let's hope they make it!" I said.

"I reckon they should land about here," he replied. "You should welcome them as befits your status."

As they came closer, we could see they were still being rowed. It seemed to be a desperate attempt to force the boats on to the shore as the wind and waves would otherwise push them further up the river. There were three loud crashes: the bottoms of the boats had hit the foreshore. The Vikings jumped off into the water and struggled to reach land and safety. Then, they stopped and lined up. They seemed apprehensive as to the kind of welcome they were going to receive. I walked forward with Penrose to my left and Rurik to my right. A giant of a man detached himself from the group of shipwrecked sailors. His shoulder-long hair was all white and as we came closer, I could see he had numerous scars on his bare arms. He seemed vaguely familiar to me but I dismissed the thought and shouted:

"Welcome! You're among friends! I am Ap Thor!"

"Where are we?" the big man enquired. "I am Eldred!"

"Eldred the Avenger from Ireland!" I exclaimed.

A smile came upon his face as he replied:

"Someone who knows me! I'm so glad! but where are we?"

"Welcome to Odin's Town!" I said. "You are on the Eastern side of Britain. Have you come back from Groendland and lost your way?"

"You know I've been there? Strange, I can't recall you."

"Perhaps, I should have cut the tip of your nose off after all."

Eldred thought for a few seconds and then burst out laughing loudly while Rurik looked astounded. This was the signal for the newcomers to advance. They knew they were among friends. Penrose chose this moment to ask me in Welsh:

"What about his nose?"

"Who is she?" Eldred asked, annoyed at hearing a foreign tongue spoken.

"This is my wife, Penrose, daughter of Penrith, late Prince of Penrith, and sister to Ulls, the current Prince. We live up there and you are welcome to stay with us. It would make my uncle very happy to meet with you again."

"Your uncle? Well! I have my son with me. Grunwald, where are you?"

"My uncle's name is Elgar. Surely, you remember him."

"That rascal! Of course, I remember him! Ah, here you are!" he said as a man of about thirty years of age joined our group at about the same time as Elgar made his appearance. While Eldred and Elgar embraced, I took the newcomer aside.

"You must be Grunwald." I said.

"I am," he replied.

"Is your mother called Grunhelda by any chance?" I asked.

"Yes, how do you know?"

"I stayed at her inn many years ago but she never revealed who your father was and I now hear Eldred is claiming to be your father."

"Shsh!" whispered Grunwald, "I'll explain later but I need to go and help drag the boats out of the water."

Later on, that evening, a relaxed and well-fed Eldred talked about his adventures in Groendland:

"This is a vast land where nobody has lived before. I was not the first Viking to settle there and settling down is not really what I wanted to do anyway. However, I did settle for a few years because of Grunwald. Most of the settlers knew me and made me welcome, they also directed me to my son. This surprises you, Elgar, doesn't it? And I am sorry, old chap, you thought that may be you were his father. It's all Grunhelda's fault by keeping it a secret for so long. Grunwald, here, had no such reticence. He knew who his father was and did not hide the fact."

"I could not tell who my father was while in Ireland," Grunwald explained, "but so far away in Groendland, it did not matter, no one was going to tell my mother."

"Well," said Elgar, "I had always hoped you might be my son but I can't say I'm surprised. At last I know for sure. I hope we'll stay friends."

"Of course," Grunwald answered, "you have been such a good friend of my mother's that I would not have it any other way."

Eldred smiled and his eyes sparkled. I could see the old man was doting upon his son. He continued:

"We sailed many expeditions to nearby islands but they too were uninhabited. The life of a settler grew pretty monotonous and I wanted to see the old country and show it to my son. I was not the only one, many other Vikings wanted to return home as well and we were doing just that when we were caught in the storm and completely thrown off course."

Penrose had learnt some Norse over the years but I could see she was struggling to follow the conversation.

"I'm sure, uncle, that you have much to catch up with Eldred," I said, "so I shall let you talk and Penrose and I will retire for the night."

"These love birds!" Elgar answered, "you would not believe they have been together for nearly ten years."

I did not want to hear any more of my uncle's smart remarks and, as the wind had relented a little, Penrose and I went back into our house where she plied me with questions. She seemed very interested to learn more about my family background which we had hardly spoken about before. I also expressed my doubts about Grunwald's claim that Eldred was his father and I told her that I would be getting to the truth of the matter. The opportunity presented itself a couple of days later when I saw him looking around the forge.

"It gets used from time to time," I said. "My father taught me the trade of a blacksmith. Do you need anything doing?"

"I lost my sword in the sea," he answered. "I could do with a new one."

"I'll be glad to cast one for you but, first, I want to know the truth about your father."

"I'd rather not talk about it."

"I owe it to my uncle to know the truth. Do you really know who your father is because Grunhelda has always maintained she does not know herself?"

"That's the truth."

"So, why say that Eldred is your father?"

"Well, promise me you won't say a word to him."

"Only if you have a good enough reason."

"I think I have. A few days after I arrived in Eisland from Ireland, some of my mates got me drunk and kept on asking me who my father was. They refused to believe I did not know. To get rid of them questioning me, I had to come up with a name. Of course the best I could come up with was Eldred but the word spread and people started to show me respect on account of who, they believed, was my father. I felt I could not retract and, to be quite honest, I rather enjoyed the attention I was getting. I then moved to Groendland at about the same time as Eldred landed there. I was relieved when he accepted me as his son and treated me as such. It would hurt the old man too much if I were to tell him now that it's not true."

"But you are living a lie."

"I know but what else can I do?"

"You can come clean. Do you really want to follow Eldred home?"

"I have no choice. I would prefer to go back to Dublin. I've tried before but I could not find a boat that would take me there from Groendland."

"Well! You can go there from here instead of boarding Eldred's boat when it's repaired."

"I'll think about it. Now, I need to go and see how we can salvage the boats."

I let him go and started the forge for I had work to do.

Nearly a month later, the boats had been made seaworthy again and Eldred was almost ready to embark when my other uncle Gwendwr arrived. He was the bearer of bad news:

"The Saxons are on the march," he said. "Ulls has been shadowing them from the South and the Scots have come from the West. I have been sent to request you to join us and attack them from the North."

"How long did it take you to reach me?" I asked.

"Two and a half days, why?"

"You go back tomorrow and I follow you the day after with as many Vikings as will come and fight under me. I should reach your Prince one day after you at around midday. Do you understand me so far?"

"Yes!"

"If we want to take the Saxons by surprise, I will attack them as I arrive. If both the Welsh and Scots were to attack at the same time, I believe victory is ours."

"How would we know?"

"I've just told you: one day after your arrival at Ulls' camp about the middle of the day. Didn't you understand?"

"Yes, it's very clever."

"Can I rely on you?"

"Absolutely!"

This was the point of no return. I went to see Rurik and together we recruited an army. Eldred offered to join us but I had something else in mind for him:

"Eldred, I appreciate your offer but your boats are ready to sail, aren't they?"

"They are!" he replied.

"Then, if you really want to help me, take them South along the coast until you reach an island that goes by the name of Lindisfarne. Only monks live there, looking after the King of Northumbria's treasures, a nice booty for you to capture on your way home."

"You want me to do that?"

"Of course, that should make them recall their army home."

Grunwald had been listening. He now made his request:

"Ap Thor, could I possibly fight alongside you? With victory, the way would be open for me to go and see my mother in Dublin. I've always wanted to do that."

I looked at Eldred. He said nothing. His face was expressing blank astonishment.

"Eldred," I said, "I could not agree without your consent."

"You have it!" he replied. Then, turning to Grunwald and in a barely audible voice, he hissed:

"You're not really my son, are you?"

As there was no reply, he continued:

"Like mother, like son! I had my suspicions for a while but I did not want to believe them. It felt good to be a father, it gave a purpose to my life and now you have robbed me of that experience."

Eldred was getting upset and really angry as he continued:

"Go back to your whore of a mother and hope to Odin that our paths never cross again."

Grunwald thought it more prudent to walk away while I was left to face him.

"Don't worry, Ap Thor," Eldred said, "I'm not angry with you and I won't let you down either. First thing tomorrow, I'll set sail South as you asked me to."

"Thanks," I replied.

Penrose had lost her interest in war a long time ago and therefore decided not to accompany me. I could not blame her. I hoped for a quick victory and an even quicker return. All of us Vikings were in high spirits and, towards the middle of the third day after we left Odin's Town, we caught sight of the Saxon army. We stopped for a brief rest before purposefully marching towards the enemy. They seemed to have been expecting us and a strong contingent moved forward to bar the way South. As far as I was concerned, this fitted into my plan since we wanted to fight them and not join up with Ulls and his army who, by now, should be ready to attack them from the other side. Soon, we were pushing them back. At the same time, we saw the Scots coming from the right but, instead of making for the Saxons, they advanced towards us. I wondered why they wanted to join us first, so it came as a total surprise when they attacked us in our rear. After some confusion, we had no choice but to fight on two fronts. I should then have given the order to withdraw but, instead, I ordered my men to break through in order to reach the Welsh. It was hard work and many a Viking was either killed or wounded so seriously that he could fight no more. Suddenly, the Scots withdrew from the battlefield. This should have given us some respite and possibly the chance to regroup except that the Saxons then sent the rest of their army against us. We stood no chance against so many. We retreated Westward as I wondered what had happened to the Welsh since they had not shown up. Had they been defeated a day or so before? I wanted to know so I ordered my men to press South and we forced our way round the enemy. We had almost accomplished that manoeuvre when I received a blow that cut part of the left side of my face and broke my shoulder. My left arm felt limp and I could not move it at all. My shield was still tied to it and somehow was offering me some protection against further blows from the left. My uncle, Elgar, who was close by, in spite of being wounded himself, managed to rescue me and we made our escape together with Rurik, Grunwald and some thirty of our men. Soon, we caught sight of the Welsh army, hastily drawn up but still not engaged with the enemy, and we made a dash for it. As we got there, I collapsed.

When I woke up, I was laying near the bend of a small river. I could hear the din of swords and shields clashing which reminded me that a battle was still going on. I tried to move but I could not and the pain was excruciating. Then, everything that had happened to me that day came flashing back. Seeing me move, Elgar spoke to me:
"Ap Thor! You did your best! I'm so proud of you!"
"Why are you not fighting?" I asked.
"I've been hurt, not so seriously as you but I can hardly stand. They got me in the legs again."
"Why did the Scots attack us?" asked Rurik, holding his belly in his hands and trying to stem the flow of blood.
"I don't know," I replied, "I thought they were our allies but obviously not."
I closed my eyes and must have dozed off for when I woke up it was night time. Ulls was sitting by me. Seeing me move, he asked:
"Where's my sister?"
"Penrose!" I exclaimed, "someone must tell Penrose! Is anyone fit enough to travel back?"
"I am," Grunwald said. "What shall I tell her?"
"The truth," I replied, "and give her any help she asks for. Go now and don't get caught. Warn her too! Wait! One more thing: tell her I love her and miss her. You won't forget, will you?"

"I won't!" he answered and went on his way.

I was feeling weak, it was as if my body was being drained of all strength.

"I'm dying, aren't I?" I said.

"The few Vikings still with us have built a boat to give you a proper send off as befits your rank," Elgar said. "You have achieved your dream: you are a Viking warrior going to Valhalla."

I tried to smile but the pain stopped me. My breathing was becoming more difficult. I was seeing everything around me in a haze. I knew the end was near. It was now an effort even to speak but I managed,

"Take me to the boat."

I felt people lifting me and carrying me, then laying me down again with my shield and sword. My hand tightened round the hilt. I looked at the faces around me but could not see Gwendwr. I closed my eyes and murmured:

"Leave me now, Odin beckons."

# EPILOGUE

A group of Saxon warriors were keeping guard over some captured Vikings. They were on top of a hill overlooking that stretch of water upon which rested the makeshift raft that was Ap Thor's funeral boat. One of them, wondering what was happening in the valley below, tried to find out from one of the prisoners in spite of the language barrier. When he was satisfied, he came back to his comrades and told them in spite of their utter indifference:

"From what I can make out, one of their leaders by the name of Arthur is going on a journey to a place called Avalon."

There was no reply but a legend was born as the boat burst into flames, which illuminated the night sky.

# THE END